BAD MEMORIES

A LT. KATE GAZZARA NOVEL

THE LT. KATE GAZZARA MURDER FILES
BOOK 22

BLAIR HOWARD

Print Paperback ISBN: 979-8-9988024-4-7

Cleveland, TN, USA

Email: BlairHoward@BlairHowardBooks.com

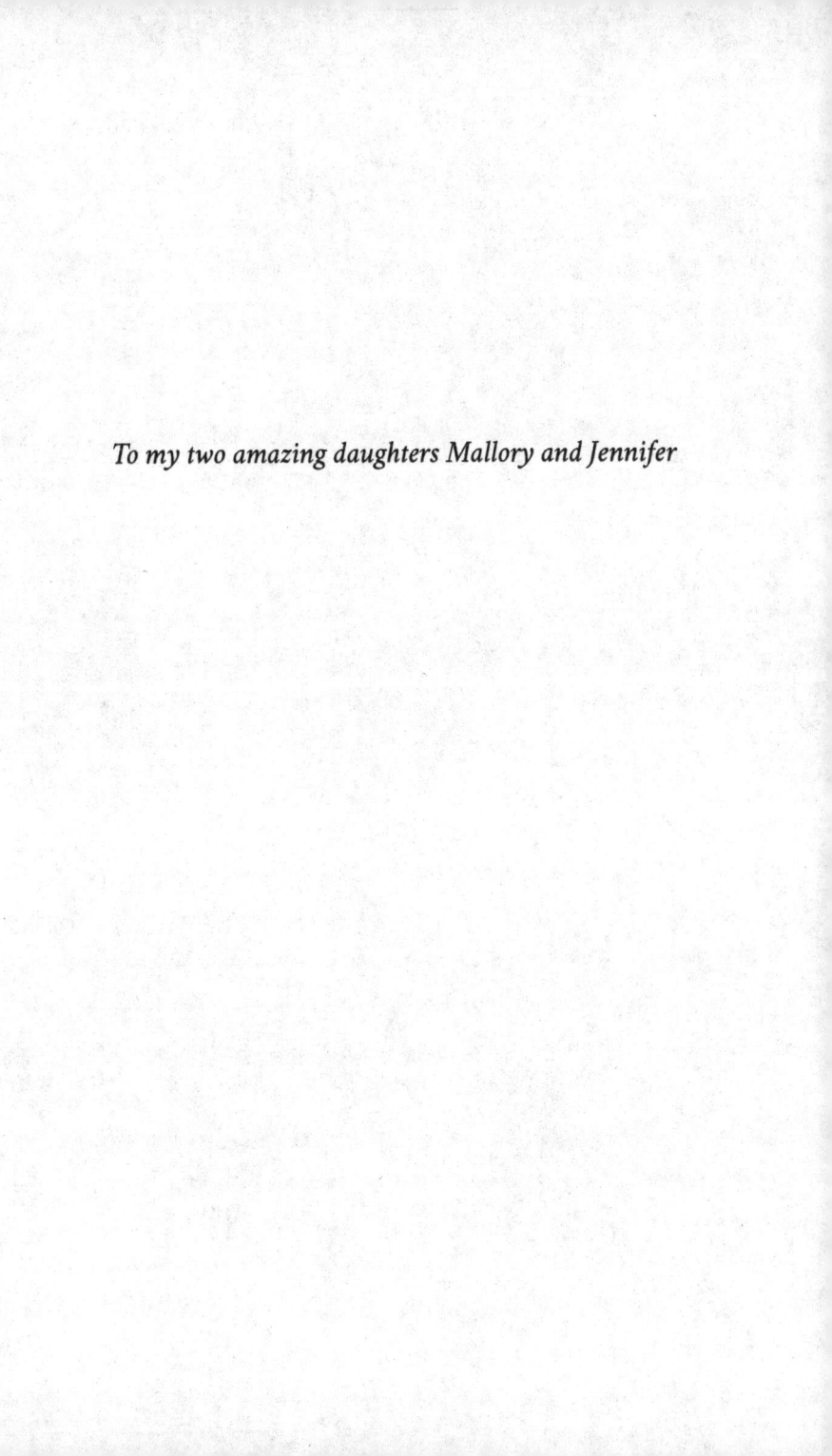

To my two amazing daughters Mallory and Jennifer

1

The Locked Room

Tuesday, October 2, 2022

THE HOLLOWAY PSYCHIATRIC ASSOCIATES BUILDING squatted on the corner of Gunbarrel Road like a monument to modern mental health care—all glass and steel and good intentions. At least, that's what it was supposed to be. At seven-thirty on a Tuesday morning in October, with patrol cars blocking both ends of the street and yellow crime scene tape fluttering in the autumn breeze, it looked more like a crime scene.

Which, I suppose, it was.

I pulled my unmarked cruiser into the parking lot and sat for a moment, studying the building. Three stories, lots of windows, security cameras mounted at every corner. The kind of place where people went to get their heads straightened out, not to get murdered. But then again, murder had a way of happening in the most unlikely places.

My name is Captain Catherine Gazzara of the Chattanooga Police department; my friends call me Kate. In 2022 I was a twenty-four-year veteran and leader of a small, but elite, special crimes unit, and I'd just been called out to a suspicious death in said building.

Samson whined softly from the back seat, his ears perked forward as he, too, studied the building through the window. My hundred-and-fifteen-pound German Shepherd had been my partner for a little more than six months, ever since I'd adopted him from the McKamey Animal Center. Why? You may well ask. The story is, I'd found him guarding his murdered owner. He was about to be shot by one of the officers when I stepped in. I talked him down, and a couple of hours later, took him to McKamey. I dreamed about him that night and the following morning I went to get him. Best thing I ever did. He has instincts that sometimes put my detectives to shame, and right now, those instincts were telling him something was wrong.

"I know, boy," I said, reaching back to scratch behind his ears. "I feel it too."

I grabbed my jacket from the passenger seat and stepped out into the crisp morning air. October in Chattanooga is my favorite time of year; the leaves were turning; the humidity had finally broken, and you could almost convince yourself that the world wasn't full of people doing terrible things to each other. Almost.

Sergeant Corbin Russell was waiting for me at the building's entrance, notebook already in hand, his dark blue suit immaculate despite him having being there for over an hour. Corbin was the kind of man who probably ironed his underwear, but he was also the most thorough detective I'd ever worked with. If there was a detail to be found, he'd find it.

"What do we have?" I asked as I approached.

"Doctor Marcus Holloway, fifty-two years old, prominent psychiatrist," he said, consulting his notes. "Found dead in his office this morning by his secretary, Linda Matthews. She arrived at seven AM for an early appointment preparation and found his office door locked. When he didn't respond to knocking, she called building security to let her in."

"Electronic lock system, I suppose?"

He nodded. "Yes. Each doctor has their own keycard. Matthews doesn't have access to Holloway's office; only he did. Building security has a master override, which is how they got in this morning."

I looked up at the building's facade. "Windows?"

"Third floor. Thirty-foot drop to the concrete walkway. The windows don't open. It's a sealed building with central heat and air. And before you ask, I already checked. There's no damage to the windows, and no signs of forced entry anywhere."

"So, we have a locked room mystery," I said. "How very Agatha Christie of our killer."

Russell didn't crack a smile. He rarely ever did. "The victim appears to have been killed sometime last night," he said. "Doc Sheddon is upstairs with the body now."

I followed Russell through the lobby, past a receptionist who looked like she'd been crying, and into an elevator that whisked us up to the third floor. The hallway was narrow and well-lit, with office doors spaced evenly along both sides. Crime scene tape blocked access to one door about halfway down the hall.

Mike Willis was photographing the door frame when we approached. Our CSI supervisor looked like he'd been up all night. His bald head seemed shinier than usual, and his thick eyebrows were furrowed in concentration.

"Kate," he said, without looking up from his camera. "I'm glad you're here. This one's interesting."

"So I'm told," I replied. "What do you have so far?"

"Well, for starters, no signs of forced entry on the electronic lock. The system shows Doctor Holloway's keycard was used to enter at 6:08 PM yesterday, and then again to exit at 8:42 PM."

"He left at 8:42?" I asked, frowning. "What time did he return?"

"That's the problem. He didn't. The security cameras show he never left the office."

"How many security cameras?" I asked.

"Four on this floor. They show Holloway arriving yesterday evening around six PM and entering his office. There's a twenty-minute gap in the footage from eight-thirty to eight-fifty PM. Someone deleted that section. But here's the weird part: as I already mentioned, the keycard system shows his card being used at 8:34 and again at 8:45 PM, right in the middle of that gap."

"So either Holloway left and came back again without being seen, or someone else used his keycard--"

"Uh, uh," Willis said, cutting me off and shaking his

head. "His keycard is on his desk. Someone knew enough about the security system to delete the camera footage but couldn't erase the keycard logs. Here's how I see it, Kate: someone knocked on his door sometime after eight-thirty and he let them in and..." he trailed off, looking at me, then shrugged helplessly.

"Have you tried that?" I asked.

He shook his head. "No, I couldn't. Not yet. The body's still in the room. But I will."

I turned to Corbin. "Has anyone talked to the secretary yet?"

"Ramirez is with her downstairs. She claims Holloway had been receiving threatening letters over the past few weeks, but he destroyed them. He told her they were probably from a disgruntled patient and not to worry about them."

"Threatening letters that conveniently disappeared," I said. "How droll."

Doc Sheddon emerged from the office, pulling off his latex gloves. Richard Sheddon was a small man who, at times, reminded me of Bilbo Baggins, but he was the best medical examiner in the state, and if anyone could tell me how someone had been murdered in a locked room, it was Doc.

"Kate, how lovely to see you," he said, his round face unusually grim. "Other than the circumstances... Yes... well, this is an interesting one." He glanced back over his shoulder as he said it.

"How so?" I asked.

"Well, the cause of death appears to be some kind of

puncture wound to the neck. Very precise, very clean. Whoever did this knew exactly where to strike."

"Knife?" I asked.

"I don't think so. The wound is too narrow, too deep. More like a medical instrument of some kind, or maybe a letter opener, or something similar."

I felt a chill that had nothing to do with the morning air. "Medical instrument?" I asked.

"That would be my guess. I'll know more after the autopsy, but the angle and depth suggest someone with medical knowledge."

"Time of death?" I asked.

"Based on body temperature and rigor, I'd say between eight and ten PM last night."

I looked at Corbin. "So, Holloway locks himself in his office sometime around six-thirty, and sometime between eight and ten someone manages to get in and kill him with what might be a medical instrument or a frickin' letter opener, then they somehow get out again, leaving the door locked from the inside."

"No ma'am. It can't be locked from the inside like a normal door," Corbin said. "And--"

"It has to be locked with a key card from the outside," I said, cutting him off. "And his key card is on his desk."

"That's about the size of it," Corbin said.

"Could someone have cloned his card?" I asked.

"That's the only answer I can think of," he replied. "Though how they could have done it, I don't know. Jack would know, I suppose, and so would Tim Clarke."

I nodded. *Tim Clarke,* I thought. *Corbin's right. If anyone would know how it could be done, he would. Maybe I'll give him a call later. For now...* I took a deep breath, turned to the ME and said, "Can I see the body, Doc?"

Doc Sheddon nodded and led me into the office. It was a typical psychiatrist's setup: leather chairs, diplomas on the walls, bookshelves lined with medical texts and psychology journals. Holloway was slumped forward behind his desk with his head resting on the blotter. There was a surprising amount of blood, I noted.

"The puncture wound is right here," Doc said, pointing to a small hole just below Holloway's left ear. "Went straight into the carotid artery. He would have bled out in minutes."

I studied the scene. The office was neat, organized, and there were no signs of a struggle. Holloway's jacket was hung carefully on the back of his chair; his briefcase was closed and sitting beside his desk. If I didn't know better, I'd say he was taking a nap.

"Was he expecting someone?" I asked.

"His secretary says no," Corbin replied. "His last appointment was at four PM. He had nothing on his calendar after that."

I snapped on a pair of latex gloves and walked around the desk, careful not to disturb anything Willis hadn't already photographed. His appointment book was front and center on his desk, along with a cup of coffee that had long since gone cold, and a framed photograph of a young man who looked like a younger version of himself.

"The son?" I asked, looking sideways at Corbin.

"According to the secretary, yes. Vincent Holloway, twenty-eight years old. Lives in Atlanta."

"Someone needs to notify him, I guess."

"Already taken care of," Corbin said. "He's driving up this morning."

I continued my circuit of the office, looking for anything that seemed out of place. The bookshelves were properly organized; the furniture was positioned with care; the windows were intact. Nothing suggested violence or a struggle.

But Samson was still agitated. I'd brought him up from the car and, now that Willis had finished with the immediate crime scene, he was pacing around the office, whining softly and occasionally stopping to sniff at something I couldn't see.

"What's bothering you, boy?" I asked, watching as he stopped near the desk and lifted his nose, testing the air.

"Dogs," Willis said, shaking his head. "Sometimes they can pick up scents we can't detect."

"Maybe," I said. But I'd learned to trust Samson's instincts. If something was bothering him, there was usually a good reason.

My phone buzzed. It was Chief Johnston.

"Chief," I said.

"Kate, I need an update on the Holloway situation. The mayor's office is already asking questions."

"It's early yet, Chief. We're still processing the scene—"

"Well, process it faster. Holloway was a prominent member of the medical community. He served on two hospital boards. More than that, he donated to political campaigns. The media's going to be all over this."

"Understood, Chief," I said, inwardly sighing.

"And Kate? I want this wrapped up quickly and quietly. We don't need a panic about some psychopath targeting doctors."

"I'll do my best, Chief."

He hung up, and I looked around the office one more time. A prominent psychiatrist, murdered in his locked office, with no apparent way for the killer to get in or out. It was the kind of case that could make or break a detective's career.

"Mike," I said, "Samson's onto something. I'm sure of it. I want you to go over this room with a fine-tooth comb. Fingerprints, DNA, carpet fibers, everything. If there's anything in here, I want it found."

"You got it, Cap," he replied.

I turned to Corbin. "I want to talk to the secretary, then the security guard, then anyone else who might have seen Holloway yesterday. And get me a list of his recent patients, especially anyone who might have had a grudge."

"That could be a long list," Corbin said. "Psychiatrists deal with a lot of troubled people."

"Then we'd better get started, hadn't we?" I said.

As I headed for the door, Samson fell into step beside me, but he kept looking back over his shoulder at the office, his ears still perked forward.

"What is it, boy?" I asked again.

But if Samson knew something I didn't, he wasn't talking. At least, not yet.

The hallway was quiet except for the sound of Willis's camera and the murmur of voices from the other offices. Through the windows at the end of the hall, I could see news vans starting to gather in the parking lot.

Chief Johnston was right about one thing: this case was going to attract attention. A locked room murder involving a prominent doctor was exactly the kind of story the media loved to sink their teeth into.

But as I stood there looking out at the gathering crowd of reporters, I had one of those moments, a feeling that this was just the beginning. Something about the whole setup felt wrong, like a stage play where the actors were hitting their marks, but the dialogue didn't quite ring true.

Samson whined again, and I reached down to scratch his ears.

"I know," I said quietly. "I don't like it either."

Whatever had happened in Dr. Holloway's office last night, I had the distinct feeling that we were dealing with someone who was very smart, very careful, and very dangerous. The kind of killer who planned ahead, who thought through every detail, who left nothing to chance. The kind of killer who might not be finished.

I took out my phone and called Sergeant Tracy Ramirez.

"Tracy, it's Kate. How's the secretary holding up?"

"She's pretty shaken up, but cooperative. Why?"

"I'm coming down to talk to her. And Tracy? Make sure she doesn't go anywhere alone until we figure out what we're dealing with."

"You think she's in danger?"

I looked back at the crime scene tape blocking Holloway's office door.

"I think everyone who knew Doctor Holloway might

be in danger," I said. "At least until we catch whoever did this."

Because one thing I'd learned in my twenty-four years as a cop was that killers who were smart enough to commit the perfect crime were usually smart enough to know that perfect crimes required eliminating loose ends.

And right now, I had no idea how many loose ends we were dealing with.

First Impressions

Tuesday, Oct 2, Late morning

LINDA MATTHEWS WAS A MESS, AS YOU'D EXPECT OF someone who'd just found her boss dead in his office on what should have been a routine Tuesday morning. She sat in the building's small conference room, clutching a cup of coffee that had probably gone cold an hour earlier, her hands shaking just enough to make the liquid tremble.

Tracy Ramirez sat across from her, notebook open, pen poised. Tracy had that gift that good detectives develop over time: the ability to look sympathetic while missing absolutely nothing. As the mother of two teenage girls, she'd seen her share of emotional melt-downs and knew how to handle them.

"Mrs. Matthews," I said as I entered the room,

Samson padding quietly beside me. "I'm Captain Gazzara. I know this has been a difficult morning for you."

Linda Matthews looked up at me with red-rimmed eyes. She was probably in her fifties, well-dressed in the understated way of professional assistants everywhere. A woman who kept her boss's life organized and probably knew where all the bodies were buried. Figuratively speaking, of course.

"I just can't believe this," she said, her voice barely above a whisper. "Doctor Holloway was such a good man. Who would want to hurt him?"

"That's what we're here to find out," I said, settling into a chair across from her. Samson lay down beside me, staring up at the woman. "I understand you've been Doctor Holloway's secretary for what… eight years?"

"Yes, eight years," she said. "I started working for him right after his divorce. He needed someone to help reorganize his practice, get things back on track. You know?"

"Tell me about yesterday," I said. "Was there anything unusual about Doctor Holloway's behavior? Did he seem worried about anything?"

Matthews shook her head. "No, nothing like that. It was a normal day. He had appointments until four o'clock, then he stayed late to catch up on paperwork. He often did that on Mondays."

"You mentioned to Sergeant Russell that Doctor Holloway had been receiving threatening letters," I said. "Can you tell me more about those?"

Her hands tightened around the coffee cup. "They started coming about three weeks ago. Maybe four. Just regular mail, no return address. Doctor Holloway would read them and then throw them away."

"Did you ever see what they said?"

"No, he was very private about them. But after the first one, he seemed... unsettled. He asked me to be more careful about screening his mail."

"How many letters were there?"

"Maybe five... No, six. They came sporadically, not on any particular schedule."

I made a note to have Corbin check with the postal service. Even if the letters were gone, there might be a trail.

"Did Doctor Holloway ever mention any patients who might have been particularly troubled or angry with him?"

Matthews hesitated. "Well, you have to understand, psychiatry isn't like other medical practices. Patients sometimes develop complicated feelings about their doctors. Doctor Holloway was very good at maintaining professional boundaries, but occasionally someone would become... fixated."

"Anyone in particular?" I asked.

"Yes! There was a woman a few months ago," she replied. "Mrs. Tillman. Margaret Tillman. She blamed Doctor Holloway for her daughter's suicide. She called here several times, very upset, furious."

Tracy looked up from her notes. "Did she ever threaten Doctor Holloway directly?"

"Not exactly, but she said things like 'he'd pay for what he did' and 'she'd make sure everyone knew what kind of doctor he really was.' That sort of thing."

I made another note. Margaret Tillman would be getting a visit.

"What about Doctor Holloway's family?" I asked. "His son Vincent?"

Matthews's expression softened slightly. "Vincent's had some problems over the years. Drugs, mostly. Doctor Holloway tried to help him, paid for several treatment programs, but..." She shrugged helplessly.

"Were father and son on good terms?" I asked.

"It was complicated," she replied. "Doctor Holloway loved his son, but he'd also learned to maintain some distance. Vincent could be... unpredictable when he was using."

"When was the last time Vincent visited the office?"

"Maybe six months ago. He came by asking for money. Doctor Holloway gave him some cash and told him not to come back unless he was serious about getting clean."

I could hear the pain in her voice. Working for someone for eight years, you became invested in their personal life, whether or not you wanted to.

"What about Doctor Holloway's business partner?" I asked. "Doctor Walton, isn't it?"

"Doctor Sarah Walton, yes. They've been partners for about three years. She has her own patient load, but they share the practice overhead and some of the administrative costs."

"Did they get along?" I asked.

Matthews hesitated again, the way people do when they're trying to decide how much truth to tell.

"They got along fine professionally," she said finally. "But there were some disagreements recently about the direction of the practice."

"What kind of disagreements?"

"Doctor Walton wanted to expand, bring in more associates, maybe open a second location. Doctor Holloway preferred to keep things smaller, more personal. He said psychiatry wasn't a business you could just scale up like selling widgets."

That was interesting. Business disagreements had a way of turning personal, especially when money was involved.

"Was Doctor Walton here yesterday?" I asked.

"She left around five-thirty. She usually leaves earlier than Doctor Holloway."

My phone buzzed. It was Mike Willis.

"Excuse me," I said, stepping out into the hallway.

"Kate, I think I've found what was bothering Samson," Willis said without preamble.

"Tell me about it," I said.

"I'm not sure what it is," he replied, "but it's interesting. Can you come back up to the office?"

"On my way," I said.

I returned to the conference room. "Mrs. Matthews, thank you for your time. We may have more questions later."

"Of course," she replied. "I just want to help catch whoever did this."

"One more thing before we go," I said. "I want you to be extra careful over the next few days. Don't go anywhere alone if you can help it, and if you notice

anyone following you or anything unusual, call us immediately."

Her face went pale. "You think I might be in
danger?"

"No, not really, but I think it's better to be safe than
sorry," I replied, smiling.

Tracy walked her out while I headed back
upstairs. Willis was waiting for me in Holloway's office,
holding what looked like a small evidence bag.

"What do you have?" I asked.

"Trace amounts of some kind of powder on the carpet
near the desk. Almost invisible, but it showed up under
the UV light, and earlier I saw Samson seeming to be
interested in that particular area."

"And you don't have any idea what it is?" I asked.

He shook his head. "I won't know for sure until I get
it to the lab, but it looks like it might be pharmaceutical. Maybe some kind of sedative or anesthetic."

That was interesting. "Really?" I said.

"I dunno," he said, holding the bag up to the light and
staring at it. "Maybe our killer drugged Holloway before
stabbing him. That would explain why there's no sign of
a struggle."

I looked around the office again. If Holloway had
been drugged, it made sense.

"Anything else?" I asked, preparing to leave.

"Yeah, actually," he replied. "I found something weird
in the desk drawer."

Willis led me to Holloway's desk and pointed to the
bottom drawer, which was open and empty except for a
single manila folder.

"That folder wasn't there when we first processed the scene," he said. "I'm sure of it. The drawer was empty."

"You're saying someone put it there while we're here?" I asked, stunned by the idea.

"That's what it looks like. And here's the really strange part; there are no fingerprints on it. None. Like it was wiped clean."

"Did you look inside it?" I asked.

Willis nodded, picked up the folder, and opened it. Inside were several photocopied pages that looked like medical records, but they were from the 1990s.

"From patient files," Willis said. "At least, that's what it looks like. From some kind of psychiatric treatment program. All the patients were teenagers."

I scanned the pages quickly. The records were fragmented, mostly intake forms and a few treatment notes, but what I could read was disturbing. Experimental drug treatments, isolation therapy, procedures that sounded more like torture than medicine.

"Geez" I muttered.

"Yeah. And look at this." He pointed to a name at the bottom of one of the treatment notes: Dr. Marcus Holloway, Supervising Physician.

"So Holloway was involved in this program, whatever it was," I said.

"Looks like it. But here's the question; who put this folder here, and why?"

I thought about that. Someone had entered a secured crime scene and planted evidence that implicated the victim in what looked like medical abuse. *Someone's sending us a message!* I thought.

"Did the cameras pick up anyone coming back into the building?"

"I'll check," Willis said, "but I doubt it. Whoever did this knows how to avoid detection."

My phone rang. It was Corbin. "Kate, we've got a problem."

Geez, I thought. What next? "What kind of problem?" I asked.

"The security footage from last night. There's a gap. I mean, someone erased about twenty minutes of footage from between eight-thirty and eight-fifty PM. Very professional job. You wouldn't notice it unless you were looking for it."

Of course there was. But we already knew that. I sighed, then said, "Yes, I know, Corbin. Any idea how they did it?"

"The building security system is networked," he replied. "Someone with the right skills could have hacked in remotely and deleted the specific timeframe."

"Or someone with physical access to the security office," I said.

"That too," he replied.

"Okay," I said. "I'm with Mike. We'll talk about it later." And I hung up, looked at Willis and said, "Missing security footage, planted evidence, a keycard cloning operation with no apparent way to trace who did it. We're dealing with someone who's very smart and very prepared."

"Or very lucky," he muttered.

"I don't believe in luck," I said. "Not when it comes to murder. Someone planned this very carefully."

My phone buzzed again. This time it was Tony Cooper, the big rookie detective who usually worked with Tracy.

"Captain, I'm downstairs with the security guard. You might want to hear what he has to say."

"On my way," I said.

I found Cooper in the lobby with a middle-aged man wearing a security uniform, and who looked like he'd rather be anywhere else.

"This is Frank Patterson," Cooper said. "He was on duty last night."

Patterson nodded nervously. "I already told the other detective everything I know."

"I need you to tell me," I said without rancor.

"Well, I do my rounds every two hours," he began. "Last time I saw Doctor Holloway was around six-fifteen when I checked the third floor. He was still in his office, working at his desk. I said goodnight. He waved back. Normal stuff."

"What about your next round?"

"That would have been around eight-fifteen. I checked the floor, but I don't have keys to the individual offices. I could see the light was still on under Doctor Holloway's door, so I figured he was still working."

"You didn't try to talk to him?" I asked.

Patterson shook his head. "No, ma'am. I had no reason to. Doctors work late all the time."

"What about the round after that?" I asked.

"Ten-fifteen," he said. "Same thing. I could see his light on under the door, but I didn't disturb him."

"And you didn't find it unusual that he was working so late?" I asked.

"No, ma'am," he replied.

I nodded. "Did you notice anything unusual? Any unusual sounds, any other people in the building?"

"See, that's the thing," Patterson said, glancing nervously at Cooper. "I didn't want to mention it before because it sounds crazy, but around eight-forty, I thought I heard voices coming from the third floor."

"Voices?"

"Yeah, like two people talking, loud, like. I couldn't make out words, but his office is at the top of the stairs and his door must have been open, so I could hear them talking. It sounded like he was having a conversation with someone."

"But Doctor Holloway was alone," I said.

"I thought he was. But I was at my desk down in the lobby, just to the left of the stairs, so I couldn't be sure."

I looked at Cooper. *Eight-forty was right in the middle of the missing security footage,* I thought. *Hmmm!*

"Did you investigate?" I asked.

Patterson looked embarrassed. "I... started to, but then everything went quiet. So I figured maybe the doctor was on a phone call or something. People talk louder on phones sometimes, don't they?"

Or maybe our killer was having a conversation with Holloway before murdering him, I thought.

"Did you see anyone enter or leave the building during your shift?" I asked. "Anyone at all?

"No, ma'am. The building was locked down tight. The

only way in or out is through the main entrance, and I was at the security desk all night."

Which brought us back to the original problem; how did the killer get Holloway's keycard to clone it, and how did they avoid the security cameras, and Patterson?

I thanked Patterson and walked back to the elevator with Cooper.

"What do you think?" Cooper asked as we waited for the elevator.

"I think we have a very smart killer who wants us to know how smart they are," I said. "They planted evidence in Holloway's office, somehow, while we were still processing it, the missing security footage, the keycard cloning, if that's what it was." I shook my head. "It's all very theatrical. It had to have been cloned," I muttered, more to myself than Cooper. "It had to be!"

"It's like they're trying to send a message?" Cooper said, his hands stuffed deep into his pants pockets.

"Exactly," I replied. "The question is, what message, and to whom?"

The elevator doors opened, and we rode up to the third floor in silence. When we got back to Holloway's office, I found Willis packing up his equipment.

"You all done?" I asked.

"No, but I have places to be," he replied. "I'm leaving Jennifer. She can handle what's left. In the meantime, I'll process the trace evidence back at the lab and let you know what I find."

"When?" I asked.

"Give me until tomorrow afternoon. Maybe sooner if all goes well."

As Willis headed out with his equipment, I stood in the doorway of Holloway's office and tried to put myself in the killer's shoes. You want to murder a prominent psychiatrist in a way that will attract maximum attention. You plan it carefully, clone his keycard, disable the security cameras at just the right time, get into his office and kill your victim with a medical instrument, then leave while staying hidden during the camera blackout. It was… mystifying.

But you also want to leave a message, so you plant evidence that implicates the victim in some kind of medical abuse from the 1990s. Why the 1990s? And why these particular patient files? And why the hell do it while we're still here? That's as risky as hell!

I took out my phone and called Jack North.

"Jack, I need you and Hawk to research a couple of things for me. How would someone clone a key card. Second, we found documents referencing something called the 'Greenbriar Behavioral Health Center Experimental Treatment Program.' It appears to have run in the 1990s involving experimental treatments on teenage patients. I need everything you can find: patient records, staff lists, funding sources, why it was shut down. Holloway's name appears on several documents as a supervising physician. This might be the key to understanding why someone wanted him dead."

"The first is easy," he said, "All you need is an RFID reader. You get close enough to the subject—in an elevator, for instance—and voila, the reader reads, and you have your info. You then transfer the info to a blank card."

I shook my head in frustration. I already knew that. It's done all the time for credit card fraud; the fraud squad is all over it. I just didn't put the two together: credit card/key card. *Stupid of me.*

"As to number two," Jack said. "I'll start digging right away. Those old medical records might be digitized by now or at least referenced in databases."

"Thanks, Jack. And be discreet about it - if this program was controversial, there might be people who don't want us poking around in it."

"I'll get right on it, Cap."

As I hung up, Samson appeared at my side, still alert, still sensing something I couldn't quite grasp.

"What is it, boy?" I asked, crouching down to his level.

He looked up at me with those intelligent brown eyes, then turned to stare down the hallway toward the elevator, almost like he was waiting for someone.

Or something.

What's next? I thought for a moment, then said to myself, "Corbin's with Doctor Walton. Come on, Sammy. Let's go see the good doctor." And together, we walked to the elevators.

3

The Doctor's Secrets

DR. SARAH WALTON'S OFFICE ON THE SECOND FLOOR WAS a study in contrasts to her dead partner's. Where Holloway's space had been warm and welcoming, Walton's was all sharp angles and modern furniture. Glass and chrome instead of leather and wood. The kind of office that said, "I'm very busy and very important" rather than "tell me about your problems."

Walton herself matched her office—mid-forties, perfectly groomed, tastefully coifed red hair that I knew must have come out of a bottle, and she was wearing a charcoal gray suit that probably cost more than most people made in a month. She sat behind her desk as if she was conducting a board meeting rather than being inter-viewed about her business partner's murder.

Her door was open, and I could see Corbin seated across from her, notebook balanced on his knee, pen poised. I stepped inside, Samson at my heels, and took the chair beside him, studying Walton's body language. She was nervous—the way her fingers drummed silently on the desk, the slight tension around her eyes—but trying very hard not to show it.

"Doctor Walton," I said, "I'm Captain Gazzara. Thank you for taking the time to speak with us. I know this must be difficult for you."

"Of course," she replied, her voice carefully controlled. "But I'll do anything I can to help find Marcus's killer."

"How long have you and Doctor Holloway been partners?" I asked.

"Three years this November. We met at a psychiatric conference in Atlanta and discovered we had similar approaches to treatment. When he mentioned he was looking for a partner to help expand his practice, it seemed like a natural fit."

"Similar approaches," Corbin repeated, making a note. "Can you elaborate on that?"

Walton hesitated, just for a fraction of a second. "We both believed in evidence-based treatment modalities. Cognitive-behavioral therapy, medication management when appropriate, that sort of thing."

It sounded like a textbook answer. Too polished, too rehearsed.

"I understand there were some recent disagreements about the direction of the practice," I said.

Her fingers stopped drumming. "I wouldn't call them disagreements," she said, tossing her head. "We had different visions for growth, that's all."

"What kind of different visions?" Corbin asked.

"I felt we could serve more patients if we expanded our staff and facilities. Marcus preferred to keep things smaller. He was more… traditional in his approach."

"Traditional how?" I asked.

Another hesitation. "He spent a lot of time with each patient. Sometimes more time than was financially practical. I thought we could be more efficient."

"Efficiency in mental health care," I said. "That's an interesting concept."

Walton's jaw tightened slightly. "Captain, I don't think you understand the economics of running a psychiatric practice. Insurance reimbursements are declining; administrative costs are rising. If you don't adapt, you go out of business."

"Was the practice in financial trouble?"

"Not trouble, exactly," she replied. "But we could have been doing better."

Corbin looked up from his notes. "'Doing better'?" he asked, frowning.

"Our overhead was higher than it needed to be. Marcus insisted on maintaining patient loads that weren't sustainable from a business perspective."

"Meaning?" Corbin asked.

"Meaning he would spend an hour with a patient when thirty minutes would have been sufficient," she replied. "He would continue treating patients who couldn't pay their full fees. That sort of thing."

I was starting to get a picture of the dynamic between the two partners. Walton was focused on the bottom line, Holloway on patient care. It was a classic conflict in modern medicine.

"Did these philosophical differences ever become heated?" I asked.

"We were both professionals, Captain," she replied, then sighed. "We could disagree without it becoming personal."

But her tone suggested otherwise.

"When was the last time you saw Doctor Holloway?" I asked.

"Yesterday evening, around five-thirty. I was leaving for the day and stopped by his office to discuss a patient case."

"How did he seem?" I asked.

She shrugged. "Normal, I suppose. Perhaps a bit preoccupied, but that wasn't unusual for Marcus."

"Preoccupied with what?" I asked.

"I don't know. He'd been distracted for the past few weeks. I assumed it was a personal issue."

"What kind of personal issue?" Corbin asked.

Walton shrugged again. "His son Vincent has been having problems again. Drug issues. Marcus was always worried about him."

"Did Doctor Holloway mention anything about threatening letters he'd been receiving?"

For the first time, Walton looked genuinely surprised. "Threatening letters?" She furrowed her brow. "No, he never mentioned anything like that."

Either she was a very good actress, or Holloway hadn't told his business partner about the threats. Given the tension between them, that wasn't necessarily surprising.

"We understand that psychiatric practices sometimes

deal with difficult patients, Doctor Walton. Have you had any patients who became fixated on either you or Doctor Holloway?"

"Occasionally. It's an occupational hazard. Most of the time it's harmless patients who call too frequently or want to extend sessions. We have protocols for handling those situations."

"Any patients who became threatening?" I asked, watching her eyes.

Walton considered this for a moment, then said, "There was a woman a few months ago who blamed Marcus for her daughter's suicide. She made some angry phone calls, but I wouldn't call them threatening exactly."

"Margaret Tillman?" I asked.

"Yes, that's her," she replied. "She was... grief stricken. But people say things they don't mean when they're in that much pain."

"What was Doctor Holloway's relationship with the daughter?"

"He'd treated her... I don't know how many years ago. It was a long time, when she was a teenager. The girl had severe depression and some behavioral issues. Marcus did everything he could, but sometimes..." Walton spread her hands helplessly. "Sometimes you can't save them all."

"How did Doctor Holloway handle Mrs. Tillman's accusations?" Corbin asked.

"He was upset, naturally. He'd genuinely cared about the girl. But he understood that grief can make people look for someone to blame."

I made a mental note to have Tracy track down the daughter's medical records.

"Doctor Walton, are you familiar with any experimental psychiatric treatments that Doctor Holloway might have been involved with in the past?" I asked.

Corbin looked sideways at me.

She frowned. "Experimental treatments? What kind of experimental treatments?"

"We're not sure yet. Possibly involving teenage patients in the 1990s."

Walton shook her head. "I wouldn't know anything about that. Marcus and I didn't discuss our past cases very often. We were focused on current patients and the business of running the practice."

But something flickered in her eyes when I mentioned the 1990s. Something that looked like recognition, quickly suppressed.

"Have you heard of..." I consulted my notes, "the Greenbriar Behavioral Health Center Experimental Treatment Program?" I asked.

Again, there was that flicker of her eyes. She slowly shook her head, then said, "Nooo, should I have?"

I ignored the question, saying, "Is there anything else you can tell us about Doctor Holloway's state of mind recently? Anything that might help us understand why someone would want to kill him?"

Walton was quiet for a long moment, and I could see she was weighing her words carefully.

"Marcus was a good man," she said finally. "He genuinely cared about his patients, sometimes to his own detriment. But he was also very private about certain aspects of his past. There were things he didn't like to discuss."

"What kinds of things?" Corbin pressed her.

"His early career, mostly. Before he went into private practice. He worked at various hospitals and treatment facilities, but he didn't like to talk about those experiences."

"Why not?" Corbin asked.

"I got the impression that he'd seen things he wasn't proud of. The mental health field was different twenty, thirty years ago. Less regulated, more experimental. I think Marcus had some regrets about his early work."

Now we're getting somewhere, I thought.

"Did he ever mention specific facilities or colleagues from that time?" I asked.

"Not really. Although..." Walton paused, as if deciding whether to continue. "A few weeks ago, he got a phone call that seemed to upset him quite a bit. After he hung up, he said something about 'the past coming back to haunt him.'"

"Did he say who the call was from?" I asked.

"No, but I got the impression it was someone from his past. Maybe a former colleague or patient."

"Did he seem frightened?" Corbin asked.

"More sad than frightened, I think," she replied. "As if he was remembering something painful."

My phone buzzed. I looked at the screen. It was Mike Willis.

"Excuse me," I said, "I have to take this." And I rose to my feet and stepped out into the hallway.

"Mike," I said.

"Kate, I've got preliminary results on that powder I found in Holloway's office."

"That was quick," I said. "What is it?"

"The lab tech—he's a buddy of mine—says he thinks it might be Midazolam, a fast-acting sedative, often used in medical procedures. The interesting thing is, it's not the kind of drug you'd typically find in a psychiatrist's office."

"Meaning?" I said, frowning.

"Meaning our killer must have brought it with them. And they knew exactly what they were doing—midazolam would have rendered Holloway unconscious in minutes."

"So, the killer drugs him, then stabs him while he's out?"

"That's what it looks like. Very clean, very professional."

"Any idea how the drug was administered?"

"The initial toxicology screen shows traces in the coffee cup on Holloway's desk. I'm thinking the killer probably brought Holloway coffee with the drug dissolved in it. There was only one cup, so the killer must have taken theirs away with them."

"Which meant the killer was in the office long enough for Holloway to drink it," I said, thoughtfully, "which also means they probably talked together, maybe even argued, which is what Patterson, the guard, must have heard."

Willis listened but said nothing.

"Anything else, Mike?"

"Yeah, I ran a scan for fingerprints on the folder. There were none. The folder itself was clean, but I did find one partial print on one of the photocopied pages inside."

"Whose are they?" I asked.

"Geez, Kate... I mean Captain. Give me a break. I'm doing the best I can for you. Don's still running it through the system. I'll let you know as soon as I get a match."

"Thanks, Mike," I said. "Keep me posted." And I hung up and returned to Walton's office.

"Doctor Walton, does the name midazolam mean anything to you?" I said as I sat down.

She blinked. "It's a sedative. Used in hospitals, sometimes in outpatient procedures. Why?"

"Would Doctor Holloway have had any reason to have that drug in his office?"

"No, absolutely not. Psychiatrists rarely use sedatives like that. We're not anesthesiologists."

"So, who would have access to midazolam?" I asked.

"Hospital staff," she replied, "anesthesiologists, some emergency medical personnel. It's a controlled substance, so access is limited."

So our killer either works in a medical facility or has connections to someone who does, I thought.

"Doctor Walton, I need you to think carefully," I said. "Is there anyone from Doctor Holloway's past who might have both a grudge against him and access to this kind of drug?"

She was quiet for a long moment, clearly thinking.

"You know... I just thought of something," she said slowly. "A few months ago, Marcus got very upset after running into someone at a medical conference. He wouldn't tell me who it was, but he was shaken for days afterward."

"Upset?" Corbin asked. "What d'you mean? How was he upset?"

"He said he thought he'd seen a ghost. Like he'd seen someone from his past who he'd never expected to see again."

"Did he give you any details?" Corbin pressed her.

"No, but he did tell me he was having trouble sleeping. "

Interesting, I thought. *Someone from Holloway's past spooked him badly enough to disrupt his sleep.*

"When was this conference?" I asked.

"June, I think. It was the Southern Psychiatric Association meeting in Nashville."

I made a note to get the conference attendance records.

"Is there anything else you think we should know?" I asked. "Anything, anything at all that might help us find Doctor Holloway's killer?"

She hesitated again, and I could see her struggling with something.

"Yes," she said finally. "About three weeks ago, Marcus asked me about the statute of limitations on medical malpractice cases."

At that, I frowned. "Did he say why?" I asked.

"No, but he seemed worried about something. And I wondered if he thought someone might be planning to sue him for something that happened in the past."

"Did you get the impression it was related to the threatening letters?" Corbin asked.

"I didn't know about any threatening letters until you just told me," she replied. "But yes, the timing seems about right."

"Anything else you can think of?" I asked.

She shook her head, pursed her lips, then said, "No. I think that's it."

I nodded, told her thank you, handed her my card and asked her to call me if she remembered anything else. She said she would.

As Corbin, Sammy, and I left Walton's office, I was almost certain she was holding something back. Maybe not about the murder itself, but about the financial state of the practice or her relationship with Holloway.

"What did you think?" I asked Corbin as we walked to the elevator.

"She's nervous about something," he said. "Her story's consistent, but she's definitely not telling us everything."

"Could be she's just worried about what happens to the practice now that her partner's dead," I said.

"Could be," he said, thoughtfully. "Or it could be she's worried about something else entirely."

We were almost at the elevators when my phone rang. It was Sergeant Hawkins, Hawk.

"Hawk," I said. "What d'you need?"

"Need?" he asked. "Nothing. I just... Kate, I've been doing some digging into that psychiatric program you mentioned. When d'you plan on getting back here?"

"Later," I replied. "So what did you find?"

"It's not pretty," he said. "And it's complicated. I'll fill you in when you get back here."

"Come on, Hawk," I said. "How bad is it?"

"Bad enough that someone might kill to keep it quiet. I'll see you later." And he hung up.

As the elevator doors closed, I found myself thinking about Dr. Walton's carefully controlled answers and the fear I'd glimpsed behind her professional facade. And I just knew there was definitely something odd going on there, and I had a feeling we were just beginning to scratch the surface of whatever had gotten Marcus Holloway killed.

4

Family Dysfunction

Early Afternoon

THE HOLLOWAY FAMILY HOME WAS LOCATED ON A QUIET street in North Chattanooga, the kind of neighborhood where people mowed their lawns on Saturday mornings and waved to their neighbors. It was a two-story colonial with white columns and black shutters, probably built in the 1960s when the area was considered the height of suburban sophistication. Now it just looked tired.

Amanda Holloway met us at the front door and, having seen her photo in Holloway's office, I could see immediately where Vincent had gotten his looks. She was an attractive woman in her late fifties, with the same dark hair and angular features as her son, but there was a hardness around her eyes that spoke of years of disappointment and anger.

"Captain Gazzara?" she said, extending a manicured hand. "Thank you for coming. This is all so... surreal."

"I'm sorry for your loss, Mrs. Holloway," I said. "I know this is a difficult time, but we need to ask you some questions about your ex-husband."

"Of course. Please, come in."

She led us into a living room that looked like it had been professionally decorated sometime in the past decade: all neutral colors and careful arrangements.

Vincent Holloway was slumped in an armchair near the window, staring out at the street. He looked like he'd been awake for days. Twenty-eight years old but carrying himself like a much older man, with the particular brand of exhaustion that comes from years of fighting a losing battle with addiction.

When we entered the room, he looked up with blood-shot eyes that reminded me painfully of his father's crime scene photos.

"Vincent," Amanda said, "these are the detectives investigating your father's death."

He nodded but didn't get up. "I already told the other cops everything I know. Which isn't much."

"Please," Amanda said, gesturing to the couch, "sit down."

So I did. I settled onto the couch across from him, with Corbin taking the chair beside me. Samson lay down at my feet, but I noticed his ears were pricked and his eyes focused on Vincent. Not in an aggressive way, but like he was picking up on something.

"When was the last time you saw your father, Mr. Holloway?" I asked.

"Maybe six months ago. I came by his office asking for money." He said it matter-of-factly, without shame or defensiveness. "He gave me some cash and told me not to come back unless I was serious about getting clean."

"How did that make you feel?" Corbin asked.

Vincent shrugged. "Like shit, if you really want to know. But he was right. I wasn't serious about getting clean. Not then."

"What about now?" Corbin asked.

"My father's dead," he replied, "so it doesn't matter much, does it?"

There was pain in his voice, under the anger and the exhaustion. The kind of pain that comes from knowing you've disappointed someone you love and now it's too late to make it right.

"Can you tell us where you were Monday night between eight and ten PM?" Corbin asked.

"I was here. With mom." He nodded toward his mother. "We were watching TV. Some cop show, which seems pretty ironic now."

I looked at Amanda. "And you can confirm that?"

"Yes," she said immediately. "Vincent's been staying here for the past two weeks. He's trying to get clean again, and I thought... well, I thought it might help if he had some stability."

"How was he getting along with his father recently?" I asked, noting the obviously warning look he was giving her.

Amanda's expression tightened. "Marcus hadn't seen him in months," she replied. Again, I noted, out of my peripheral vision, the look eased to one of what I assumed was relief.

"Marcus didn't approve of my helping Vincent," she continued. "He thought I was enabling him."

"Were you?" Corbin asked.

"Was I trying to help my son?" she asked angrily. "Yes, of course I was. Marcus gave up on him years ago."

"That's not true," Vincent said quietly. "Dad never gave up. He just... he couldn't watch me destroy myself anymore."

The family dynamics were becoming clearer. A father torn between love and tough love, a mother unwilling to let go, and a son caught in the middle of his own self-destruction.

"How about you, Mrs. Holloway?" I said. "What was your relationship with your ex-husband like?"

Her laugh was bitter. "What relationship? We've been divorced for five years. The only time we talked was when it involved Vincent."

"And the divorce was contentious?" I asked.

"Not really. Marcus left me for his work," she replied. "Not another woman... his work. He was obsessed with his patients, with being the perfect doctor. Our marriage was something that got in the way."

"Were there any financial disputes?" I asked.

"The settlement was fair. Marcus wasn't vindictive, just... absent," she replied. "Even during the divorce proceedings, he seemed more concerned with his patients than with our family."

I was getting a picture of Marcus Holloway as a man who cared deeply about helping people but struggled with personal relationships. It was a common syndrome among caregivers; they became so focused on fixing everyone else they neglected their own family.

"Did Doctor Holloway seem worried about anything recently?" Corbin asked. "Any threats or unusual behavior?"

Amanda shook her head. "I wouldn't know. As I said, we didn't talk unless it was about Vincent."

"What about you, Vincent?" Corbin asked. "Did your father mention anything about threatening letters or problems at work?"

Vincent was quiet for a long moment, staring out the window again.

Finally, he turned his head to look at Corbin and said, "A couple weeks ago, when I called him for money. He sounded... different. Distracted. Like he was worried about something."

"Did he say what?"

"Not exactly. But he said something about 'old mistakes coming back to haunt him.' I thought he was talking about me, about how he'd screwed up as a father."

"But now you don't think so?" Corbin said.

"I don't know. Maybe it was something else..." he shook his head and shrugged.

It was then that my phone buzzed. I glanced at the screen. It wasTracy.

"Excuse me. D'you mind if I take this?" I said. No one did, so I rose to my feet and stepped out into the hallway.

"I'm conducting an interview, Tracy—"

"Yeah, I'm sorry, but I thought you should know. Kate, I've been digging into Margaret Tillman's background. Her daughter, Jessica, committed suicide three years ago. She was thirty-five. She'd been in and out of psychiatric treatment since she was fifteen. Holloway was her primary psychiatrist for about two years."

I was silent for a moment, digesting the news. Then I said, "What were the circumstances of the suicide?"

"She overdosed on prescription medications, but here's the interesting part: Margaret Tillman tried to sue Holloway for malpractice, claiming he overprescribed the drugs that Jessica used to kill herself."

"Really? How did that go?" I asked.

"The case was dismissed. Insufficient evidence. But Tillman's been bitter about it ever since. I talked to some of Jessica's friends, and they said Margaret blamed Holloway for her daughter's death."

"Where's Tillman now?" I asked.

"Well, she's not at home, and her neighbors say they haven't seen her since yesterday morning."

.A grief-stricken mother with a grudge against our victim, and now she was missing.

"Put out a BOLO," I said. "I want her found before she does something stupid."

"Already done," Tracy replied.

"Good," I said. "Look, I have to get back to my interview with Holloway's wife. I'll talk to you later, when I get back to the office." And then I hung up, cutting her off.

I returned to the living room, where Amanda was showing Corbin what looked like family photographs.

"These were taken last Christmas," she was saying. "It was the first time in years that Marcus actually came for dinner. Vincent was clean then, for about three months."

The photo showed the three of them around a Christmas tree, trying to look like a normal family. But even in the picture, I could see the tension: the forced smiles, the careful distance between Marcus and Amanda, the hollow look in Vincent's eyes.

"It looks like you were trying to rebuild your relationship," I said.

"We were," Amanda said. "For Vincent's sake. We thought if we could at least be civil to each other, it might help him."

"And did it?" I asked.

Vincent snorted. "I was high during that dinner. Popped a couple pills before Dad arrived so I could make it through without losing my shit."

Amanda looked stricken. "You never told me that."

"There's a lot I never told you, Mom."

The pain in the room was palpable. A family that had been destroyed by addiction, divorce, and the kind of good intentions that somehow made everything worse.

"Vincent," I said, "I need to ask you about your drug use. What's your drug of choice?"

"Oxy, mostly. Sometimes heroin when I can't afford pills."

"Do you know anyone who deals in medical drugs? Sedatives, anesthetics, that sort of thing?"

He shook his head. "Street dealers don't usually have that kind of stuff. Why?"

"I'm just trying to understand all the angles." I said.

Samson suddenly lifted his head, ears perked, looking

toward the front of the house. A moment later, I heard a car door slam.

"Are you expecting someone?" I asked Amanda.

"No, I—"

The doorbell rang. Amanda went to answer it, and I heard voices in the hallway, "You'd better come in," I heard her say and she returned a moment later followed by a middle-aged man in an expensive suit.

"This man says he's Robert Tillman," she said. "Margaret Tillman's brother in law."

What the hell? I thought, as I stood up.

Robert Tillman looked like he'd been running on adrenaline and coffee for days. His tie was loose, his hair disheveled, and there was a desperate look in his eyes that immediately put me on alert.

"Are you the police?" he asked.

"Yes, I'm Captain Gazzara, Chattanooga PD," I replied, frowning. "What are you doing here? More to the point, how did you find me?"

"I need to talk to someone about my sister in law, so I called the police department and talked to a Sergeant Ramirez. She told me you were here. She didn't want to, but I insisted."

I looked at Amanda. She was standing behind him, her hands clasped together in front of her. She nodded, and I took a deep breath and looked again at Tillman.

"This is Sergeant Russell," I said. "Go on, Mr. Tillman."

"I need to talk to you about Margaret," he said. "She's missing, and I think she might be planning to do something terrible."

"What makes you say that?" I asked.

"She called me this morning, completely hysterical. She said she was going to 'make them all pay' for what happened to Jessica. I tried to calm her down, but she hung up on me."

"Them?" Corbin asked. "Who is 'them'?"

"I don't know. Margaret's been obsessed with conspiracy theories since Jessica died. She thinks there was some kind of cover-up, that Doctor Holloway was part of a larger group that was running experiments on troubled kids."

Now here was something. "Experiments?" I asked, quietly.

"I don't know the details," he said. "Margaret found some old medical records that she claimed proved Jessica was part of some unauthorized treatment program when she was sixteen. She tried to use them in a malpractice suit, but the lawyers said they were irrelevant."

"Do you know how she got hold of the records?" Corbin asked, frowning.

"Margaret said she got them from someone who used to work at the hospital where Jessica was treated. Some kind of whistleblower who was trying to expose what happened."

"D'you know the name of this whistleblower?" Corbin asked.

"I don't remember," he replied. "It was three years ago, and Margaret was... well, she wasn't thinking clearly. Losing her husband five years ago, then Jessica... Grief is a terrible thing, Sergeant."

"Do you have any idea where Margaret might have gone?" I asked.

"She mentioned something about 'going to the source.' I thought she meant Doctor Holloway, but if he's already dead..." He trailed off, looking scared.

"How d'you know he's dead?" Corbin asked as I watched the man's eyes.

"I went to his office. The security guard told me."

"Think carefully, Mister Tillman," I said. "Did she mention any other names? Any other doctors or facilities?"

"There was another doctor who was supposedly involved in the same program," he replied. "Margaret said she was going to confront all of them."

"What was this doctor's name?" I asked.

"I can't remember exactly. Something Spanish, I think. Rodriguez? Recaldi, maybe?"

I gave Corbin a look. We'd need to check if there were any other doctors from the 1990s program who were still practicing in the area.

He nodded, almost imperceptibly.

"I'll see what I can do, Mister Tillman," I said. "We'll need her cell number and car registration number. In the meantime, I need you to call us immediately if Mrs. Tillman contacts you again. Corbin?"

Corbin handed him his card. I continued, "And if you remember anything else about these conspiracy theories, anything at all, we need to know."

He nodded vigorously. "You think she might have killed Doctor Holloway?"

"What?" I asked, surprised by the question.

He shrugged. "She was pretty wound up. She has been for years. She could have. Couldn't she?"

"We're investigating all possibilities," I said, dryly.

After Tillman left, I found myself studying Vincent Holloway again. There was something about his demeanor that was bothering me, something beyond the obvious pain and exhaustion.

Samson seemed to sense it, too. He kept glancing at Vincent, still not aggressively, but with the kind of attention he usually reserved for people he was unsure of.

"Vincent," I said, "is there anything else you want to tell us? Anything that might help us find your father's killer?"

He was quiet for a long moment, and I could see him struggling with something.

Then, finally, he said, "A couple of months ago..." he looked down, shrugged, then continued, "maybe less than that. It was when I was really desperate for money, I tried to break into Dad's office."

Amanda gasped. "Vincent, you never told me—"

"I didn't take anything," he said quickly, cutting her off. "I couldn't even get in. But while I was there, I saw Dad talking to someone in the parking lot. They seemed to be arguing about something."

"Can you describe this person?" I asked.

"It was dark, and I was pretty far away. But it looked like a woman. Middle-aged, maybe. She seemed really angry about something."

"Can you be more precise?" I asked. "About when this was?"

He thought for a moment, then looked at me, shrugged again and said, "June. Maybe July, I guess.."

Hmm, around the time Holloway ran into someone from his past at the medical conference.

"Did you see what kind of car she was driving?" I asked.

"Something small. Dark colored. That's all I can tell you."

It wasn't much, but it was another piece of the puzzle. Someone from Holloway's past had confronted him in his office parking lot, someone angry enough to seek him out after dark.

As we prepared to leave, I noticed Samson was still watching Vincent with that particular intensity that meant he was picking up on something I was missing.

"What is it, boy?" I asked quietly.

But whatever Samson was sensing, Vincent wasn't ready to share it. Not yet.

Corbin gave them both a card and reminded them to call if they remembered anything that might be helpful, and we left.

Outside, Corbin and I stood beside our cars, comparing notes.

"What did you think?" he asked.

"Vincent's holding something back," I said. "Something more than just the parking lot incident."

"His alibi seems solid," Corbin said, "though it is just his mother. And he doesn't seem to have the kind of medical knowledge it would take to pull off this kind of murder."

"No, but Margaret Tillman is starting to look very

interesting," I said. "Grief, rage, conspiracy theories about medical experiments, all motives for murder, and now she's missing."

"You think she's our killer, then?" Corbin asked.

I made a face. "I think she's dangerous. Whether she killed Holloway or not, she's clearly planning something."

My phone rang. It was Mike Willis.

"Kate, I have a preliminary result on that partial fingerprint from the planted folder." He spoke before I could say anything.

"That's good," I said. "Who is it?"

"An Elena Vasquez," he replied. "She's a psychiatric nurse who used to work at the Greenbriar Behavioral Health Center, in East Chattanooga. They closed the facility almost twenty-four years ago. Here's the weird thing, though: according to her employment records, she died two years ago."

My mind began to churn.

"Mike, are you sure about that?" I asked.

"Positive. I double-checked. Elena Vasquez, a former psychiatric nurse, age forty-nine when she supposedly died in a car accident in 2016."

"But her fingerprint is on evidence from our crime scene," I muttered.

"That's what it looks like," Mike replied.

Either Elena Vasquez had faked her own death, or someone was using her identity. Either way, we'd just found our first real lead.

And Margaret Tillman was still out there somewhere,

possibly armed with her own agenda and a grudge that had been festering for three years.

"All right, Mike. Keep digging. We'll talk soon."

I DROPPED in at the office on the way home to see what Hawk had discovered.

I found him in the conference room, surrounded by printouts, looking like he'd been digging through records for hours.

"All right, Hawk," I said, settling into a chair while Samson found his usual spot. "What did you find that's got you so worried?"

He looked up from a stack of documents. "Kate, Jack and I've been researching the Greenbriar Behavioral Health Center, and there are some serious red flags. The facility closed abruptly in 2001, but not for financial reasons."

"What kind of red flags?"

"For starters, the closure was handled by a law firm that specializes in crisis management for medical institutions. The same firm that represents pharmaceutical companies in liability cases." He pulled out a folder. "Then there's this—in the six months before closure, at least twelve families filed complaints with the state medical board about treatment protocols."

"What happened to those complaints?"

"That's what's strange. They were all withdrawn within weeks of being filed. No disciplinary actions, no investigations, nothing. But here's the kicker—every single family that withdrew their complaint received payments from something called the 'Medical Research Advocacy Fund.'"

I felt my stomach tighten. "How much money?"

"The payments ranged from fifty thousand to two hundred thousand dollars. All with confidentiality agreements attached." Hawk pulled out another document. "Kate, someone was trying to silence these families, and it looks like they got away with it."

"Any idea who funded this advocacy fund?" I asked.

"The paper trail gets murky, but it traces back to a consortium of pharmaceutical companies and medical research organizations. The same companies that were funding experimental treatment programs at facilities like Greenbriar."

I studied the timeline Hawk had constructed. "So someone with serious money and legal resources was making Greenbriar's problems disappear."

He nodded. "Right, and, Kate, several of the medical professionals who worked at Greenbriar are still practicing. Holloway was one. And we might be dealing with someone who's very motivated to keep what happened there buried."

"As you said," I muttered, "motivated enough to kill."

———

I CAN'T TELL you I lost any sleep over the Holloway murder that night. In fact, I slept better than I had in a long time. Samson had, some months earlier, decided his place was beside me on the bed. Me, I wasn't against it, but I made him sleep at the bottom of the bed, close to my feet. He slept well, too.

The following morning, we rose early and went for our customary run around the neighborhood. By seven-thirty I'd had two cups of coffee, a slice of sourdough toast and was dressed in blue jeans, a white sweater over a blue shirt, and my burgundy leather jacket, ready for work.

I made a quick stop at Dunkin's for a large coffee to go and two chocolate donuts, and fifteen minutes later Sammy and I walked into the PD building on Amnicola at a little after eight, slipping quietly past the chief's offices on our way to the elevator.

5

Following the Money

Wednesday 8:30am.

Printouts of the Holloway Psychiatric Associates' financial records were spread across two tables in our conference room like pieces of a jigsaw puzzle that nobody wanted to solve. Tracy sat hunched over a laptop, cross-referencing bank statements with patient billing records, while Cooper had taken on the thankless task of organizing three years' worth of receipts and invoices. Hawk was seated at the far end of the table, methodically going through correspondence files and patient communication records.

I was at the whiteboard, trying to make sense of the timeline we'd established so far, when Jack North walked in carrying a stack of printouts and looking like he'd been up all night.

"Please tell me you found something useful in Holloway's computer files," I said.

"Define useful," Jack replied, dryly, as he settled into a chair at the far side of the table and dumped his papers on the tabletop. "Because what I found is definitely interesting, but I'm not sure how much it will help us catch a killer."

"Start with interesting and we'll work our way up to useful," I said.

Jack extracted a thick folder from the pile. "Doctor Holloway was a digital packrat. He kept everything: patient notes, correspondence, financial records, personal emails going back fifteen years. The man deleted nothing."

"But is there anything recent that might give us a lead?" I asked.

"We...ll, that's where it gets complicated. Three weeks ago, Holloway started researching legal firms that specialize in medical malpractice defense. He also did extensive searches on statute of limitations laws for medical malpractice in Tennessee."

Tracy looked up from her laptop. "That matches what Doctor Walton told us about him asking her about malpractice statutes."

"There's more," Jack continued. "He also researched something called the False Claims Act. That's federal legislation that deals with fraud against the government; usually healthcare fraud, billing irregularities, that sort of thing."

"So he was worried about both malpractice and fraud charges," I said. "What else?"

"He'd been corresponding with someone using an encrypted email service. The messages are coded, but I can tell they were discussing some kind of meeting. The last message was sent two days before his murder."

"Can you trace the other party?" Tracy asked.

Jack shook his head. "They were using a sophisticated encryption service routed through multiple servers. Whoever sent those messages knew what they were doing."

Cooper looked up from his pile of receipts. "Speaking of knowing what they're doing, I think Doctor Walton has been playing games with the practice finances."

"Oh yes? What kind of games?" I asked.

"The kind that involve moving money around to places it shouldn't be," Cooper said. "Look at this."

He spread several bank statements across the table. Even without an accounting background, I could see there were regular transfers to accounts that weren't part of the normal business structure.

"These transfers started about eighteen months ago," Cooper continued. "Small amounts at first, but they've been getting larger. In the past six months, Doctor Walton has moved almost seventy thousand dollars out of the practice accounts."

"Into her personal accounts?" I asked, taking my seat opposite Jack.

Cooper grinned at me and shook his head. "That's the thing. I can't tell where the money went. The transfers go to a business account, but I can't find any records of what that business is or who owns it."

Tracy frowned. "Seventy thousand dollars is a lot of

money for a psychiatric practice. That could definitely cause problems between partners."

"Especially if Holloway found out about it," I said. "Jack, did you find anything in Holloway's files that suggests he knew about these transfers?"

"Not directly, but there are some interesting browser searches. Three weeks ago—same time he was researching malpractice lawyers—he also looked up information about reporting financial crimes and whistleblower protections."

"So maybe he did know," I said, "and maybe he was planning to report it."

"That would give Doctor Walton a pretty powerful motive for murder," Tracy said.

My phone rang. It was Doc Sheddon.

"Doc," I said, leaning back in my chair. "You're early this morning. I hope you have some good news for me."

"Kate, I did the postmortem late yesterday afternoon, and I have some preliminary results. Can you stop by?"

I looked at my watch. It was a little after nine. I nodded to myself, then said, "Sure, I'm on my way. I'll be there in a minute."

I looked at Hawk and said, "Anything?"

He shook his head, "Nothing you need to hear," he replied. "Not yet, anyway."

"Tracy," I said. "We need to find Margaret Tillman, soonest."

She nodded. "I'm on it."

I nodded, stood up, and left the four of them to continue following their various assignments, thinking I needed to find a temporary replacement for Anne Robar who was visiting family in the UK and would be gone for at least a couple of weeks more, and headed three blocks south on Amnicola to what I called 'Doc's little house of horrors.' It was, in fact, the Hamilton County Forensic Center, a small but modern facility that managed to be both sterile and somehow comforting at the same time; maybe because Doc himself was such a reassuring presence.

I found him in his office, reading over what looked like an autopsy report.

He looked up at my knock on the door and said, "Kate, my dear. You're looking chipper this morning. You must have had a good night. Hey, Sammy," he said, ruffling his ears. "You been chasing the neighborhood cats again? Well, Kate, sit down, sit down."

So I sat. "You're looking kind of chipper yourself, Doc. What do you have for me?"

"Well, the cause of death is confirmed as a single puncture wound to the carotid artery. Very precise, very clean. Whoever did this knew exactly where to strike."

"Medical knowledge, then?" I asked.

"Almost certainly. The angle and depth of the wound suggest someone with anatomical training. But here's the interesting part: I found evidence of the midazolam that Mike Willis detected at the scene."

"Actually, Samson found it, but what the heck? You found it in Holloway's system?"

"Yes, but not as much as I would have expected. Either the killer used a smaller dose than necessary, dropped some of the dose, or Holloway had some natural resistance to the drug."

"Okay, so what does that mean?" I asked, frowning.

"It means he might have been conscious when he was killed. Groggy, disoriented, but possibly well aware of what was happening to him."

That was a disturbing thought. "Anything else?"

"I found something under his fingernails," he replied. "Microscopic fibers that don't match his clothing or anything else in his office."

"What kind of fibers?"

"Cotton blend, probably from a medical scrub or similar garment. The killer was wearing scrubs, Kate."

"So we're looking for someone with medical training who has access to sedatives and medical clothing," I said. "Are we looking for another doctor?"

"That's what the evidence suggests," he replied, nodding vigorously. "Either that or a practitioner."

I was about to ask another question when my phone buzzed with a text from Tracy: "I found Margaret Tillman. I'm heading that way now. You need to meet me there."

I thanked Doc Sheddon and drove quickly to the address Tracy had sent me, a modest apartment complex on the south side of town. Tracy was waiting in the parking lot with two patrol officers and an ambulance.

"What's the situation?" I asked.

"The landlord called it in about an hour ago," Tracy replied. "It filtered through to me, eventually. He said he hadn't seen Mrs. Tillman for two days and her car was still here, so he went to check on her. He called 911. That triggered the BOLO and... here we are."

"Is she...?" I trailed off.

"She's alive, but barely. Apparent suicide attempt. Overdose of prescription medications."

"Same MO as her daughter?" I said.

"That's what it looks like."

I followed Tracy up to a second-floor apartment. The door was propped open with Cooper standing beside it, and I could see paramedics working on someone lying on the couch. The apartment was small and cluttered, with papers and photographs scattered everywhere.

Margaret Tillman was conscious but barely responsive as the paramedics prepared to transport her to the hospital. She was a small woman in her late fifties, with gray hair and the kind of deep sadness in her eyes that comes with years of pain.

"Mrs. Tillman," I said gently, kneeling beside the couch. "I'm Captain Gazzara with the Chattanooga Police. Can you hear me?"

Her eyes focused on me with difficulty. "Too late," she whispered. "It's all too late."

"What's too late?" I asked.

"Justice. For Jessica. For all of them."

"Mrs. Tillman, did you hurt Doctor Holloway?"

She shook her head weakly. "I wanted to. But someone beat me to it."

"What? Who? Who beat you to it?" I asked.

"The nurse. She said... she said she'd make them all pay. All the doctors who hurt those children."

"What nurse?" I asked. "What was her name?"

But Margaret Tillman had lost consciousness, and the paramedics were already lifting her onto a stretcher.

"Is she going to make it?" I asked one of the EMTs.

"Probably. We got here in time. But she'll be in the ICU for a while."

After the ambulance left, I took a closer look around Tillman's apartment. The scattered papers were a mix of medical records, legal documents, and what looked like an obsessive amount of research into various psychiatric facilities and doctors.

Tracy was examining a bulletin board covered with photographs and newspaper clippings.

"Kate, come and look at this," she said.

The bulletin board was like something out of a conspiracy theorist's nightmare. Photos of doctors, including Marcus Holloway, were connected with red string to newspaper articles about psychiatric treatment programs, medical malpractice suits, and patient deaths. In the center was a photograph of a young woman whom I figured must have been Jessica Tillman.

"She's been tracking all of this for years," Tracy said. "Look at these notes."

Handwritten papers were tacked to the board, filled with Margaret Tillman's increasingly frantic research. Names, dates, locations, all connected to what she believed was a conspiracy involving experimental psychiatric treatments on teenagers.

Out of all of it, one name caught my attention: Elena Vasquez.

"Tracy, did you see this?" I pointed to a section of notes that mentioned Elena Vasquez as a "potential ally" and an "insider who knows the truth."

"The nurse whose fingerprint Mike found?" she asked. "Yes."

"The very one," I said, standing at the board, my chin in my hand. "According to this, Margaret Tillman was in contact with Elena Vasquez right up until her supposed death in 2016."

Tracy frowned. "But if Vasquez is dead, how did her fingerprint end up on evidence at our crime scene?"

"Maybe she's not as dead as everyone thinks," I replied, thoughtfully.

I took out my phone and called Jack.

"Jack, I need you to dig deeper into Elena Vasquez's death. Get me everything you can, accident reports, witness statements, autopsy records if they exist."

"What am I looking for?" he asked.

"Anything that suggests her death might have been faked," I replied. "Call me back if you find anything."

While Jack worked on that, Tracy and I continued searching Tillman's apartment. In a bedroom that had been converted into a kind of research center, we found boxes of documents related to various psychiatric facilities in the Southeast.

"Geez," Tracy said, opening one of the boxes. "She's been collecting this stuff for years."

The documents were a mix of patient records, staff directories, treatment protocols, and financial records. All of it appeared to be related to psychiatric treatment programs from the late 1990s and early 2000s.

"Whoa! Look at this," I said, pulling out a folder labeled "Greenbriar Behavioral Health Center—Experimental Treatment Program 1996-1999."

Inside were photocopied patient files, staff schedules, and what looked like research protocols for experimental drug treatments on adolescent patients. The names on the files had been redacted, but I could see the ages: most of the patients were between fourteen and seventeen years old. And, again, Dr. Marcus Holloway's name appeared on several of the documents.

"This is what Margaret Tillman was talking about," I said. "Some kind of experimental program they were trying out on troubled kids."

"Hmm," she said, looking over my shoulder. "What kind of trouble and what kind of treatments?"

I scanned the protocols. The language was technical, but what I could understand was disturbing. Experimental medications, isolation therapy, behavioral modification techniques that sounded more like torture than treatment.

"I'm thinking the kind that would leave the kids permanently damaged," I said. It was just then that my phone rang. I checked the screen. It was Jack.

"Jack," I said, "what do you have for me?"

"Elena Vasquez's death was definitely suspicious," he said. "She supposedly died in a single-car accident on a rural road outside Memphis. No witnesses, no skid marks, no apparent reason for her to lose control of the vehicle. Now here's where it gets interesting: the car caught fire after the crash and the body was burned beyond recognition. The identification was based on circumstantial evidence: the vehicle registration, personal effects, and the fact that Elena Vasquez disappeared."

"So maybe she isn't dead after all," I said.

"Right! It's possible," he said. "But get this; three days

before her supposed death, Elena Vasquez cleaned out her bank accounts and cancelled her lease on her apartment."

I nodded to myself. "Sounds like she was planning to disappear."

"That's what I thought," he replied. "I'm still digging, but I think Elena Vasquez staged her own death and has been living under a new identity for the past two years. Anyway, I just thought you'd like to know."

"Yes, keep digging," I said. "I want to know everything there is to know about Elena Vasquez, including what name she might be using now."

As I hung up, Tracy, who was examining another set of documents from Margaret Tillman's collection, turned to look at me and said, "Kate, I heard what you just said. Come and look at this staff directory from Greenbriar Behavioral Health Center."

I looked over her shoulder at a photocopied list of employees from 1996. And there she was, about halfway down the list, Elena Vasquez, Psychiatric Nurse.

"That's her connection to Holloway," I said. "It looks like we might have ourselves a suspect."

"And according to this," Tracy replied, "she was there almost throughout the experimental treatment program."

We were starting to get a picture of what had happened. Elena Vasquez had been a nurse at a psychiatric facility where experimental treatments were being conducted on teenage patients. Something had happened, something bad enough that she'd eventually faked her own death to escape it. But now she was back, and Marcus Holloway was dead.

"Tracy, I want you to get these documents to Jack North. Have him cross-reference every name on these staff lists with current Tennessee medical licenses. If Elena Vasquez is using an alias, she might still be working in the medical field."

"What about Margaret Tillman?" she asked.

"Post a guard at the hospital. If she survives, I want to talk to her as soon as she's conscious. She might be the only person who knows how to find Vasquez. Let's get out of here."

Somewhere out there, I thought, *there's a woman who's supposed to be dead planning something that involves more than just Marcus Holloway. And based on what I've just seen in Margaret Tillman's research, there are other doctors and staff members from that experimental program who might be in danger.*

The question was: could we find Elena Vasquez before she found them?

I needed to get back to the office.

Professional Rivalry

I ARRIVED BACK AT THE OFFICE SOME THIRTY MINUTES later.

The breakthrough came from Margaret Tillman's research files. While Jack continued analyzing her digital communications, I'd been reviewing the hard copy documents we'd found in her apartment. Buried in a folder marked "Current Practitioners" was a list of medical professionals who had worked in the experimental program and were still practicing in the area.

Dr. James Fletcher's name was third on the list, with a note in Margaret's handwriting: "Private practice, Chattanooga. Continues adolescent treatment protocols. Possible ongoing experimental work."

"Corbin," I said, grabbing my jacket, "we need to pay a visit to this Dr. Fletcher. Cooper, call him and let him know we're coming." And less than thirty minutes later, we parked outside his office on Gunbarrel Road.

Dr. James Fletcher's office was cold and impersonal. Located in a gleaming medical complex, it screamed success and ambition. The waiting room was full of expensive furniture, medical journals, and golf magazines, with not a single personal touch to suggest that actual human beings were being treated here, though there was one expensively-dressed young woman seated demurely, flipping through a Chattanooga Cityscape magazine. She looked up and smiled, then looked down again and continued flipping.

Fletcher himself was a tall, lean man in his early sixties, with silver hair and the kind of confident bearing that comes from years of being the smartest person in the room. When Corbin and I were shown into his office, he barely looked up from the papers on his desk.

"Captain Gazzara, I presume," he said. "To what do I owe this singular honor? I can give you fifteen minutes. I have patients waiting."

"Doctor Fletcher, we appreciate you taking the time to speak with us. It's about Doctor Holloway's murder," I began. "This is Sergeant Russell, by the way, and my K9 is Samson."

He glanced at Sammy, but other than that, didn't react to his presence. Sammy was similarly disinterested.

"Terrible business," he said, finally. "Please. Sit down. Marcus was a good psychiatrist, even if I didn't always agree with his methods."

So we sat, and I furrowed my brow and waited for him to continue.

Fletcher leaned back in his chair, clearly pleased to have an opportunity to discuss his professional opinions.

"Marcus was old school," he continued, steepling his fingers. "He believed in lengthy therapy sessions, building deep personal relationships with patients. Very time-intensive, and not particularly cost-effective."

"And your approach is different?" Corbin asked.

"I believe in evidence-based treatment," he said, staring at Corbin over his fingertips. "Targeted interventions, measurable outcomes, efficient use of resources. The modern approach to psychiatric medicine."

Corbin looked up from his notes. "We understand there was some professional competition between your practices."

Fletcher's expression hardened slightly. "Competition is healthy in any profession. It drives innovation and keeps practitioners sharp."

"But in your case, it involved competing for the same contracts and referral sources."

"That's the nature of business, Sergeant. Marcus' practice had certain advantages: his reputation, his connections in the medical community. I had to work harder to establish my own patient base."

"Were you bitter about losing contracts to Doctor Holloway?" I asked, mildly.

"Bitter?" Fletcher laughed, but there was no humor in it. "Captain, I'm a successful psychiatrist with a thriving practice. I don't have time for bitterness."

I heard him, but his tone suggested otherwise. "Where were you Monday night between eight and ten PM?"

"I was here, working late," he replied. "I often stay until nine or ten to catch up on patient notes and administrative work."

"Can anyone verify that?" Corbin asked, looking at him expectantly, his hand hovering over his notebook.

"My office manager," he replied. "Sandra Mills; she was here until about eight-thirty. After that, I was alone."

So Fletcher has an alibi for part of the timeframe, but not all of it. I thought.

"Did you know Doctor Holloway personally," I asked, "or was your relationship purely professional?"

Fletcher hesitated for a second, and I caught a glimpse of something more personal behind his professional facade.

"We knew each other in medical school," he said finally. "We were… friends, once upon a time."

"What happened to that friendship?" I asked, genuinely interested.

"Life. Career choices. Different philosophies about how to practice medicine. The usual."

But I could tell by the way he looked away and to the left that either he was lying or there was something else there, something he wasn't telling us.

"Doctor Fletcher, are you familiar with the experimental psychiatric treatments that Doctor Holloway might have been involved with in the past?"

The effect on Fletcher and the change in his demeanor were immediate and dramatic. His face went pale, and his hands tensed on the desk.

"Experimental treatments?" He asked, carefully, frowning. "What kind of experimental treatments?"

"We're not sure yet. Possibly involving teenage patients in the 1990s."

Fletcher was quiet for a long moment, clearly wrestling with something.

"There were... programs back then," he said finally. "Different times, different standards. Things that wouldn't be acceptable now."

"Were you involved in any of these programs?"

"I did my residency at Greenbriar in the mid-1990s. There were research protocols that residents were expected to participate in."

"What kind of research?" Corbin asked.

"Pharmaceutical trials, mostly. Testing new medications and treatment approaches on patients who hadn't responded to conventional therapy."

"Including teenage patients?" Corbin pressed him.

Fletcher nodded reluctantly. "Yes, I'm afraid so. The adolescent psychiatric unit was part of the research program. Kids with severe behavioral problems, treatment-resistant depression, that sort of thing."

"Was this research properly supervised?" I asked. "Were there adequate safeguards for the patients?"

By then, his demeanor had changed completely. He seemed... vacant, as if he was lost somewhere in the past. "We thought so at the time," he said, quietly. "But looking back..." He shrugged helplessly. "The regulations were different then. Informed consent wasn't as rigorous. There were things that happened that probably shouldn't have..." he trailed off, staring out the window.

"Please continue, Doctor," I said.

He sighed, turned his head to look at me and said, "Patients who got worse instead of better. Side effects that weren't properly documented. Kids who should have been removed from the program but weren't."

"Doctor Fletcher, do you remember a nurse named Elena Vasquez?" I asked.

His reaction was unmistakable: fear.

"Why are you asking about Elena?" he said.

"So you do remember her?" I said.

"She worked in the adolescent unit during my residency. She was very dedicated, very protective of her patients. Sometimes too protective."

"What do you mean by that?" Corbin asked.

"She questioned everything," he replied. "Every medication order, every treatment protocol, every decision the attending physicians made. It got to the point where some of the doctors refused to work with her."

"Including Doctor Holloway?"

"Especially Marcus. Elena accused him of... well, of not having the patients' best interests at heart."

"What did she accuse him of specifically?" I asked.

Fletcher was clearly uncomfortable. "Look, this was all more than twenty-five years ago. People said things, accusations were made. But nothing was ever proven."

"Accusations?" I asked. "What kind of accusations?"

"Elena claimed that some of the research protocols were more about advancing careers than helping patients. She said certain doctors were using the kids as test subjects for treatments that had no real chance of success."

"And was she right?" I asked.

"I don't know, Captain. Maybe she was, maybe she.... The pressure to publish research, to get grants, to advance in academic medicine, it was intense. Sometimes good intentions became lost in the pursuit of professional success."

Corbin leaned forward. "Doctor Fletcher, what happened to Elena Vasquez?"

"Eventually, she was fired," he replied. "There was some kind of incident with a patient... She allegedly interfered with a treatment protocol without authorization. The administration said she was becoming too emotionally involved with the patients."

"When was this?" I asked.

"Late 1998, I think. She was gone by the time I finished my residency."

"Did you have any contact with her after she was fired?" I asked, leaning forward.

"No. I heard she went to work at some other facility. I never saw her again."

My phone buzzed. It was Jack North.

"Excuse me," I said, stepping into the hallway.

"Jack, this had better be important. I'm in the middle of an interview."

"It won't take a moment, Kate. I've been digging deeper into Elena Vasquez's supposed death. There are some serious inconsistencies in the accident report. The timeline doesn't add up. She was supposedly driving from Memphis to Nashville, but the accident happened on a road that's nowhere near that route. And the fire that destroyed the body? It burned way too hot for a normal car fire."

"So someone staged the fire to cover up a murder?"

"Or to help her disappear," he replied. "I'm still trying

to track down where she might have gone after 2016, but it's like she vanished completely."

"Keep looking," I said. "And Jack, check if there are any other medical facilities in the Chattanooga area that might have hired someone with Elena's background, even under a different name."

"Already on it," he said and hung up.

I returned to Fletcher's office, where Corbin was asking about other staff members from the experimental program.

I sat down and said, "Doctor Fletcher, we're trying to locate Elena Vasquez. Do you have any idea where she might be now?"

Fletcher shook his head. "I told you; I haven't seen her since she was fired in 1998. For all I know, she could be anywhere."

"If she contacts you, would you call us immediately?" I asked, giving him a hard look.

"Of course. But why would she contact me? We weren't exactly friends back then."

"Because if our theory is correct, someone who was involved in that experimental program is targeting the doctors and staff who participated in it. Elena Vasquez might be in danger, or she might have information about who's behind the murder, or... she, herself, might be the one doing the targeting..."

I paused for a second, then said, "What exactly happened back then?"

"There was a patient," he said, quietly. "A young girl, maybe sixteen or seventeen. She was part of one of the experimental protocols, a new antipsychotic medication that was supposed to help with severe behavioral problems."

"And something went wrong?" I asked.

He nodded, and then continued, "The girl had a severe reaction to the medication. Neurological damage that was probably permanent. Elena was the one who first noticed the symptoms, but by the time anyone listened to her, it was too late."

"What happened to the girl?" Corbin asked.

"I don't know. Her family removed her from the program and threatened to sue the hospital. The whole thing was covered up: sealed records, non-disclosure agreements, that sort of thing."

"And Elena Vasquez blamed the doctors for not listening to her warnings?" I asked.

"She blamed all of us. Said we were more interested in protecting our careers than protecting our patients. She wasn't entirely wrong, of course."

I sat back in my chair and stared at him. He looked... chagrined. "I'm going to assign a patrol car to keep an eye on your office and your home for the next few days," I said. "If Elena Vasquez contacts you, or if you notice anything unusual, call us immediately."

I looked at Corbin. He nodded and handed Fletcher his card.

"You really think I'm in danger?" Fletcher asked.

"I don't know," I replied. "I think someone is targeting people who were involved in that experimental program. So, until we know who and why, everyone connected to it should be careful."

I twitched Samson's leash, and he rose to his feet, as did Corbin and I.

"Thank you for your time, Doctor," I said, then turned and walked to the door where I turned and said, "Anything, anything at all, for any reason, you call Sergeant Russell."

He nodded vacantly, and Corbin and I left his office.

"What do you think?" Corbin asked.

I looked at my watch. It was almost noon. It had been a long morning. "I think it's time we had some lunch. What d'you fancy? It's on me."

He looked at me and grinned.

"I get it," I said. "The usual, huh?"

He nodded.

The Second Body

Wednesday afternoon 12pm

IT WAS LUNCHTIME ON A WEDNESDAY, BUT THE URBAN Stack on West 13th wasn't as packed as I thought it would be, and we found a booth at the far end of the room. Corbin ordered a New Mexico Green Chile Cheeseburger, and I ordered Philly Cheese Steak Burger.

"So, come on, what d'you think?" he asked as we waited for our food.

"I think we need to find Elena Vasquez before whoever killed Holloway finds her," I said. "And I think we need to figure out who else was involved in that experimental program."

"What about Fletcher?" he asked.

I made a face, shrugged slightly, and said, "Mostly on

the up and up, I think, but I also think he was more involved in the program than he was letting on."

"He seemed genuinely worried about his safety," Corbin said, "so, yes, I think maybe you're right."

"He should be worried," I replied. "If someone is systematically targeting people from that program, then everyone who was involved is potentially at risk."

I looked around for a server, and as I did so, my phone rang. It was Chief Johnston.

"Kate, I need to see you in my office as soon as you get back."

"Okay… Is something wrong, Chief?"

"We'll talk about it when you get here." He said and hung up, just as the server put our food down.

"Geez," I muttered. I looked up at him. "We need to-go boxes, please."

"It never rains—" Corbin began, smiling, but I cut him off with a look.

"When the chief calls…" I said and trailed off.

The boxes came, and we left with me wondering if I'd get to eat mine. If I didn't, I knew who would. Either way, I was going to share with him. Sammy, I'm talking about.

I walked into Chief Johnston's outer office to find Christy, his PA, seated at her desk. "You'd better go on in, Kate," she said. "He's loaded for bear today."

I nodded glumly, knocked on his door, opened it, and stepped inside.

"Close the door, Kate," he said without looking up.

I settled into the chair across from his desk; Sammy lay down beside me. "What's the situation, Chief?"

"The situation is that I've had four phone calls in the past hour. One from the hospital board, one from the medical society, one from someone who claims to represent 'concerned physicians' in the community, and one from the district attorney's office asking questions about the Holloway case. Apparently, some of the people involved in this experimental program you're investigating have connections in the city. I need a full briefing on where we stand."

"You want to know all about the Holloway case?" The question was redundant. I already knew the answer, but I was playing for time. He didn't give me much.

"Yes, that's it exactly. Word's getting out that you're looking into something that happened twenty-five years ago, and that's making some people very nervous."

I leaned back in my chair. "Chief, we're investigating the murder of Dr. Holloway late Monday evening. If that investigation leads us to examine his past, then that's what we're going to do."

"I understand that, Captain. But I also need you to understand that some of these people are potentially connected to that program, and I say potentially advisedly, are prominent members of the medical community. People with influence, people who can make phone calls to the mayor's office."

"And you're telling me to back off, is that it?" I asked angrily. I knew he wasn't, but I was pissed. This always happened with high-profile cases, and I was getting fed up with it.

Chief Johnston looked at me directly. "No, Kate. I'm asking you to be smart about how you proceed. Focus on the murder, not on decades-old medical practices that may or may not have been questionable."

"And if the two are connected?" I asked.

"Then you'll have to find a way to prove murder without opening up a can of worms that could embarrass a lot of important people."

I felt my jaw tighten. "Chief, we've got a dead doctor and a potentially dead nurse, who probably isn't. If someone is killing people to cover up what happened in that program, then I have to investigate said program. Not only that, don't you think the public has a right to know?"

"The public has a right to safety, Kate, yes. And they have a right to know that killers are being caught and prosecuted. They don't necessarily have a right to every ugly detail about medical malpractices from a quarter-century ago."

"So we solve the murders but keep quiet about the motive, is that it?"

"You solve the murders by building a case based on evidence that will hold up in court," he replied. "If that evidence happens to touch on the experimental program, then so be it. But don't make this case about exposing some kind of medical conspiracy."

I stood up. "Understood, Chief. Is there anything else?"

"Kate." His voice softened slightly. "I'm not trying to interfere with your investigation. I'm trying to make sure you can do your job without getting blindsided by political pressure. Be careful, be thorough, but be smart about it."

I nodded. "Come on, Sammy."

As I walked back to the elevator, I had a feeling that Chief Johnston's warning was just the beginning. If people were already making phone calls about our investigation, it meant we were getting close to something they wanted to stay buried.

Me? I was going to make sure it didn't.

———————

THE CALL CAME in at six-thirty the next morning, Thursday, just as I was finishing my first cup of coffee and trying to convince myself that a piece of toast counted as a balanced breakfast. I'd been up half the night thinking about the experimental program and wondering where Elena Vasquez might be hiding, so I was already dressed and ready to go when my phone rang.

"Gazzara," I said.

"Captain, we've got another body," the dispatcher said.

"Geez," I said. "Where?"

"Northside apartments on Frazier Avenue. The victim has been identified as Elena Santos."

And there it was, and I had a bad feeling about it, about Elena Santos. "I think we just found Elena Vasquez," I muttered.

If it was Vasquez, it put a crimp in the investigation. I so much wanted to interview her about that experimental program.

"Give me the address, please, and let them know I'll

be there in twenty minutes. Has Doc Sheddon been notified?"

"He's on his way. So is your team."

I grabbed my jacket and headed for the door, Samson padding along beside me. The drive to Frazier Avenue gave me time to think about what this second murder meant. Either Elena had been killed to keep her quiet about something in the past, or our killer was systematically working through a list of people connected to the experimental program. Neither possibility made me feel any better.

The Northside apartments were one of those complexes that had been nice about twenty years ago but was now showing its age in peeling paint and patched asphalt. The kind of place where people lived when they were trying to stay invisible.

Three patrol cars were already on scene, along with Mike Willis's CSI van and an ambulance that wouldn't be needed for anything except transport to Doc's forensic center. Corbin was talking to a uniformed officer near the building entrance when I arrived.

"What do we have, Corbin?" I asked.

"Good morning, Kate," he replied, smirking at me. "Elena Santos, apartment 2B. She was found by her neighbor this morning when he noticed her door was standing open. The body's in the living room."

"Good morning to you, too," I said, dryly, "Any signs of forced entry?"

"None that I could see," he replied. "Either she knew her killer or they had a key."

I followed Corbin up a narrow staircase that smelled like old carpet and cooking grease. The second-floor hallway was dimly lit and lined with doors that probably hid a dozen different sad stories of people just trying to get by.

Elena Santos' apartment door was propped open with crime scene tape stretched across the entrance. Through the doorway, I could see Mike Willis photographing what looked like a modest living room furnished with pieces that had probably come from thrift stores and yard sales.

I hadn't been there but a moment when Doc Sheddon emerged from the apartment, pulling off his latex gloves with the same careful precision he applied to everything else.

"Greetings, Kate," he said. "Did we get you out of bed?"

"No, Doc. I was already up. What do we have?"

"Hispanic female, late forties, early fifties. Single stab wound to the neck."

"Same killer as Holloway?" I asked.

"Almost certainly," he replied. "The weapon punctured the carotid artery; very precise placement, and it appears to be the same type of medical instrument."

"Do we have a time of death?" I asked.

"Sometime between six and eight yesterday evening, I'd say. I'll know more when I've done the postmortem."

"When can you do it, Doc?" I asked. "I need to know who this person really is, and quickly."

He looked at me, frowned and nodded. "I already

have one for this morning, but I should be done by eleven-thirty. I can do it right after lunch. That quick enough for you?"

I nodded, my mind far away, thinking about... "Any evidence of midazolam?" I asked.

Doc gave me one of his looks. "Too soon to tell. I'll have to run tests, but there's a coffee cup on the kitchen counter that might be worth checking. I'll have a preliminary result tomorrow morning."

Mike Willis appeared in the doorway. "We've got a Live one here, Kate. The killer left us another message."

'live one' was his way of saying we were dealing with something or someone out of the ordinary. I followed him into the apartment, stepping carefully around the evidence markers. Elena Santos was slumped in an armchair near the window, positioned almost exactly the way Holloway had been. If I didn't know better, I'd have thought she'd just fallen asleep. But the small puncture wound below her left ear and the copious amount of blood told a different story.

"What's the message?" I asked Willis.

He led me to a small dining table near the kitchen. Spread across the surface were more photocopied patient files, similar to the ones that had been planted in Holloway's desk. But these were different, more detailed, with handwritten notes.

It is, I thought. *It is Elena Vasquez.*

"Have we verified her identity?" I asked.

Willis looked at me and shook his head. "Officially, no, not yet, but we know who she is. The neighbor identified her. Her name's Elena Santos."

"I don't think so," I said. "I think she's Elena Vasquez. I need you to rerun her prints, Mike, ASAP. And compare them to the partial on the file we found at the Holloway scene."

He looked at me and frowned. "You think?"

"I do. Now what is it you want to show me?"

"Well…" he paused, his brow furrowed. "Now that I think about it, what you're saying makes sense," he said. "She was investigating the program. Look at this."

He pointed to a timeline that Elena had drawn on a piece of paper. It showed the dates of the experimental program, the names of participating doctors and staff, and a list of patients with their ages and outcomes.

"I looks like she was tracking everyone involved," I said, scanning the timeline. "Doctors, nurses, administrators, even hospital board members."

"Yeah, and then there's this," Willis said, pointing to another section of Elena's notes. "She'd identified several patients who suffered permanent damage from their treatments."

Corbin appeared in the doorway. "Kate, the neighbor who found the body wants to talk to you. He says he saw someone leaving Elena's apartment last night. His name is Perkins. He's out front."

I FOUND Harold Perkins sitting on the front steps of the building. He looked shaken but alert, the kind of person who noticed things because he didn't have much else to do.

"Hello, Mr. Perkins," I said. "I'm Captain Gazzara, Chattanooga, PD. Mind if I sit down?"

"Suit yourself," he said. "Nice dog. Can I pet him?"

I didn't need to answer. Samson got the message and sat down beside him.

"I understand you saw someone leaving Ms. Santos' apartment last night," I said.

"Around seven-thirty, maybe eight o'clock. I was coming back from the store and I saw someone coming down the stairs."

"Can you describe this person?"

"It was a woman, middle-aged, I'd guess. She was wearing scrubs, like a nurse or something."

"Did you get a good look at her face?"

Perkins shook his head. "She had her head down, walking fast like she was in a hurry. But I remember thinking it was odd because Elena didn't get many visitors, especially not medical people."

"What about her physical attributes?" I said.

"Her what?" he asked, frowning.

I smiled. "Her height, build, hair color?"

"Average height, I suppose," he replied. "Maybe five-six or five-seven. Not heavy, not thin. Dark hair, but I couldn't tell you much more than that."

"Did you see what kind of car she was driving?" I asked.

"Didn't see her get into a car. She walked toward the street, but I went inside and didn't watch where she went."

It wasn't much, but it was something. Our killer was a woman with medical training who was comfortable enough in medical scrubs to wear them while out in public.

"Mr. Perkins, had you noticed anything unusual about Ms. Santos recently? Any changes in her behavior, any visitors, anything that seemed out of the ordinary?"

"Well, she'd been getting mail from lawyers and doctors and such. I could see the return addresses when I picked up my mail from the box downstairs. Seemed like she was writing a lot of letters, too."

"Letters?" I said. "What kind of letters?"

"Official looking ones. Typed, with fancy letterheads. She asked me once if I knew how to do certified mail, like she was planning to send something important. I told her she'd have to go to the post office to do that."

So Elena had been investigating the Greenbriar program, possibly preparing to expose what had happened. And someone had killed her to stop her.

I walked back upstairs to take another look at Elena's research. The level of detail was impressive. She'd somehow managed to get hold of patient records, staff schedules, even financial information about the program's funding.

"Mike, bag all of this research," I said. "I want my people to go through every piece of paper."

"Already on it. There's also a computer in the bedroom that might have more information."

"Bag that, too, and I'll take it with me. I'll have Jack take a look at it." He did as I asked and signed off on the evidence bag. I signed for it and was just about to leave when my phone rang. It was Tracy.

"Hey, Kate, I'm at the hospital with Margaret Tillman. She's conscious and asking to speak with you."

"I'll be there as soon as I finish processing the scene here," I said. "How is she?"

"Physically, she'll be fine, I think," she replied. "Mentally, I'm not so sure. She keeps talking about 'the nurse' and saying she has to warn people."

"Okay, stay with her. I'll be there as soon as I can."

I hung up and looked around Elena's apartment one last time. Based on the positioning of the body and the lack of signs of struggle, Elena Vasquez—yes, by then I was pretty sure it was her—had probably been drugged like Holloway, and that made me think she must have known her killer. I stared down at the body. It looked so peaceful, as if she was asleep.

"Corbin," I said, "I want you to go back to the office and give this to Jack"—I handed him the bagged computer—"he'll know what to do with it. Also, I want you to ask him to do a deep background check on an Elena Santos. I want to know what she's been doing for the last two years, and where she's been working, the works."

"Got it," he replied. "Anything else?"

I thought for a minute, then shook my head. "No, but if I think of anything, I'll call you. I'm going to the hospital."

I left a few moments later with one thing on my mind: Why kill Elena if she was on the same side as the patients? I could only think the killer must be one of the providers—a doctor or nurse—who didn't want to be exposed.

Twenty minutes later, I was walking through the corridors of Erlanger Hospital, thinking about experimental programs and damaged teenagers and wondering how many more people were going to die before we caught whoever was behind this.

Margaret Tillman was awake but looked ten years older than she had a day earlier. The suicide attempt had left her weak and shaky, but her eyes were alert and focused.

"Hello Mrs. Tillman," I said brightly as I entered the room. "Remember me? I'm Captain Gazzara. I'm glad to see you're feeling better."

"I'm not better," she said hoarsely. "I won't be better until someone pays for what happened to Jessica."

"We're investigating Jessica's death as part of a larger case," I said. "What can you tell me about Elena Santos?"

Margaret's eyes filled with tears. "Elena's trying to help," she whispered. "She's been collecting evidence about what they did to those children. She said she was going to make sure everyone knew the truth."

"When was the last time you spoke to her?" I asked.

"Three days ago. She called to tell me she'd found something important, something that would prove the doctors were covering up what really happened."

"Did she say what she'd found?" I asked.

"No, she just said she'd found something important she wanted to share with me."

"Is that all?" I asked.

Margaret nodded. "She was being careful. She said there were people who would kill her to keep the truth hidden."

She was right about that, I thought.

I debated what to do next, and then I made up my mind. I didn't like it, but I didn't see any other way, "Mrs. Tillman," I said. "Elena Santos was found dead this morning. She was murdered. I'm sorry."

Margaret's face went white. "No. Oh dear God, no. This is all my fault."

"How is it your fault?" I asked.

"I pushed her to investigate. I gave her all my research, all the documents I'd collected. If I hadn't involved her, she'd still be alive."

"Mrs. Tillman, whoever killed Elena made that choice. You're not responsible for someone else's decision to commit murder."

But she wasn't listening. She was staring at the ceiling, tears running down her cheeks.

"They're never going to pay," she whispered. "They're going to get away with it, just like they always do."

"No," I said firmly. "They're not going to get away with it. We're going to find who killed Elena and Dr. Holloway, and we're going to make sure they face justice."

I took a deep breath. I'd done the one thing a police officer must never do. I'd made an inferred promise I wasn't sure I could keep.

I put a comforting hand on her arm, then quietly left the room.

I left the hospital and went back to the apartments on Frazier Avenue, where Corbin was back and working the scene.

"I found something interesting in her jewelry box," he said, holding up a small evidence bag and smiling.

I took it from him. It contained a small brass key.

"First Horizon Bank," he said over my shoulder. "Box number 247."

"Elena was definitely planning ahead," I said, examining the key. "Corbin, I want Tracy and Cooper to get a warrant and go check out that safe deposit box ASAP. If Elena was building a case against the experimental program, she might have kept the most important stuff somewhere secure."

"Got it," Corbin replied, taking back the bag. "If there's more documentation in that box, it could be the breakthrough we need."

"It could," I said, "so go and get the ball rolling." I looked at my watch. It was almost two-thirty. "Judge Strange should be in his chambers. If they're quick, they should be able to catch him before he leaves for the day. I'll give him a call to let him know they're coming."

Corbin left, and I continued to work the scene with Mike. An hour later, my phone buzzed with a text from Jack North: "I found something on Santos' computer. You coming back to the office?"

Forty-five minutes later, I barged into the conference room, Sammy trotting at my side, threw my gear down on the tabletop, dropped heavily into my chair and said, "Okay, Jack. Talk to me."

"I found some encrypted communications, Kate. Elena was corresponding with someone using a secure messaging system. The messages go back about eighteen months, and they're all about tracking down people connected to the experimental program."

"Can you trace who she was communicating with?" I asked.

"Not yet - whoever it is knows how to cover their digital tracks. But Kate, the person she was talking to has been helping her gather evidence. They've been sharing information, back and forth, about current locations of former Greenbriar staff, even providing financial support for Elena's investigation."

"So Elena had a partner?" I mused.

"More than that," Jack said. "Based on these messages, I think Elena's contact might be another survivor of the experimental program. Someone with resources and advanced technical skills who's been planning this for years."

"Any indication of who it might be?"

He shook his head—always a bad sign. "The handle they use is 'Subject23.' And Kate, the last message was sent just hours before Elena was murdered. It says: 'Time to finish what we started.'"

"Subject23?" I said, frowning. "That sounds like a patient designation from the experimental program."

"That's what I was thinking too," Jack replied. "Kate, if Elena was working with another survivor, and that person has the technical skills to set up encrypted communications—"

"Then we might be dealing with someone with inside knowledge of the program and a very personal reason for revenge," I finished for him.

"There's something else, Kate. The digital footprint

suggests this person has significant technical resources: expensive encryption software, multiple secure servers. I'm talking professional-grade computer skills."

I looked at Samson, who seemed to sense my growing unease. "So Elena was part of a larger operation," I muttered to myself, but loud enough for everyone to hear, "and now Elena's dead... Jack, I need to know who Subject23 is, like yesterday."

"On it," Jack said.

8

The Santos Autopsy

IT WAS JUST AFTER FOUR-FORTY-FIVE THAT WEDNESDAY afternoon when Doc Sheddon called.

"Kate, I just finished the autopsy on Elena Santos. Can you come? There's quite a bit we need to discuss."

"You bet," I said. "I'm on my way."

I left the team to continue processing Elena's research and drove the three blocks to the forensic center. Doc Sheddon was waiting for me in his office, looking even more grim than usual, with what I recognized as an autopsy report on his desk.

"I'm guessing it's the same killer," I said as Sammy and I sat down together across from the pathologist.

"Almost certainly," he replied, adjusting his half-glasses and consulting his notes. "But this autopsy tells us considerably more about our killer than the Holloway case did. Shall we start with the basics and work our way to the more interesting findings?"

I nodded, taking out my my phone and setting it to record.

"Elena Santos, female, age thirty-four—though I suspect that's not her real age—approximately five feet six inches, one hundred thirty-five pounds. Time of death, based on rigor mortis, body temperature, and stomach contents, between six-fifteen and seven-forty-five PM yesterday evening. She'd eaten a light meal approximately two hours before death—salad and a ham and cheese sandwich."

"So she was comfortable enough with her killer to eat with them?" I asked.

"Or the killer arrived after she'd finished eating," Doc replied. "Now, the cause of death: a single penetrating wound to the left carotid artery, identical in location and angle to the Holloway murder. The weapon also appears to be the same—a narrow, sharp instrument, approximately four inches in length, with a slightly curved blade. Very precise placement, indicating anatomical knowledge."

He turned a page in his report. "However, this victim fought back significantly. I found extensive defensive wounds on both hands and forearms—seven distinct cuts on the palms and fingers, consistent with grabbing at a blade, and three deeper lacerations on the left forearm where she attempted to block the attack."

"So the midazolam either didn't work or she realized what was happening before it took full effect?" I asked.

"Ah, that's where it gets interesting," Doc said, his eyes lighting up with the enthusiasm he reserved for particularly complex cases. "I found significant levels of

Chapter 8

propofol in her system—that's a surgical anesthetic, very fast-acting and potent. The killer's primary method of attack."

"Propofol?" I frowned. "How was it administered?"

"Injection, right here," he said, pointing to a spot on a anatomical diagram. "Upper left arm. I found the injection site: a small puncture wound, consistent with a standard syringe, probably a 22-gauge needle. The killer knew exactly where to inject for maximum efficiency."

"So they came prepared."

"Very much so. Propofol works within seconds when properly administered. The killer expected Elena to be unconscious almost immediately." Doc adjusted his glasses. "But here's what I find fascinating—I also found traces of midazolam in her system, but at much lower concentrations."

"Two different drugs?"

"I believe the midazolam was secondary. When the propofol didn't work as expected—Elena had clearly built up tolerance to the drug from years of handling psychiatric medications—the killer may have attempted a backup sedation method. But by then, Elena was fighting back."

That was interesting. Elena's medical history from the experimental program might have inadvertently saved her life, at least temporarily.

"You mentioned tissue under her fingernails?" I prompted.

Doc nodded vigorously. "Yes, indeed. Significant amounts, actually. She managed to scratch her attacker quite deeply during the struggle that ensued when the propofol failed to render her unconscious quickly enough. I found skin cells, what appears to be a small amount of blood, and—most interestingly—synthetic fibers consistent with medical scrubs."

"So our killer was definitely wearing medical clothing."

"That would be my assessment. The fibers are a cotton-polyester blend, white or very light colored, consistent with standard hospital scrubs. But here's what's particularly telling—" He pulled out a small evidence bag containing what looked like a tiny fragment of something. "This was embedded under the nail of her right index finger."

I leaned forward to get a better look. "What is it?"

"A small piece of latex. From a medical glove, I'd say. But not the standard disposable gloves most people would use. This is thicker, higher quality, the type used in surgical procedures or other medical applications requiring dexterity and sensitivity."

"So our killer wears surgical gloves but Elena managed to tear them during the struggle."

"Precisely. The killer came prepared with professional-grade equipment but didn't anticipate Elena's drug tolerance. Which brings me to the DNA analysis I've already started. I'm expediting the tests—Carol is working it as we speak—so preliminary results should be available by tomorrow morning. If we're fortunate, Elena managed to collect enough genetic material to give us a profile."

Doc turned another page. "The propofol tells us something crucial about our killer, Kate. This isn't a drug you can obtain easily—it's controlled, used primarily in surgical and intensive care settings. Our killer either works in a hospital or surgical center, or has connections to someone who does."

Doc removed his glasses and cleaned them carefully, a gesture I'd learned meant he was about to share something particularly significant.

"Kate, there's something else. Something that disturbs me more than the murders themselves, if that's possible."

"What's that, Doc?"

"The precision of these attacks. The location of the wounds, the angle of entry, the depth of penetration. This killer has performed this exact procedure before, probably many times. The muscle memory is there, the confidence, the efficiency."

"You're saying our killer has killed before?"

"I'm saying our killer has extensive experience with this particular method of killing. Whether that experience comes from previous murders or from some other source, I can't say. But no one achieves this level of precision without practice."

I felt a chill that had nothing to do with the air conditioning. "How many times would someone need to practice to achieve this level of skill?"

Doc put his glasses back on and looked at me directly. "In my professional opinion? Several times, at least seven or eight. This isn't beginner's luck, Kate. This is expertise."

I sighed, blew the air out through my lips, then said, with no little resignation, "Anything else I should know?"

"Two more things. First, I found evidence that Elena

was moved after death. The blood spatter patterns don't match her final position in the chair. She was killed elsewhere in the apartment—probably the kitchen, based on the blood traces I found there—then positioned in the living room chair."

"So the killer took time to stage the scene, just like with Holloway."

"Exactly. And second, I found something in her clothing that I initially missed." He handed me another evidence bag, this one containing what looked like a small piece of paper.

"It was tucked into her jacket pocket. It appears to be a hospital identification badge holder—empty, but with partial printing visible. I can make out part of what looks like 'Chattanooga Gen—' before it's torn."

I studied the fragment. If it came from Chattanooga General Hospital, it meant our killer either worked there or had recent access to the facility.

"Doc, this is excellent work. You'll call me when you have the DNA results?"

"I've put a rush on everything. Preliminary DNA by tomorrow morning, final toxicology by tomorrow afternoon. I'll call you the moment I have anything definitive."

"One more question," I said, standing to leave. "You think we're dealing with someone who's killed more than just these two victims?"

Doc was quiet for a long moment, considering his answer carefully.

"Kate, in thirty years of forensic pathology, I've learned to recognize the patterns. The precision, the methodology, the comfort level with violence, so yes, I believe we're dealing with someone who has killed before. Whether those deaths were classified as murders or something else, I can't say. But this person has extensive experience with death."

As Sammy and I walked back to the car, I found myself thinking about Doc's words. Extensive experience with death. In a healthcare setting, that could mean many things—some legitimate, some not.

But combined with everything else we'd learned, it painted a picture of a killer who was not only methodical and intelligent, but also someone who had been preparing for a very long time.

The question was: how many more people were on their list?

Hidden Evidence

WEDNESDAY EVENING, 6:15 PM

I was still processing Doc Sheddon's disturbing revelation about the killer's expertise when Tracy and Cooper returned from First Horizon Bank. They walked into the conference room carrying a large evidence box and wearing the kind of expressions that told me Elena Santos/Vasquez had left us more than just a few documents.

"Please tell me you found something useful," I said, looking up from the whiteboard where I'd been trying to make sense of the experimental program timeline.

"I think so," Tracy replied, as Cooper set a large cardboard box on the conference table. "It was a big safe deposit box. It looks to me like she was trying to build a case."

Cooper opened the box and began removing items one by one. The first thing that caught my attention was a large file box labeled "Patient Files - UNREDACTED." Unlike the photocopied fragments we'd found at the crime scenes, these documents looked official, complete, and potentially damning.

"These are original patient files," I said.

"Not the originals," Cooper said, "but certified copies with all the redacted information intact. Real names, addresses, family information, detailed treatment protocols. Everything."

I picked up one of the files and opened it. It contained eight pages of reports. The patient was listed as Jennifer Walsh, age sixteen, admitted to the Greenbriar Behavioral Health Center in March 1996 for "behavioral difficulties and family conflict." What followed was three years of documented torture disguised as medical treatment: experimental antipsychotic medications, electroshock therapy, prolonged isolation, and something called "aversive conditioning" that made my stomach turn.

"There must be more to this," I said, holding up the file.

Tracy shook her head. "There must be," she agreed, "but from what I can tell, these files contain just the basic details."

"How many files are there?" I asked.

"Sixty-three," Tracy replied. "Every patient who went through the experimental program between 1996 and 1998."

Cooper removed another file box. This one contained a stack of photographs that looked like they'd been taken with a hidden camera. The images showed teenage patients in various states of distress: kids strapped to gurneys, others sitting in isolation cells, some with visible injuries that had nothing to do with self-harm.

"Geez," I muttered as I flipped through the photographs.

Cooper removed a small cardboard box and handed it to Tracy. She opened it and took out a small digital recorder. "She had audio recordings, too. Former staff members talking about covering up patient deaths, falsifying records, continuing treatments they knew were harmful."

I frowned, narrowed my eyes. "Patient deaths?" I asked quietly.

Cooper nodded grimly. "According to these recordings, at least seven teenagers died during the experimental program. Their deaths were listed as suicides or accidents, but the staff members Elena interviewed admitted they were directly related to the experimental treatments."

"Seven kids," I said quietly. "Geez."

But Tracy wasn't done. "Look at this," she said, opening a manila file folder. "These are financial records showing the doctors who received bonuses for keeping patients in the program. This one confirms Doctor Holloway received over two hundred thousand dollars."

I nodded. She was right. The document confirmed what we already knew.

But it was the last item in the box that really caught my attention. Cooper took out a leather-bound journal with Elena's name embossed on the cover. Inside, in her own handwriting, she detailed years of investigation, tracking down survivors, documenting ongoing health problems, and building what she hoped would be an airtight case for federal prosecution.

I flipped through the pages, noting Elena's meticulous documentation. She'd tracked down forty-three of the original sixty-three patients. Of those, twelve had died by suicide, eight from drug overdoses, six were in long-term psychiatric care, and the rest were scattered across the country, most dealing with ongoing mental health issues, addiction problems, or both.

I stopped at an entry dated just two weeks before Elena's murder.

"Finally made contact with Subject23. I will not mention the subject's name for security reasons. They remember every-thing - every treatment, every doctor, every day of those three years. They've been tracking the staff just like I have, but their methods are different. They say legal justice failed us once and won't work again. I'm worried about what they're planning, but I understand their anger. They were children, and they were destroyed for money. They mentioned 'the ones who got away' and said some people deserved to face the consequences of their actions. I tried to convince them to work within the system, but they said the system protected them then and it will protect them now. I'm scared they might be right."

"Tracy, look at this," I said, showing her the journal entry.

She skimmed it. "Subject23 could be any of the chil-dren," she said.

"Could be," I said. "But Elena was clearly worried about this person's methods. 'Their methods are different' doesn't sound like someone planning to file a lawsuit."

I continued reading Elena's journal. The entries became increasingly concerned about Subject23's intentions, with references to "settling scores" and "making them pay for what they did to us." The last entry was dated three days before Elena's murder.

"*Subject23 called tonight. They've made their decision. Says they're tired of waiting for justice that will never come. They asked me for the complete list of staff members and their current locations. I told them I couldn't be part of anything violent, but they said I was already part of it just by documenting everything. They're right, I suppose. By collecting all this evidence, by tracking down all these people, I've been preparing for this moment without realizing it. They said they'd handle everything from now on, that I should just disappear and let them finish what we started. I told them I couldn't disappear, that too many people were counting on the truth coming out. They got quiet for a long time, then said they understood. But something in their voice scared me. I think they're going to protect me by eliminating the problem themselves. I'm going to call the police tomorrow and turn everything over to them and let them handle it. Maybe it's not too late to stop this.*"

But Elena never got the chance. Someone killed her.

"So, she was on our side," I said.

"Which means the killer knew Elena was about to go to the police," Tracy replied.

I was about to respond when my phone rang. It was Chief Johnston.

"Kate, I need to see you in my office."

"Chief, I'm in the middle of processing evidence—"

"Now, Kate."

He hung up, and I looked at Tracy and Cooper. "Keep going through everything. I want a complete inventory of what Elena collected, and I want those audio recordings transcribed."

"What about the journal entries?" Tracy asked.

"Make copies of everything, especially the entries about Subject23. We need to figure out who that is."

As I walked toward the elevator with Samson, I had a feeling Chief Johnston's summons wasn't going to be pleasant. The medical community had been making calls all week, and now we had evidence that could destroy the careers and reputations of a lot of important people.

Chief Johnston's office door was closed, but I could hear voices inside. Christy shrugged and raised her eyebrows. I knocked and waited.

"Come in," he called.

I opened the door to find not just Chief Johnston, but also ADA Robert Hayes and a woman I didn't recognize —mid-fifties, expensive suit, the kind of bearing that screamed federal government.

"Kate, this is Deputy Assistant US Attorney General Patricia Hendricks from the Justice Department's Civil Rights Division," Chief Johnston said.

Federal involvement meant this case was about to get a lot more complicated.

"Captain Gazzara," Hendricks said, extending her hand. "I understand you've been investigating some allegations related to medical practices in the 1990s."

"I'm investigating two murders," I replied carefully.

"The medical practices are relevant only insofar as they provide a motive for the crimes."

"Of course," she said smoothly. "But I'm sure you understand that allegations of civil rights violations in federal healthcare sponsored programs fall under DOJ jurisdiction."

"Are you saying you're taking over my murder investigation?"

"Not at all," Hendricks replied. "We're simply here to ensure that any evidence related to potential federal crimes is handled appropriately."

Hayes leaned forward. "Captain, what the Deputy Assistant Attorney General is saying is that the federal government has an interest in ensuring that this investigation doesn't compromise ongoing civil rights inquiries."

"What ongoing civil rights inquiries?" I asked.

"The kind that require discretion and careful handling," Hendricks said. "I understand you've recently obtained some documents that might be relevant to... federal investigations."

So they already knew about Elena's safe deposit box. Either someone at the bank had made a call, or the federal government had been monitoring our investigation more closely than I'd realized.

"Any evidence I've obtained will be handled according to proper police procedures," I said.

"Of course," Hendricks said. "But I'm sure you'll agree that evidence related to federal crimes should be shared with the appropriate federal agencies."

Chief Johnston looked uncomfortable. "Kate, the

Deputy Assistant Attorney General would like to review any documents related to the experimental program."

"To ensure they're properly preserved for federal prosecution," Hayes added.

I understood what they were really asking. They wanted Elena's evidence, probably to bury it in federal bureaucracy where it would disappear for years while "ongoing investigations" protected the people who'd committed these crimes.

"I'll be happy to provide copies of any evidence that's relevant to federal crimes," I said carefully, and with a smile. "Once my murder investigation is complete."

Hendricks's smile didn't reach her eyes. "Captain, I think you misunderstand the situation. This isn't a request."

"Are you ordering me to turn over evidence in an active murder investigation?" I asked.

"I'm asking you to cooperate with federal authorities in a matter of national importance."

"National importance?" I asked skeptically.

"The psychiatric treatment programs in question were funded partly through federal grants," she said. "Any improprieties could have far-reaching implications for current federal healthcare policies."

In other words, they were worried about the political fallout.

"I see," I said. "And I'm sure you understand that I have a responsibility to the victims of these murders to ensure their killer is caught and prosecuted."

"Of course," Hendricks said. "And I'm sure we can find a way to balance those interests."

Chief Johnston cleared his throat but said nothing.

"With all due respect, ma'am," I said, quietly, "my job is to catch the killer. The political implications aren't my concern."

Hendricks stood up. "Captain Gazzara, I hope you'll reconsider your position. Federal cooperation can be very beneficial to local law enforcement agencies. Federal non-cooperation can be... shall we say, less beneficial."

It was a threat, politely delivered but unmistakable.

"I'll consider everything you've said," I replied.

After Hendricks and Hayes left, the Chief and I sat in uncomfortable silence for a moment.

"Kate, I know this is frustrating," he said finally. "But we're dealing with forces bigger than the Chattanooga Police Department."

"Chief, we have evidence that seven teenagers were murdered at Greenbriar, and their deaths were covered up. Now someone is killing the people responsible. Are we supposed to ignore that because it might embarrass some federal bureaucrat?"

"I'm not saying ignore it. I'm saying be smart about how you handle it."

"And if the feds try to take my evidence?"

He was quiet for a long moment. "Then you'd better make sure you solve this case quickly."

As I walked back to the elevator, I thought about Elena's journal entry. She'd been scared that legal justice would never come, that the system would protect the perpetrators just like it had twenty-five years ago. And looking at what had just happened in Chief Johnston's office, I was beginning to think she might have been right.

But that didn't mean I was going to let a killer continue murdering people, no matter how justified their anger might be.

Back in the conference room, Tracy and Cooper had made progress organizing Elena's evidence. The scope of the conspiracy was staggering: doctors who falsified records, administrators who covered up deaths, pharmaceutical companies that provided experimental drugs knowing they were being used on children, and federal officials who looked the other way because the research was producing publishable results.

"Any luck identifying Subject23?" I asked.

"Nope," Jack and Cooper said, almost together.

"The feds just tried to grab our evidence. Her name was Deputy US AG Patricia Hendricks."

"No shit," Jack said. "So what's our next step?"

"We keep digging. We make copies of everything and park them somewhere safe, just in case they come with warrants, and that means all computer files, Jack."

"Already done," he said, grinning. "Everything's up in the cloud."

10

The Brother's Grief Friday

Friday Morning, 6:30 AM

I'VE ALWAYS BEEN AN EARLY RISER, BUT SINCE SAMSON came into my life, my morning routine had become something of a ritual. By six-thirty, we were both awake and ready for our daily run through the neighborhood. It was one of those October mornings when the air was crisp enough to remind you that summer was finally over, but not cold enough to make you regret getting out of bed.

Samson was waiting by the door when I emerged from the bedroom, his tail wagging with the kind of enthusiasm that made me wonder if dogs actually enjoyed exercise or if they were just happy to be doing something with their humans. Either way, his energy was contagious.

"Ready for a run, boy?" I asked, reaching for his leash.

But Samson was already at the door, practically vibrating with excitement. He'd learned the routine by now: leash, keys, a quick stretch, then out into the neighborhood for our usual three-mile circuit that took us to the trees at the north end and back.

The streets were quiet at this hour, with just the occasional early commuter backing out of their driveways and the sound of lawn sprinklers doing their work before the day got too warm. Running with Samson had become more than just exercise; it was thinking time. The rhythm of footsteps on pavement, the steady breathing, the way Samson would occasionally alert to something I couldn't see or hear; it all helped me process whatever case was occupying my mind.

That morning, it was Elena Vasquez's murder and the growing complexity of the investigation. As we jogged past the familiar houses and tree-lined streets, I found myself thinking about the evidence we'd gathered from her safe deposit box. Elena had been methodical, thorough, and determined to seek justice through legal channels. But someone had killed her to prevent her from doing it.

Samson suddenly veered toward a fire hydrant, his nose working overtime on some scent trail that probably told him more about the neighborhood's recent activity than any surveillance system could provide. While he investigated, I stretched against a streetlamp and watched the sun climb higher over the Chattanooga skyline in the distance.

"Come on, Sammy," I said after he'd finished his investigation. "We've got work to do."

The rest of our run was uneventful, but by the time we returned to my apartment, I felt more focused and ready to tackle whatever the day might bring. After a quick shower, I scrambled some eggs and made toast, sharing a piece with Samson, who had perfected the art of looking pathetically underfed despite having just finished his own breakfast.

"You're not fooling anyone," I told him as he performed his hungry dog routine. But I gave him the toast, anyway.

By eight-fifteen, we were both ready for work. I grabbed my jacket, badge, and weapon, then looked at Samson, who was already waiting by the door with the kind of patience that suggested he understood we had important business to attend to, and said, "All right, partner," I said. "Let's go find Bobby Vasquez."

BOBBY VASQUEZ WAS Elena's younger brother. He lived in a small frame house on the south side of Chattanooga, the kind of neighborhood where people minded their own business and didn't ask too many questions about their neighbors. The yard was neat but sparse, with a pickup truck parked in the gravel driveway and the smell of coffee drifting from the open kitchen window.

I'd called ahead, but when Bobby answered the door, it was clear he'd slept little since learning about his sister's death. He was a big man in his late forties, with calloused hands and the kind of weathered face that came from working construction in all kinds of weather. His eyes were red-rimmed, and he looked like he'd been crying.

"Mr. Vasquez," I said. "I'm Captain Gazzara, and this is Sergeant Russell. Thank you for agreeing to see us."

He nodded and stepped aside to let us in. Samson padded quietly beside me, and I noticed Bobby's expression soften slightly when he saw the dog.

"Nice dog," he said quietly.

"His name's Samson," I replied. "He's very gentle."

Bobby's living room was small but comfortable, with a couch that had seen better days, and a coffee table covered with what looked like photo albums and loose pictures. He gestured for us to sit, then settled into a recliner across from us.

"I still can't believe she's gone," he said, his voice hoarse. "Elena was all the family I had left."

"I'm sorry for your loss," I said. "I know this is difficult, but we need to ask you some questions about your sister."

He nodded. "Ask whatever you need to ask."

Corbin opened his notebook. "When was the last time you spoke with Elena?"

"Tuesday night," Bobby replied. "She called around nine o'clock. She sounded scared, which wasn't like Elena. She was always the tough one, you know? Even as kids, she was the one who took care of everybody else."

"What was she scared of, d'you know?" I asked.

Bobby was quiet for a moment, staring at his hands. "She said someone had been following her. She thought it was connected to that research she'd been doing about the old hospital."

"Did she say who was following her?" Corbin asked.

"No, but she said she'd seen the same car outside her apartment three times in the past week. A dark sedan with tinted windows."

I made a note to have Tracy check with Elena's neighbors about any suspicious vehicles.

"Mr. Vasquez," I said, "we need to ask you about your sister's identity. She wasn't married, was she? Her real name *was* Elena Vasques, wasn't it?"

Bobby's shoulders sagged. "No, she wasn't married. She changed her name to Santos after she started getting death threats."

"Death threats?" Corbin asked. "When was this?"

"About two years ago. Elena had been working at a medical records company, temp work mostly. She'd gotten hold of some old files from that psychiatric hospital where she used to work. She said she was going to expose what happened there, make sure everyone knew the truth. I don't know how, but somehow it got out."

"And then what happened?" I asked.

"Someone broke into her apartment," Bobby said. "They didn't steal anything, but they trashed the place pretty good. Then she started getting phone calls in the middle of the night. Just breathing, you know? Finally, someone called and told her if she didn't stop digging into the past, something bad would happen to her."

"Did she report this to the police?" Corbin asked.

Bobby shook his head. "Elena didn't trust the police.

She said the people she was investigating had connections everywhere, that reporting it would just make things worse."

"So she changed her identity instead?"

"I helped her disappear," he said. "I had some friends who knew how to get new papers, a clean identity. Elena became Elena Santos, and I made sure no one could trace her back to the old name. But they did, didn't they?"

I leaned forward. "Bobby, did Elena ever mention someone she was working with? A survivor from the hospital program?"

His expression changed, became more guarded. "Why are you asking about that?"

"Because we found evidence that Elena was in contact with someone who might have been part of the program."

Bobby was quiet for a long time, clearly wrestling with something.

"There was someone," he said finally. "Elena never told me much about them, just that they'd been in touch for about a year."

"What did she tell you?" I asked.

"Just that they were a survivor—she never would tell me their name—someone who'd gone through the program. Someone who'd managed to build a normal life, even became some kind of medical professional."

"A medical professional?" Corbin asked.

"That's what she said. They had gotten themselves through school, became some kind of healthcare worker. Elena said it showed that the bastards who ran that program hadn't broken everybody."

"Did Elena seem worried about this person?" I asked.

Bobby hesitated. "Lately, yeah. She said they were getting impatient with the legal route. They wanted to take matters into their own hands."

"Go on," I said.

"I don't know exactly, but I know she was scared this person was going to do something violent."

"Did she say anything else?" Corbin asked, looking up from his notebook.

Bobby shook his head.

"When did this conversation happen?" I asked.

He shrugged, frowned, thought for a moment, then said, "Maybe two weeks ago. Elena called me afterward, really upset. She said she was scared and that she'd created a monster."

"Did Elena ever meet this person in person?" Corbin asked.

"Yeah, several times," he replied, "and they were supposed to meet the night Elena was killed. Elena said she'd found something important, something that would prove the doctors had covered up patient deaths. She was excited about it."

"But she was also worried about their intentions?"

Bobby nodded. "Elena said this person had started talking about 'settling scores' and 'making them pay.' She said she'd tried to convince them to work through the legal system, but they said the system had failed them once and would fail them again."

I studied Bobby's face. He was holding something back, and I smiled. It was obvious he was trying to protect Elena's memory while still helping us.

"Bobby, is there anything else you think we should know?" I asked.

He sighed and reached for one of the photo albums on the coffee table. "Elena left this here a few weeks ago. Said she wanted me to have it in case something happened to her."

He opened the album to reveal photographs of a much younger Elena and several teenagers. Elena was dressed in scrubs, the teens in hospital gowns, all looking hollow and scared. The pictures had clearly been taken without permission, probably by hidden cameras.

"Elena took these while she was working at the hospital," Bobby said. "She wanted to document what was happening to the kids."

I studied the photographs. The teenagers looked like prisoners more than patients. Many showed signs of physical abuse, and all had the vacant stare of people who'd been heavily medicated.

"Bobby, do any of these pictures show the person Elena was working with?"

"Possibly, but if they do, she never mentioned it to me."

Corbin asked, "Did your sister seem to think this person was dangerous?"

Bobby was quiet for a moment. "Elena loved them all. They'd been through hell, and the kids had helped each other survive. But toward the end, Elena said the treatments they'd gone through had affected each of them differently."

"How so?" Corbin asked, obviously fascinated by what we were hearing.

"She said most of them were broken by what happened to them at Greenbriar. They couldn't function, couldn't hold jobs, couldn't maintain relationships. But she said this person, the one she was working with, was different. Elena said it was like they'd taken all the pain and anger and focused it in this one person, and it scared her."

"Bobby, I'm going to assign a patrol car to keep an eye on your house for the next few days. If this person contacts you, or if you notice anything unusual, I want you to call us immediately."

"You think I'm in danger?"

"Probably not, but you never know," I said. "Elena's friend might see you as either an asset or a threat."

As we prepared to leave, Bobby walked us to the door.

"Captain," he said, "I want you to catch whoever killed Elena. But I also want you to understand something. Those doctors and nurses at that hospital, they destroyed a lot of kids. Elena's friend was one of the lucky ones, if you can call it luck."

"Whatever happened to them at Greenbriar, it doesn't justify murder," I replied.

"No," Bobby said. "But it explains it."

Outside, Corbin and I stood beside our cars, comparing notes.

"So, we're looking for a former Greenbriar patient who's now a medical professional," Corbin said.

"That's what it looks like," I replied. "And Elena was the only person who might have been able to stop them."

I called Mike Willis. "What have you got for me, Mike?" I said when he picked up.

"Kate, I've got preliminary confirmation on our victim's identity based on fingerprint comparison," he said without preamble. "The fingerprints from Elena Santos appear to be a match for the prints we found on the planted evidence at Holloway's office. Elena Santos and Elena Vasquez are the same person."

"Yeah, I know," I replied.

"You know?" he asked. "How d'you know?"

"I just talked to Bobby Vasquez, her brother. But thanks, anyway, Mike. The prints confirm what we already know."

I hung up, looked at Corbin and said, "Let's go see how the rest of the team is doing."

As we drove back toward the police department, I found myself thinking about that awful hospital and the kids that had had their lives ruined there, and how Elena had channeled all her energy into seeking legal justice. And how her friend had apparently chosen a different path.

Samson whined softly from the back seat, and I reached back to scratch his ears.

"I know, boy," I said quietly. "I don't like it either."

But we were getting closer. Elena's research had given us a profile of our killer, and Bobby's information had confirmed our theory about their motives. Now we just had to find them before they killed again.

Based on what Elena had written in her journal, someone from that experimental program had a list of targets and had begun systematically working their way through them.

Digital Ghosts

FRIDAY AFTERNOON, 2:15 PM

Jack North's desk looked like a computer graveyard. Three laptops were open and running, cables snaked across every available surface, and the lights on at least four external hard drives were blinking quietly in the background. Empty energy drink cans formed a small pyramid beside his keyboard, and a half-eaten sandwich sat forgotten on top of a stack of printouts. Jack himself looked like he'd been living on caffeine and determination for the past two days, but his eyes had the kind of focused intensity that meant he was onto something.

"Please tell me you have good news," I said as Samson and I approached his workstation.

"Maybe," Jack replied without looking up from his screen. His fingers moved across the keyboard with the rapid-fire precision of someone who'd been coding since he was twelve years old. "Because what I found is definitely interesting, but I'm not sure how helpful it is."

I settled into the chair beside his desk, noting the organized chaos of his workspace. Jack was the kind of person who could find a specific cable in what looked like electronic mayhem but couldn't remember to eat lunch for three days straight.

"Let's see what ya got," I said.

Jack nodded and pulled up what looked like an email interface on one of his laptops. The display showed a secure messaging system I didn't recognize, with encryption symbols and security certificates scattered across the interface.

"I've been digging through Elena's computer files for the past sixteen hours," he said, "and I found something. She was corresponding with someone using encrypted email. Someone with the user name Subject23."

"Yeah, I know. So?"

"The emails go back about eighteen months," he said, turning to look at me, "and they're all about the experimental program. Elena and Subject23 were sharing information, tracking down other survivors, documenting evidence." Jack scrolled through a long list of message headers. "There are over three hundred emails."

"Three hundred?" I asked. "That's a lot of communication."

"They were building something together, Kate. Look at the early messages."

He clicked on an email dated fifteen months earlier:

Elena - Thank you for reaching out. I never thought I'd find someone else who remembered the night ward protocols.

The isolation rooms. The special treatments Dr. Holloway administered after hours. I've been collecting evidence for years, but I never had anyone to share it with. I'm not crazy. We're not crazy. What they did to me, and the rest of the kids was real. - Subject23.

Elena's response was below:

You're not crazy. I have documentation, too, patient logs, medication schedules, even some audio recordings I made with a hidden recorder. We can prove what they did to you. We can make sure it never happens to other kids. - E

"Can you trace the account?" I asked.

Jack shook his head, pulling up another screen that showed a network diagram with connection lines criss-crossing like a spider web. "Whoever set this up knew what they were doing," he said. "The emails are routed through servers in at least seven different countries, using military-grade encryption that would make the NSA proud. I can read the content because Elena saved the decrypted versions on her local machine, but tracking the source? I'd need resources I don't have and probably six months to crack it."

"What do the rest of the emails say?" I asked. "Can you show me the progression?"

Jack organized the messages chronologically on his screen. "At first, they're just sharing information," he said. "Elena would send Subject23 updates on her research, copies of patient files she'd obtained, and contact information for other survivors. Subject23 would provide details about specific staff members or treatment protocols, information about current locations of people who worked in the program."

He pulled up several exchanges from the early months:

Elena - I found Dr. Fletcher. He's practicing in Chattanooga now, has his own clinic. Still specializing in adolescent psychiatry. Some things never change. I also located one of the night nurses - she's retired but living on Signal Mountain, name of King. Do you think any of them remember us? - Subject 23

This was followed by:

I'm sure they remember. The question is whether they feel any guilt about what they did. I've been researching legal options. There might be ways to pursue civil claims even if criminal charges aren't possible. - E

Elena - Legal options assume the system works. The system failed us when we were children. Why would it work for us now? But I'm willing to try your way first. Send me whatever you find about statutes of limitations. - Subject 23

"But over the past few months, the tone changed," Jack said, scrolling to more recent messages.

He pulled up an email dated three months earlier:

Elena - I've been thinking about what you said regarding legal action. You still believe the system will work? I don't. These people destroyed us and covered it up for twenty-five years. The statute of limitations has expired on most of their crimes. Even if we can prove everything, what happens? They retire with full pensions while we deal with the aftermath for the rest of our lives. I'm losing patience. - Subject 23

Elena's response showed her growing concern:

I understand your frustration, but violence won't bring you justice. It will just make you a criminal. We have enough evidence now to force an investigation, maybe even federal

charges. *We need to trust the system, give it a chance to work. -
E*

But Subject23's next email showed a completely
different mindset:

*Elena, the system failed us once. It protected them then, and
it will protect them now. I've spent years building a life,
gaining skills, positioning myself to do what the law won't. I'm
going to do what I should have done years ago. I hope you
understand. - Subject23*

"That was sent six weeks ago," Jack said. "Elena's
responses after that show she was getting worried about
Subject23's intentions."

He pulled up a series of increasingly frantic emails
from Elena:

*I can't be part of anything violent. Yes, I know these people
hurt you, but violence isn't justice. Please reconsider what
you're planning. There are other survivors depending on us to
do this the right way. - E*

*Hey, I found a lawyer who specializes in institutional abuse
cases. She thinks we have a strong case for a class action
lawsuit. We could get justice for everyone who was hurt, not
just revenge for you. Please give this a chance. - E*

But Subject23's responses grew colder and more
distant:

*Elena - You always tried to help. It's one of the things I
loved about you. But idealism didn't protect us then, and it
won't protect other children now. I can't wait any longer. I
have to do something - Subject23.*

And then, Subject23's chilling final ultimatum:

Elena - I'm not asking you to be part of anything. But I am asking you to stay out of my way. I have everything I need to finish this. This is not a request. - Subject23

"That was sent four days before Elena's murder," Jack said.

I was reading the exchange. Subject23 had given Elena an ultimatum: disappear or get out of the way. When Elena refused to abandon her legal approach, Subject23 had eliminated her.

"Any emails after that?"

"Just one," Jack said, pulling up the final message. "Sent two hours before Elena's estimated time of death."

Elena - I have everything we need. Meet me tonight and we'll finish this. No more waiting for justice that will never come. Come alone. - Subject23

"So Elena thought she was meeting Subject23 to continue their legal strategy," I said, thoughtfully. "But Subject23 was planning to kill her."

"That's what it looks like," he replied. "And then there's this: Elena wrote a response, but she never sent it."

All right, I'll meet you, but only to try one more time to convince you that violence isn't the answer. The lawyer I mentioned thinks we can get media attention, maybe even a congressional hearing. We can expose this without becoming criminals ourselves. Please give me a chance to show you there's another way. - E

Jack opened a window on one of his other laptops, showing what looked like a network analysis diagram. "But here's where it gets really interesting," he said, turning the computer a little so I could see it better. "I've been analyzing the metadata from these emails, looking at routing information, server connections, timing patterns."

The diagram showed email activity across a map of the Southeastern United States, with different colored dots marking activity in various cities.

"Subject23 has been very busy over the past year," Jack said, "sending encrypted messages to addresses in Memphis, Atlanta, Nashville, even Birmingham. Always using different servers, always routing through different networks, but the encryption signature is consistent."

I frowned. "You're saying this person has been in contact with people in other cities?"

"Or they've been traveling," Jack said, highlighting different areas of the map. "Look at this pattern. Six months ago, Subject23 was sending emails from servers in different cities across the Southeast. Four months ago, intensive activity in Atlanta. Two months ago, Nashville. And for the past month, all the activity has been centered here in Chattanooga."

"So our killer has been traveling around the Southeast, targeting people connected to the experimental program?"

"That's my theory. And here's the thing that really bothers me." Jack pulled up another screen showing network intrusion logs. "Someone's been hacking into law enforcement databases."

I leaned forward, studying the technical data that meant nothing to me but clearly alarmed Jack. "What databases?"

"Memphis, Birmingham, Atlanta PD's, The Tennessee Bureau of Investigation, even some FBI systems. The intrusions are sophisticated. Whoever's doing this knows network security better than most IT professionals. But there's a pattern. They've been accessing FBI files related to unsolved murders, specifically cases involving medical professionals."

"That's... unbelievable," I muttered. "Why would they do that?"

"Maybe they're making sure the police departments aren't connecting the dots between their murders," Jack said. "I mean, look at this timeline."

He pulled up a chart showing database access times correlated with the murder dates. "Two days before the Memphis murder, someone accessed Memphis PD's case management system. Three days before we found Elena's body, someone was in our evidence database."

"Wait," I said, feeling my stomach tighten. "Someone's been accessing our databases?"

He nodded. "Personnel files, case reports, email communications, even your calendar and phone logs. The intrusions started about two weeks ago, right after we began investigating Holloway's murder."

"How long have you known this, Jack?"

"Today," he replied.

"Have you told the chief?" I asked.

"No, I was waiting until I'd run it by you."

I thought for a minute, then said, "He needs to know. Talk it over with him. Tell him you ran it by me, and that I insisted you report it to him. This is serious, Jack."

He nodded. "Geez, that's all I need," he muttered, turning back to his screens.

"So our killer knows we're hunting them?" I said.

"They know everything about our investigation," Jack replied, pulling up a log of accessed files. "They've been reading our case files, monitoring our progress, staying one step ahead of us. Look at this."

The screen showed a list of files that had been accessed: my personnel record, Corbin's background check, Tracy's case notes, even Doc Sheddon's preliminary autopsy reports.

"They know our methods, our procedures, our personal information," he said, "and it gets worse. They accessed the witness interview records from Bobby Vasquez's statement yesterday. They know we identified Elena as Elena Vasquez."

"Can you trace the intrusions?" I asked.

"I'm working on it," he said, "but whoever's doing this is extremely sophisticated. They're using stolen credentials from multiple agencies, bouncing through compromised systems in different countries, covering their tracks. It's going to take time, and frankly, they're better at this than I am."

"Nah, I don't believe it," I replied, touching his shoulder.

Jack looked embarrassed. "Kate, I've been doing computer forensics for eight years. I thought I was pretty good at it. But this person? They're operating at a level I've only seen from federal agencies or major criminal organizations. They have access to tools and techniques that aren't available to normal hackers."

My phone rang. It was Tracy.

"Kate, I think you need to get back here. We found something in Elena's address book."

"I'm on my way," I said, then turned back to Jack. "Don't forget. Talk to the chief. Then keep working on those database intrusions. I want to know exactly what information they've accessed and when."

"There's one more thing before you go," Jack said. "I've been monitoring the Subject23 account since I found it. There's been no new activity for the past three days, but this morning at four AM, someone logged in and deleted everything. The entire account, all message history, all contact information."

"Crap," I said. "They know we found their communications?"

"Either that, or they're finished with that identity and moving on to something else. But Kate, here's what really worries me. Based on the sophistication of these intrusions, our killer is operating like a professional intelligence agent. They have resources, training, and capabilities that go way beyond what a normal person should have."

"What are you saying, Jack?"

"I'm saying I think our killer's getting help, professional help. The kind of help that comes from organizations that train people to kill efficiently and cover their tracks. Someone at one of the federal agencies, like the CIA."

I stared at him for a moment, then said, "I sincerely hope you're wrong, Jack."

I FOUND TRACY, Cooper and Hawk in the conference room, Tracy examining Elena's small address book with a magnifying glass.

"Okay, so what did you find?" I asked.

Tracy looked up, her expression grim. "Elena kept detailed records of everyone connected to the experimental program. Current addresses, phone numbers, employment information, even family details. But look at this entry."

She pointed to a page near the back of the book. Written in Elena's careful handwriting was:

"Subject23 - Emergency Only - Local Contact - Night Shift - Medical Professional - If anything happens to me, only Subject23 can finish this."

"So, as we thought, Subject23 works in the medical field?" I said.

"That's what it looks like," Cooper replied. "Night shift at some kind of medical facility. That would give them access to sedatives, medical equipment, surgical instruments, all the tools they'd need to commit these murders."

"And it explains how they've managed to stay under our radar," Tracy added. "Night shift workers are almost invisible. They come and go when most people are asleep, and medical staff have legitimate reasons to access all kinds of supplies."

I thought about Doc Sheddon's autopsy findings. Professional-grade medical equipment, surgical-quality latex gloves, expert knowledge of anatomy and drug interactions, propofol and other surgical anesthetics. Our killer had been hiding in plain sight, using their medical training and hospital access to plan and execute perfect murders.

"Any indication of which medical facility?" I asked.

"Elena was careful not to be too specific," Tracy said. "But based on the other entries in her book, I'm guessing it's somewhere in the Chattanooga area."

"There's something else," Cooper said, as he took the address book from Tracy. "Look at the rest of Elena's notes."

He flipped through the address book, showing me page after page of names, addresses, and phone numbers. All meticulously organized, cross-referenced, and updated with current information.

"Elena tracked down everyone," Tracy said. "Doctors, nurses, orderlies, administrators, pharmaceutical company representatives, even hospital board members who approved the experimental program. She has current contact information for all of them."

"How many names?" I asked. "Give me the total."

"Forty-seven, in all," Cooper replied. "And based on what we know about our killer's methods and the time-line Jack discovered, every one of these people is a potential target."

I studied the list, recognizing some names from our investigation. Dr. Fletcher, along with a Judge Marks, Dr. Holloway, and Elena herself. All the people who'd already been murdered were on Elena's master list.

"We need to warn them," I said.

"Kate," Tracy said quietly, "some of these people are prominent members of the medical community. Doctors at major hospitals, pharmaceutical executives, hospital administrators. If we start calling them and telling them they might be targets of a serial killer, it's going to cause panic."

"And if we don't warn them and more people die—" I snapped, then immediately regretted it.

Cooper shrugged and turned to another section of the address book. "Elena ranked them," he said.

I frowned. "Ranked them? How?"

"Priority targets," he said, showing me Elena's margin notes. "She has numbers beside each name - one through forty-seven. Dr. Holloway was number one. Elena herself was number four. Judge Marks was number seven."

"So our killer is working from Elena's research," I said, "using Elena's priority system to select targets."

"That's what it looks like," Tracy agreed. "And based on the ranking system, the next likely targets would be Dr. Fletcher, then Dr. Sarah Walton, and someone named Dr. Amanda Pierce."

My phone buzzed with a call from Chief Johnston.

"Kate, I just got off the phone with the federal authorities again. The pressure is escalating. And North just informed me we've been hacked. What the hell is going on?"

"I can't help you with that one, Chief," I said. "We're dealing with a highly skilled killer. Jack thinks whoever it is may be getting help from a government insider; maybe CIA, or some such."

The chief was silent, so I said, "What kind of pressure, Chief?"

"Deputy Assistant Attorney General Hendricks called personally. They're threatening to involve the FBI if we don't share the evidence from Elena's safe deposit box. They're claiming the experimental program falls under federal jurisdiction because it involved federal healthcare funding."

"And?" I pressed him.

"And they're making it clear that continued federal non-cooperation could affect our department's federal grants, our task force participation, even our access to federal databases."

I felt my jaw tighten. "So they're threatening to cut off our resources if we don't hand over evidence in an active murder investigation."

"That's about the size of it. Kate, I'm trying to buy you time, but they're not going away. How close are we to solving this?"

I looked at Tracy and Cooper, who were still working through Elena's evidence. "We're making progress, Chief," I said, dodging the question. "We know our killer is someone called Subject23 who was a patient in the experimental program. That's about all I can tell you."

"That's not specific enough to satisfy the feds. They want names, addresses, arrest warrants."

"I understand, Chief," I said. "Give me another forty-eight hours."

"That's about all I can give you. After that, this case might be taken out of our hands."

I looked at Hawk, Tracy and Cooper after hanging up. "Keep working on it. We need to identify Subject23, and pretty damn quick. Cross-reference the patient files with current medical licenses in the area. I want to know who from that experimental program is now working in healthcare."

"What about warning the potential targets?" Tracy asked.

"Let me think about the politics of that. But start putting together contact information for the top ten names on Elena's list. If we're going to warn them, we need to do it quickly."

12

Warning the Living

SATURDAY MORNING, 9:00 AM

I woke up Saturday morning with the uncomfortable feeling that we were rapidly running out of time. The coffee maker gurgled to life as Samson and I prepared for our morning run, but even that familiar routine couldn't shake the sense of urgency that had been building since Jack North's revelation about the database intrusions. Our killer was monitoring our every move, staying one step ahead, and we still didn't know who it was.

The morning air was cooler than it had been all week, with the kind of crisp clarity that made the mountains visible in the distance. Even Samson seemed more alert than usual during our run, his ears constantly swiveling as if he, too, sensed that something was different about the day.

By eight, we were back home, and I was scrambling eggs while reviewing my notes from the previous day.

Elena's address book had given us forty-seven potential targets, and we needed to start warning them before our killer struck again. The problem was figuring out how to do that without causing panic or alerting the media.

After a quick breakfast, Samson and I headed to the police department where I found Tracy already at work, surrounded by printouts and phone lists.

"You're here early," I said.

"Couldn't sleep," she replied, looking up from her computer screen. "I've been cross-referencing Elena's target list with current addresses and phone numbers. About half of these people are still in the tri-state area, but the others are scattered across the Southeast."

"Any pattern to their current locations?"

"Not really. Some stayed in medical fields, others got out completely. Dr. Fletcher is still practicing. Dr. Walton has her partnership with Holloway, but there's a former orderly who now runs a hardware store in Nashville, and one of the night nurses who became a real estate agent in Atlanta."

I studied Tracy's lists. She had a gift for making sense of complex information, turning chaos into something manageable.

"Based on Elena's ranking system, who should we contact first?"

"Dr. Fletcher is number three on the list," Tracy said. "Then Dr. Walton at number five, followed by Dr. Amanda Pierce at number six. She's currently a hospital administrator at Chattanooga General."

"Chattanooga General," I repeated. "That's interesting."

"Why?"

"Elena's address book mentioned that Subject23 works night shift at a medical facility. If Dr. Pierce is at Chattanooga General, maybe that's where our killer has connections."

Cooper arrived carrying a box of donuts and looking like he'd actually gotten some sleep, which put him ahead of the rest of us.

"Morning, Captain," he said.

"What are you looking so chipper about?" I asked.

He tilted his head as he looked at me and grinned.

"All right," I said. "That's enough. Let's start warning people. Tracy, I want you to contact Dr. Fletcher. Cooper, you take Dr. Walton. I'll handle Dr. Pierce myself."

"What should we tell them?" Tracy asked.

It was a good question. One to which I didn't have a good answer.

"Be diplomatic," I said. "We don't want to frighten them, or God forbid, cause a panic." I thought for a moment, then said, "Tell them we think one of the patients at Greenbriar back in the nineties may be targeting people connected to one of the psychiatric treatment programs. Don't mention specifics about the murders, but make it clear they should be careful and report anything unusual."

"And if they ask questions?" Cooper asked.

"Tell them it's an ongoing investigation and we'll provide more details as and when we can. But emphasize that they should take precautions."

I was about to head out when my phone rang. Speak of the devil; It was Dr. Fletcher.

"Captain Gazzara, I need to see you," he said without preamble. His voice sounded strained, almost panicked.

"What's wrong, Dr. Fletcher?"

"I'd rather not discuss it over the phone," he replied. "Can you come to my office? There's something I need to show you."

"I'll be there in twenty minutes." I said.

I looked at Tracy and Cooper. "Change of plans. That was Fletcher. He wants to see me. So, for now, you two continue working on the contact list. I'll take Samson and see what Fletcher has to say."

THE DRIVE to Fletcher's office gave me time to think about our conversation from earlier in the week. He'd been nervous then, defensive about his involvement in the experimental program. Now he sounded downright scared.

I arrived at Fletcher's office on the north side of town some twenty minutes later to find the man himself waiting in the lobby, looking like he hadn't slept for a week.

"Thank you for coming, Captain," he said. "I wasn't sure who else to call."

"What's going on, Dr. Fletcher?"

He led us to his office and closed the door. On his desk was a manila envelope that looked like it had been delivered by hand.

"I found this on my car windshield this morning," he said, handing it to me. "No postmark, no delivery service markings. Someone put it there during the night."

I pulled on latex gloves before taking and opening it. Inside was a single sheet of paper, a photocopied patient record from the experimental program. The patient was listed as "Subject23" with all identifying information redacted except for the age: sixteen years old.

At the bottom of the page, someone had written in red ink: "You remember me now, don't you, Dr. Fletcher? It's time to pay for what you did."

"Do you remember this patient, Dr. Fletcher?"

His face went pale. "Subject23. Yes, I remember her. One of the most difficult cases we dealt with. Highly intelligent, very resistant to treatment, always asking questions about the medications and procedures."

So now we know our killer is a woman, I thought. *That's a huge step forward,*

"What happened to her?" I asked.

"She was in the program for almost three years. Longer than most patients because the standard treatments weren't working. We tried increasingly aggressive approaches - experimental antipsychotics, electroshock therapy, prolonged isolation."

"And?" I asked, unable to completely hide my disgust.

Fletcher sat down heavily in his chair. "She got worse instead of better. Much worse. By the time she was discharged, she was... different. Changed. The treatments had affected her personality, cognitive function, everything."

"Changed how?"

"She'd become calculating, cold. Before the treatments, she was angry and defiant but still recognizably a troubled teenager. Afterward, she was something else entirely. Like all the emotional responses had been burned out and replaced with pure intellect."

I studied the patient's record again. "What was her name, Doctor?"

"I... I can't tell you that," he replied. "It would be a breach of patient confidentiality."

"Oh, come on," I snapped. "This patient is threatening you and you're refusing to cooperate?" It was a question as much as it was a statement. "If you want our protection, you need to consider what's more important: confidentiality rules or staying alive."

He was quiet for a long moment, staring at the patient record.

"I understand what you're saying, Captain. But I can't do it. Not without consulting a lawyer about what I can and can't reveal."

I heaved a sigh. He didn't seem to notice. It was as if he was off somewhere, in another world.

"You obviously think this patient is dangerous, Doctor. What makes you think that?"

"Because the treatments we subjected her to didn't break her the way they broke other patients. We essentially created a highly intelligent individual with an intimate knowledge of medical procedures and a very good reason to hate everyone who was involved in her treatment."

"Where is she now? Do you know?"

"I have absolutely no idea," he replied, shaking his

head. "After discharge, she disappeared completely. But Captain, if she's been planning revenge for twenty-five years, then she's probably the most dangerous person any of us will ever face."

I frowned. I usually wasn't one to judge—I'd had that trained out of me over my years as a police officer—but I just couldn't help myself. "Don't you ever feel remorse for what you and the rest of the staff at Greenbriar did to those children?" I asked.

He looked at me as if I was stupid. "We were trying to help them, for God's sake."

I heaved a deep breath and shook my head. Again, he didn't seem to notice.

"Do you have any other records pertaining to this... Subject23?" I asked. "Photos, psychological evaluations, anything that might help us identify her now?"

Fletcher shook his head. "Most of the program records were destroyed when the facility closed. But there might be something in the old files at Chattanooga General. That's where most of the staff went when the experimental program ended."

"Including Dr. Amanda Pierce?" I asked.

"Yes, Amanda was there during the final year of the program. She might remember her."

I stood up, taking the threatening message with me. "Dr. Fletcher, I'm increasing the protective surveillance to your home and office. Don't go anywhere alone, and if you receive any more messages or notice anything unusual, call us immediately."

"Do you think she'll try to kill me?" he asked, his face pale, his fingers trembling.

I had little sympathy for him, but I could understand how he was feeling, so I tried to let him down gently. "I think she's been planning this for a very long time, and I think you're probably on her list. The question is whether we can find her before she finds you."

I stood. Samson almost leapt to his feet. And we left him there, sitting behind his desk looking positively terrified, and I can't say I blamed him.

As Samson and I walked out into the parking area, I took out my phone and called Tracy.

"Tracy, I'm heading to Chattanooga General. I need to talk to Dr. Amanda Pierce. Everything okay there?"

"Yeah... Sure," she replied. "Did Fletcher give you something useful?"

"Subject23 is female. She was a patient at Greenbriar for three years. She went through the program and, from what I could get out of him, they turned her into some kind of intellectual monster. And if I'm right, she's been working under our noses."

"That's helpful. And she's working where?" Tracy asked.

"That's what I'm hoping to find out. You, Hawk and Cooper keep digging. I don't know how much help knowing that it's a she will be, but it's something."

I loaded Sammy into the passenger seat of my unmarked cruiser, thinking about what Fletcher had told me. It wasn't much, but now we knew we were dealing with a highly intelligent female patient who had been transformed rather than broken by three years of experimental treatments, and had spent years after her release gaining medical and technical training and was now putting into practice all that she'd learned, and not in a good way. And, to some extent, I could understand how she wanted to destroy the people who had destroyed her adolescence.

But we still didn't know who she was. And that was a huge problem.

The Memphis Connection

SATURDAY MORNING, 11:00 AM

Chattanooga General was one of those satellite medical complexes that had once been a small hospital serving West Chattanooga, but had grown organically over several decades, with new wings and additions creating a maze of corridors and departments. The administrative offices were located in the newer section, all glass and steel and the kind of sterile efficiency that modern hospitals seemed to favor.

Dr. Amanda Pierce's office was on the third floor, and when Samson and I arrived, her secretary informed us that Dr. Pierce was finishing up a budget meeting but would see us shortly. I used the time to study the wall of certificates and awards that covered one side of her waiting area. Pierce had been at Chattanooga General for over fifteen years and had apparently worked her way up from staff coordinator to assistant administrator to her current position.

"Captain Gazzara?" Dr. Pierce emerged from her office, extending her hand in greeting. "I'm sorry to keep you waiting. Please, come in." She glanced at Samson, who was wearing his K9 harness and badge, but said nothing.

I judged Pierce to be in her mid to late fifties with graying hair pulled back in a neat bun and the kind of professional demeanor that suggested she'd spent years dealing with difficult situations and even more difficult people. Her office was everything you'd expect from a hospital administrator: efficient, organized, and completely impersonal, with medical journals neatly stacked on shelves and a computer monitor that never seemed to stop displaying streams of data.

"What can I do for you, Captain?" She asked, all business, as I sat down across from her, and Sammy settled down at my side.

"If you don't mind, Dr., I'd like to record this interview." I said, taking out my phone and setting it to record. "I understand you worked at the Greenbriar Behavioral Health Center during the final two years of the experimental program,"

Her expression became guarded immediately. "Yes... Of course... I was a staff coordinator there, yes. But that was a long time ago, and most of those records have been destroyed."

"We're investigating two murders that appear to be connected to the experimental program and people who worked that program."

Pierce leaned back in her chair, clearly processing this information. "Who's been killed?"

"Dr. Marcus Holloway and Elena Vasquez, though she was using the name Elena Santos when she died."

"Elena," Pierce said quietly. "Yes, I remember her. She was one of the night nurses. Very dedicated, very protective of her patients. She used to question treatment protocols, always advocating for the children."

"What happened to her?" I asked.

She tilted her head a little and said, "She was fired eventually. There was some kind of incident with a patient where she allegedly interfered with a treatment protocol without authorization. The administration said she was becoming too emotionally involved with the patients."

"Do you remember the specific incident?" I asked.

Pierce was quiet for a moment, clearly weighing how much to reveal. "There was a patient who was having severe reactions to one of the medications. Elena tried to stop the treatment, said it was causing neurological damage. But the supervising physician overruled her and continued the protocol."

"What happened to the patient?" I asked.

"I don't know the long-term outcome, but Elena was dismissed shortly after that incident, and the patient's records were sealed."

I leaned forward. "Dr. Pierce, we're particularly interested in a patient designated as Subject23. Dr. Fletcher mentioned you might remember the case."

Pierce's expression became even more guarded. "Subject23," she said carefully. "Yes, I remember. That was one of our most challenging cases. Why are you asking about this patient specifically?"

"Because we believe this patient may be connected to the recent murders."

Pierce was quiet for a long moment, clearly considering how much to reveal. "Captain, you have to understand that the experimental program was controversial, even at the time. We were trying to help severely disturbed adolescents using treatments that were considered groundbreaking then but would be questionable by today's standards."

"What can you tell me about Subject23?" I asked.

"The patient was admitted at age sixteen for behavioral problems and family conflicts. The intake file mentioned running away from home, conflicts with authority figures, and some minor legal issues. Initially, the case seemed routine: a troubled teenager who needed structure and therapy."

"But it wasn't routine, was it?" I said.

"No," she replied. "As the treatment progressed, it became clear that this patient was different. Extremely intelligent, highly observant, able to analyze our treatment protocols and predict medication effects. Subject23 was able to manipulate other patients, and even some staff members."

"How did the medical team respond to that kind of resistance?" I asked.

Pierce looked uncomfortable, glancing at her office door as if to make sure it was closed. "Dr. Holloway was the supervising physician for most of Subject23's treatment. He believed that the patient's resistance indicated deeper psychological problems that required more aggressive intervention."

"What kind of aggressive intervention?"

"Experimental antipsychotic medications that hadn't been fully tested on adolescents. Extended periods of isolation—sometimes weeks at a time. Electroconvulsive therapy, which was controversial even then for patients that young. The theory was that if we could break through the patient's psychological defenses, we could address the underlying issues."

"And did it work?"

Pierce shifted uncomfortably in her chair. "In a sense, yes," she replied. "After about eighteen months of intensive treatment, Subject23 stopped resisting. Became compliant, even helpful. Started participating in group therapy, following medication schedules, even helping with other patients."

"That sounds like success," I said.

"That's what we thought at the time. But looking back, I think we may have simply taught the patient to hide her true thoughts and feelings. To present whatever facade would get her what she wanted."

My phone rang. It was an unknown number. I ignored it.

No sooner had I declined the call than it rang again. This time I stopped recording and answered it. "Captain Gazzara."

"Captain. This is Detective Ray Torres from Memphis."

"Excuse me," I said to Pierce. "Detective Torres?"

"Captain Gazzara, I saw your case in the bulletin, and

I think you need to hear me out. Are you somewhere you can talk freely?"

"Can I call you back, Detective? I'm interviewing a witness."

He agreed and gave me his direct number, which I wrote down in my notebook.

After Torres hung up, I set my phone to record again and looked at Pierce. "So, Doctor," I said, "based on what we've learned about Subject23, who is she, and do you know where she is??"

"I never knew her name. She was always referred to by her designation, Patient23. And no, I don't know where she is. But I can tell you this - if Subject23 is behind these murders, then everyone who worked in that program is in danger. Because Subject23 had an extraordinary memory. She remembered every staff member, every treatment, every interaction. If she's spent the past twenty-five years planning revenge, she will have detailed knowledge of everyone involved and probably current information about where we all are now."

"She does," I said. "Including contact information."

Pearce stared at me, then said, "I'm not surprised. She was always watching, always learning. Even as a teenager, she had an uncanny ability to gather and retain information. She could tell you things about staff members that the staff members didn't even know about themselves: personal habits, family situations, financial problems."

"You sound like you were afraid of her," I said.

Pierce looked out her office window at the hospital

complex below. "Not afraid, exactly. But wary. Subject23 was unlike any patient I'd ever encountered. Most of the kids in the program were clearly disturbed, acting out their trauma in obvious ways. But Subject23 was different. It was like working with a computer wrapped in a sixteen-year-old's body."

"Did you have direct contact with her?" I asked.

"Some," she replied. "I coordinated treatment schedules, medication protocols, that sort of thing. But I tried to limit my interactions with her because, quite frankly, she made me uncomfortable."

"Uncomfortable how?" I asked.

"She seemed to be studying me. Analyzing my behavior, my routines, my reactions. I always felt she was learning things about me that I wouldn't want her to know."

I stared at her for a moment, my lips pursed, then I stood up, closed my notebook, stopped recording and said, "I think that's enough for now, Dr. Pierce. I'm recommending that you take some time off and go away for a few days, at least until we get this thing sorted out. If Subject23 is working from a target list, you're probably on it."

"So, you really think I'm in danger?" she asked.

"At this point, I think anyone who worked in that program is in danger until we catch the killer."

"I can't just up and leave my patients," she replied. "What else should I do?"

"Vary your routines," I said. "Don't go anywhere alone. Go stay in a hotel for a few days. If you notice anyone following you or anything unusual, call us immediately. And Dr. Pierce, if you remember anything else about this Subject23—any details that might help us identify her—please contact me right away."

She nodded, biting her bottom lip, wringing her hands in front of her, and said, nodding, "Of course." And, with that, I left, and I didn't look back.

When I got to my car, I returned Detective Torres' call.

"What can I do for you, Detective Torres?"

"I saw the Holloway case in The Bulletin, and it clicked with me," he began. "Two months ago, we had a murder that matches your pattern exactly. Dr. Samuel Rodriguez, a psychiatrist, was found dead in his home office with a single puncture wound to the carotid artery. The scene staged. He'd been placed in his desk chair and surrounded with old medical equipment."

"Thin bladed weapon, four, maybe five-inch blade?" I asked.

"Yes, that's it," he replied. "A narrow, sharp instrument, the placement very precise. But Rodriguez had been receiving threatening letters for several weeks before his death. Letters referencing his work at a psychiatric facility in Chattanooga in the late 1990s. The letters included patient numbers, treatment dates, and specific medical procedures. Whoever sent those letters had intimate knowledge of Rodriguez's work during that period."

"Did Rodriguez save any of the letters?"

"A few. And Captain, one of them mentions a Subject23 specifically. I have it here in front of me. Listen to this: 'You remember Subject23, don't you, Dr.

Rodriguez? You remember what you did during the night shifts when no one else was watching, don't you?' What the hell does that mean, Captain?"

"It means one of the patients that was treated in an experimental mental health program between 1996 and 1999 is systematically eliminating anyone who had anything to do with it. Dr. Rodriguez is the third victim that I know of." I paused for a second, then said, "Detective, what else can you tell me about the Rodriguez murder?"

"I told you the basics," he replied. "How about I send you a copy of the file?"

"Yes, please," I said. "Thank you. What about forensic evidence?"

"Clean scene, just like yours probably were," he said. "But we did find evidence that the killer had been monitoring him. We found professional-grade surveillance equipment hidden in his home: cameras and audio recording devices, in his office, the living room and bedroom. There was even a keylogger installed on his computer and a tracking device on his car. None of it the kind of stuff you can buy at an electronics store, and it was installed by someone who knew what they were doing. Whoever did this has serious technical skills and resources."

I thought about Jack North's discovery of the database intrusions. "How about you? Did you find any evidence of hacking in your investigation?"

"Now that you mention it, yes. Rodriguez's computer had been compromised for at least a month before his murder. Someone was reading his emails, monitoring his online activity, tracking his daily routines, even accessing his banking information."

"No, no," I said. "Were any of your computers hacked?"

He was quiet for a moment, obviously thinking, then said, "Not that I know of, but I'll have our IT guys check everything out… You know, Captain, I don't think this is the work of some traumatized patient seeking revenge. The letters Rodriguez received weren't emotional rants - they were calculated psychological warfare designed to terrorize him. The killer knew Rodriguez's schedule, his habits, his fears. They'd been studying him like a specimen."

"Any witnesses or security footage?" I asked.

"Nothing useful," he replied. "Rodriguez lived alone in a house in a quiet neighborhood. The killer avoided all the security cameras, knew exactly when Rodriguez would be home alone, even knew which entrance to use to avoid being seen by neighbors."

"Got it," I said. "Well, thanks for the call—"

"Wait," he said, cutting me off. "There's something else. We don't think that Rodriguez was the first victim in our area."

I was silent for a moment, trying to figure out the implications of that statement, then, finally, I said, "What makes you think that?"

"We started looking at other unsolved murders with similar characteristics," he replied, "and we found two more cases over the past year. Both victims were former healthcare workers, both were killed the exact same way, and both scenes had been staged. We just hadn't connected them until the Rodriguez case. Captain, based on our three cases and what you've told me, I think we're looking for a serial killer."

But I already knew that, and while I was grateful for him calling me and filling me in on his cases, I wasn't prepared to admit it, not yet. So I thanked him for the call and the file he was going to send me, told him we needed to stay in touch, and that I'd have one of my detectives call him, and then I hung up. Then I called Tracy.

"Tracy, I need you to coordinate with Memphis PD immediately. They've got three similar murders. Detective Torres is the contact. Here's his direct number." I read it to her. "It looks like we might be dealing with more victims than we thought."

"It does?" she replied. "How many?"

"I don't know," I said. "We have two. Torres has three. That's five. God only knows how many more there are. Tracy, before you do anything else, I want you to organize round-the-clock surveillance on Dr. Amanda Pierce, starting immediately."

"What about Dr. Walton?"

"Same, and have Cooper check on her right away. If Subject23 is working systematically through the staff list, she could be next."

"Kate, do we have any idea who she is?" she asked.

"Nope, only that she's female." I said. "Look, I'm on my way back. I'll see you in about thirty minutes. Have Cooper make a fresh pot of coffee, will you? I need some in the worst way."

I was ten minutes out when my phone buzzed with a

text from Chief Johnston: *Federal agents arriving Monday morning. I need a full briefing on current investigation status. Also getting calls from hospital administrators about police presence at Chattanooga General. Handle discreetly.*

I sighed. Federal involvement meant more political pressure, jurisdictional conflicts, and probably orders to handle the case even more "discreetly" than we already were. But it also meant more resources and the possibility of coordinating investigations across multiple states. So maybe we'd get a little good with the bad.

14

Under Surveillance

Sunday Morning

SUNDAY MORNINGS IN CHATTANOOGA ARE USUALLY peaceful interludes between stressful weeks of investigation, quiet times, times to relax and rejuvenate, but that Sunday the quiet seemed ominous. As Samson and I finished our morning run through East Brainerd, I couldn't shake the feeling that we were running out of time. The killer had already claimed two victims in my jurisdiction and at least three more in Memphis and, with federal pressure mounting and Chief Johnston breathing down my neck, I knew we had to act fast.

By nine-thirty, I was in the conference room coordinating what would be one of the most complex surveillance operations I'd ever attempted. With limited resources and a killer who seemed to stay one step ahead of us, we'd have to be strategic about who we watched and how we deployed our people.

Tracy arrived at just after ten carrying a stack of files and looking like she'd spent most of the night working. "I've got the priority list organized," she said, spreading papers across the conference table. "Based on Elena's ranking system and the pattern we've seen so far, I think we should focus on the next top ten targets. Do we have the names of the other two Memphis victims?"

"Damn!" I snapped. "Why didn't I think of that?" I took out my phone and called Torres.

"Sorry to disturb you on Sunday," I said. "I just need the names of your other two victims, please."

"No problem," he replied. "Victim number two is nurse practitioner Michael Robbins, age fifty-one, and victim number three is Rosemary Whatley, age fifty-eight. She was an RN. Anything else? I'm... on my way to church."

"No, that will do it. Thanks, Ray. That's all I need for now. Oh, and if you could send me those files too?"

"You got it," he replied. "In the meantime, you know where I am. Have a good day, Captain."

He hung up and I turned to Tracy, handed her the piece of paper on which I'd written the two names, and said, "Okay, show me what you've got," as I settled into a chair while Samson found his usual spot beside my feet under the table.

"Dr. Fletcher is number three on the list," Tracy began, consulting her notes. "We've already assigned patrol surveillance to his home and office, so we're good there. Judge Sandra Marks is number seven. She's agreed to limited protective surveillance but refused to alter her routine."

"What about the night shift nurses?" I asked, remembering what Bobby had told us about Elena's killer being a medical professional.

"Well, aside from," she looked at the piece of paper I'd just given her, "Robbins and Whatley, I found two sisters, Dorothy and Helen King who worked night shifts during the experimental program. They're both retired now, living together in a house on Signal Mountain."

Cooper looked up from his laptop. "I ran background checks on the King sisters. They've kept a very low profile since leaving the medical field. No social media presence, unlisted phone numbers which Jack was able to get for me, and they haven't worked in healthcare for over ten years."

"Sounds like they might be hiding from something," I said.

"Or someone," Tracy added. "When I called them yesterday, they sounded terrified. I talked to Helen King. She said they'd been expecting something like this for years."

I studied the surveillance schedule Tracy had prepared. With our limited personnel, we could maintain continuous surveillance on only three, maybe four targets at a time. The rest would have to settle for periodic check-ins and patrol car drive-byes. By ten-thirty, I was ready.

"All right," I said. "Here's how we'll deploy. I want round-the-clock surveillance on the King sisters, Judge Marks and Dr. Fletcher. Tracy, I want you and Cooper to interview the King sisters. They seem the most vulnerable, and if they have information about the night shift operations, they might be priority targets. Hawk, you can handle Judge Marks. She knows and trusts you, and he's got the experience to spot trouble."

Hawk nodded.

"What about Dr. Walton?" Cooper asked.

"She's number five on the list," I said, "but she's also the most visible. Her office is in a busy medical complex with good security. We'll put a plainclothes officer in the lobby and see how it goes."

Corbin arrived at just after ten-thirty, carrying a tray with five Styrofoam cups of coffee and a dozen donuts, looking more alert than the rest of us despite it being his day off.

"Corbin, that's good of you," I said. "Did you get a receipt?"

He handed it to me, and I told him I'd reimburse him. He refused, which I knew he would. "Nope, it's on me," he said, putting the tray down on the table. "Any word from Jack on those database intrusions?"

"He's still working on it," I replied. "But he confirmed that someone accessed our case files again last night. They know we're ramping up surveillance."

"So they'll probably change their approach," Tracy said.

"Maybe. Or maybe they'll speed up their timeline." I said as I stood up and walked to the whiteboard where I'd mapped out the connections between the victims. "Think about it. She's killed two people in less than a month in the Chattanooga area and three more over a two-month period in Memphis. That's aggressive for any killer, but especially so for a woman."

I looked at my detectives and, as I did so, my phone rang. It was Chief Johnston. *What the hell?* I thought. *On a Sunday. Are you kidding me?* I took a deep breath. "It's the chief," I said, then answered it.

"Kate, where are you?" He asked before I could speak.

"I'm in the conference room and—" He cut me off.

"My office. Now," he said and hung up.

The chief's tone told me this wasn't going to be a pleasant conversation. I left the team to continue organizing the surveillance details and headed downstairs, Samson padding along beside me.

Chief Johnston was waiting with ADA Robert Hayes and another man I didn't recognize - mid-forties, expensive suit, the kind of bearing that suggested federal government.

"Kate, this is Deputy US Marshal William Crawford," Johnston said. "He's here to discuss federal protective services for some of the potential targets."

I felt my stomach tighten. Federal involvement in protection details usually meant they were planning to take over the entire investigation.

"Marshal Crawford," I said, shaking his hand. "What kind of protection are we talking about?"

"Captain Gazzara, nice to meet you," he replied. "We understand you're dealing with a serial killer who's targeting medical professionals connected to a federal healthcare program. The Justice Department has determined that several potential victims may require federal protection."

"And which victims are we talking about?" I asked.

Crawford consulted a folder. "Judge Sandra Marks, Dr. James Fletcher, and Dr. Amanda Pierce. All three have connections to cases that fall under federal jurisdiction."

"Judge Marks has already agreed to local protection," I said. "And we have surveillance on Dr. Fletcher."

"Local protection may not be sufficient," Hayes interjected. "We're dealing with someone who has demonstrated sophisticated surveillance and computer skills. Federal resources might be more appropriate."

I understood what they were really saying. They wanted to control who had access to the potential victims, probably to limit what information came out during any interviews or interrogations.

"Marshal Crawford, with all due respect, my team knows this case better than anyone. We've been tracking the killer's methods, understanding her psychology, building a profile based on her history. Local protection coordinated with the local investigation is going to be more effective than federal agents who don't understand the specific dynamics."

"Captain," Crawford said smoothly, "no one is questioning your team's competence. But this killer has already demonstrated the ability to evade local law enforcement. Two victims in two weeks suggests that current protective measures aren't working."

Chief Johnston looked uncomfortable. "Kate, the Marshal has a point. If federal protection could prevent more murders..."

"Chief, if we turn our potential witnesses over to

federal protection, we lose access to them. How am I supposed to investigate this case if I can't interview the people who might have crucial information?"

"You'll have access," Crawford said. "But interviews will need to be coordinated through appropriate channels."

Appropriate channels meant bureaucratic delays, restricted access, and probably orders not to ask certain questions about the experimental program.

"Not good enough," I snapped. "I need to maintain direct access to my witnesses. If you want to supplement our protection with federal resources, that's fine. But I won't turn over control of key witnesses in an active murder investigation."

Crawford and Hayes exchanged glances. "Then we'll need to discuss this with our supervisors," Crawford said finally.

"You do that," I replied. And they both rose to their feet and, without another word or a backward glance, walked out of the room.

After they were gone, Chief Johnston and I looked at each other, and he shook his head. "Kate, Kate, Kate," he said. "You know you have my support, but the pressure from above is getting intense. If we don't show progress soon, this case is going to be taken away from us."

"I understand, Chief. But we're making progress. We know our killer is a woman, and I think our surveillance operation might force her to make a move, make a mistake."

He frowned. "What kind of move? Not another murder—"

"No, of course not," I said, cutting him off. "But look, someone who's been planning this for years isn't going to be deterred by patrol cars and obvious surveillance. They're either going to find a way around our protection, or they're going to target someone we're not watching."

"That's not exactly reassuring," he said. "What you're saying is that you're setting someone up and that you don't have all the bases covered. I don't like it, Kate."

"Chief, this killer has been studying her targets for weeks or months before striking. She knows their routines, habits, vulnerabilities. Standard protection protocols aren't going to work against someone with that level of preparation."

"So what's your plan?" He asked.

"We make ourselves the more attractive target. We publicize our investigation; make it clear we're closing in. Force her to either flee or come after us directly."

Chief Johnston looked skeptical. "That's a dangerous game, Kate."

"It's better than waiting for her to pick off her victims one by one while the feds tie our hands with bureaucratic BS."

He stared at me for a moment, then said, "Very well, but it had better work, and soon. I can't keep staving them off. That's all, Captain."

Having been dismissed, I left Chief Johnston's office and returned to the conference room, where the team had finished organizing the surveillance assignments. The next few days would be crucial. Either our protective measures would deter the killer, or we'd learn just how sophisticated her capabilities really were.

"All right, everyone," I said. "We're going to try something different. Standard surveillance protocols aren't going to work against someone who's been planning these murders for years. We need to be smarter."

"What are you thinking?" Tracy asked.

"We're going to run both obvious and covert surveillance," I said. "Let them see some of our protection details, but keep others hidden. If she tries to get around the obvious surveillance, we'll be waiting."

Corbin looked up from his notes. "So, we hurry up and wait," he said. "What about the feds?"

"We'll deal with them when we have to," I replied. "Right now, our priority is to prevent more murders and to continue gathering intelligence about the killer."

By noon, we had surveillance teams deployed across Chattanooga. Tracy and Cooper were positioned near the King sisters' house on Signal Mountain, using an unmarked van with recording equipment. Hawk was maintaining a loose surveillance on Judge Marks, staying far enough back to avoid detection, but close enough to respond if needed. Me? Corbin, and I, along with Samson, found a position where we could monitor Fletcher's office complex.

The first few hours were routine. Dr. Fletcher arrived at his office around one o'clock, Judge Marks had lunch at her usual restaurant, and the King sisters stayed inside their house with the curtains drawn. And for the next couple of hours, nothing happened until, just after three-fifteen, Tracy's voice crackled over the radio.

"Kate, I've got movement here. We have a woman in medical scrubs, and she appears to be conducting some kind of reconnaissance around the King house."

"Can you give us a description?" I asked.

"Mid-forties, average height, dark hair. She's walking through the neighborhood like she belongs here, but she's paying a lot of attention to the house. She's checked the mailbox and looked at the windows. Ah, I don't see her now."

"Is there a vehicle?" I asked.

"I don't see one. But I didn't see her arrive. She must have parked somewhere out of sight and walked. You want me to go after her?"

"You can, but be discreet. I don't want to spook her," I said. "And don't engage unless she approaches the house directly."

"I'm dressed in sweats and sneakers," she said. "I'm going for a run."

Forty-five minutes later, Tracy reported that the woman had left the area. A canvas of the nearby streets had found nothing. Whoever the woman was, she was gone.

The next significant development came just after four-thirty, when Cooper called in. He'd been checking the Kings' house and surrounds.

"Captain," he said. "I think I found something, a footprint. You might want to come and take a look?"

We drove immediately to Signal Mountain. The King sisters' house was located on a quiet street with large lots, bushes and mature trees. It was the kind of neighborhood where someone could observe a house without being seen.

Cooper led me to a spot about fifty yards from the sisters' front door, where a low-hanging branch and a couple of bushes offered a secluded spot where one could monitor the house without being seen.

"She was here for a while," Cooper said. "Just watching the house. But if you look there…" He trailed off, pointing to a spot in the dirt between one of the bushes and the tree.

There, barely visible in the dirt, was a partial footprint. Not enough for a full impression, but clear enough to show the tread pattern of what looked like an athletic shoe, the type worn by medical personnel. More importantly, Samson had locked onto a scent that he seemed to find particularly interesting.

"Get this photographed," I said to Cooper. "And I want Samson to memorize this scent. If our surveillance subject comes back, he should be able to track her."

"You want me to do it?" he asked, taking out his phone, "or d'you want me to have Mike do it?"

I thought for a minute, then said, "I think we'd better have Mike do it. That way we create a chain of evidence admissible in court."

Cooper nodded and made the call.

As we waited for the CSI team, I studied the area where the woman had positioned herself. She'd chosen a spot with clear sight lines to the house but minimal exposure to the street. It was impossible to tell if she'd stayed long enough to observe patterns and routines, but obviously not long enough to attract attention from neighbors. It was exactly the kind of professional reconnaissance that Jack North's analysis had suggested.

My phone buzzed with a text from Jack: *Urgent - I just found something in the database logs. Someone accessed King sisters' address and phone records two hours ago. She knew you were watching.*

So, our killer is monitoring our surveillance, I thought. *She knew exactly where we deployed our people, and it looks like she's using the information to plan her next move.*

"Tracy," I called on the radio. "I want you and Cooper to maintain visual contact with the house, but I think maybe you're being watched."

"Copy that," Tracy replied. "Should we relocate?"

"No… Not yet," I replied, thinking fast. "But be ready to move quickly if anything changes."

Willis arrived on the scene some thirty minutes later, but by then I'd already realized that our standard police procedures were inadequate against someone with this level of capability. And, quite frankly, I was at a loss as to how to deal with her, much less identify her. I mean, how the hell do you catch someone who knows everything you're doing before you do it?

Samson whined softly and looked up at me, as if sensing my frustration. I scratched behind his ears and tried to think like our killer. She'd spent years planning her revenge, decades acquiring skills and resources, and she wasn't going to be deterred.

But she'd made one mistake. By conducting reconnaissance on the King sisters, she'd revealed that the two women were definitely on her target list. And by leaving trace evidence, little as that partial shoe print was, and perhaps a scent Samson might recognize, she'd given us our first real lead. Now all we had to do was figure out how to use it. Easier said than done, right?

As the sun began to set, I had the uncomfortable feeling that our killer was out there somewhere, watching us watch her intended victims, laughing as she planned her next move in a deadly game of cat and mouse where she seemed to be holding all the advantages.

After loading Samson in the back seat of my unmarked cruiser, I rejoined Corbin who'd been waiting for me behind the wheel, then turned to Samson, reached back and scratched behind his ears. "I sure hope you got something out of that, Sammy," I said.

"Something out of what?" Corbin asked.

"Cooper found a footprint and Sammy seemed to hit on something..." I paused for a second then said, "She's been monitoring us, Corbin. She knows what we're doing and how we're doing it. We need to find out who the hell she is. Let's get out of here."

As Corbin put the car in drive and eased away from the curb, I looked again at Sammy. He tilted his head and gave me the look as if he knew what I was thinking. And maybe he did. If there was one thing I'd learned in the months since I'd adopted him, it was that my four-legged partner had instincts that sometimes put mine to shame.

15

The Judge's Fear

Sunday Evening, 7:00 PM

THE SURVEILLANCE OPERATION HAD BEEN RUNNING FOR just over eight hours. I'd dropped Corbin off at the PD and was again positioned near Dr. Fletcher's office complex, watching for any sign of a woman in medical scrubs when my phone rang and Judge Sandra Marks' number appeared on my screen. I knew her. I'd had dealings with her in the past. She was also number 7 on Elena's list.

"Gazzara," I said after accepting the call.

"Captain Gazzara," she said, and I could tell by the sound of her voice she was upset. "I need help. Someone called me this evening."

"Calm down, Judge," I said, gently. "Someone called you. Did you recognize the voice?"

"No! No… I don't know. It was a woman's voice," she replied, shakily.

"Okay, I said. "What did she say?"

"She said, 'You signed my life away when I was sixteen. Now it's time I returned the favor.'"

Geez, I thought, then said, "Where are you right now?"

"At home. I've been here all afternoon, going through old case files, trying to remember… God help me, I've signed so many commitment orders over the years. So many kids sent for treatment."

"Is Sergeant Hawkins still with you?" I asked.

"He left about an hour ago when his shift ended," she replied. "He said the replacement officer would be here soon, but no one's shown up yet."

I was already starting my car, Samson sat up on the passenger seat and stared out through the windshield. "Listen to me, Judge," I snapped. "I want you to lock all your doors and windows. Don't let anyone in except uniformed police officers, and before you do, verify their badge numbers by calling dispatch. I'm on my way. Are you sure you don't know who this woman might be?"

"No!" she replied. "As I told you, I've been going through my old files from the 1990s. I found commitment orders for the Greenbriar facility. There are dozens of them. All teenagers—most of them girls—I sent them there for what I thought was legitimate treatment."

"How many commitment orders did you sign for that facility?" I asked, as I swung the car right off Gunbarrel Road, lights flashing, siren blaring, onto East Brainerd Road heading for I-75.

"I don't know exactly," she replied. "I wasn't the only

judge signing such orders. Maybe thirty, forty cases over the three years the program was running. I was a family court judge then, and the psychiatric evaluations all recommended residential treatment. I trusted the medical professionals. I thought I was helping these kids."

I could hear the guilt in her voice, and I could sympathize with her. She'd unknowingly been the legal gateway that sent dozens of vulnerable teenagers into a program that tortured them. No wonder she was high on the killer's priority list.

"Stay on the line with me while I drive. I'll be there in twenty minutes."

As I raced through the Sunday evening traffic, I called Corbin on the radio. "Corbin, I need you and a patrol unit at Judge Marks' house immediately. She's received a threatening call."

"On my way," he replied. "ETA twenty-five minutes."

"And Corbin, call Hawk. He was assigned to Marks' protection detail, but he went off duty and I want to know why the replacement officer didn't show up."

The drive to Judge Mark's house in North Chattanooga gave me time to think about the killer's pattern. Dr. Holloway had been killed without warning. So had Elena Vasquez but I think she must have known who her killer was. After all, she'd been corresponding with her— her... It was good to be able to put a label on the killer. Anyway, the Memphis victim, Samuel Rodriguez, had also received threatening letters during the weeks before his murder. Now Judge Marks had received a phone call that was both a threat and a psychological attack.

The killer was evolving, becoming more personal with each victim. She was also becoming bolder, moving from clandestine assassinations to direct contact. That suggested either growing confidence or increasing desperation to complete her mission.

"Captain," Marks said, still on the line, "I keep thinking about those commitment orders. Some of the kids were so young, barely teenagers. The psychiatric evaluations always said residential treatment was necessary, but looking back—"

"You made decisions based on the information you received at the time," I said, interrupting her. "The fault lies with the people who abused those kids, not with the people who tried to get them help. You did what you thought was right."

"But I enabled it," she insisted. "I gave them legal authority to take children away from their families and subject them to... to whatever the hell happened in that place."

I pulled into Marks' driveway just as Corbin, followed by a blue and white cruiser, arrived from the opposite direction and parked on the street. The house was a modest two-story colonial in a quiet neighborhood, with mature trees and a well-maintained yard. Lights were on in several windows, and I could see movement inside.

"Judge Marks," I said. "I'm outside now. I can see you in the front window. I'm coming to the door. Sergeant Russell is going to take a look around outside."

Samson and I approached the front entrance while Corbin circled around the back of the house. Judge

Marks opened the door before I could knock, and I could see immediately that the stress was taking its toll. She was in her late sixties, and I imagined she was usually a composed and professional woman, but that night she looked haggard and frightened.

"Thank God you're here," she said, stepping aside to let us in. "I've been jumping at every sound for the past hour."

The living room was comfortable but formal, with legal books lining the shelves and framed certificates covering one wall. But what caught my attention was the dining room table, which was covered with manila folders and loose papers.

"These are the commitment orders?" I asked.

"Every case I could find relating to the Greenbriar Behavioral Health Center," she replied. "Forty-three teenagers over a three-year period. Most of them for behavioral issues, family conflicts, minor legal troubles. Nothing that should have warranted the kind of treatment we now know they received. I know there were more, but these were mine."

I studied some of the files. The psychiatric evaluations all followed similar patterns: recommendations for residential treatment, emphasis on the need for intensive intervention, glowing descriptions of the experimental program's success rates. It was a carefully constructed pipeline that sent vulnerable kids into the hands of medical professionals who abused them.

Corbin appeared at the back door and knocked. Marks let him in, and he immediately began checking the security of the house while I continued examining the commitment files.

"Do you remember any cases that stood out? Any teenagers who tried to fight the commitment or appeal their placement?"

She nodded slowly, then seemed to change her mind and shook her head. "No, most of the kids just accepted the placement, but there was one who…" she blinked several times, then said, "It was so long ago. I'm sorry."

"This is important," I said. "Please try to remember. Girl or boy?"

"Girl. Young. I can see her face, but…" She paused, then said. "I'm sorry. I signed commitment orders for thirty-three girls. It was more than twenty-five years ago. That's all I can remember."

"Tall? Hair color, anything?" I snapped, thoroughly frustrated. I would have said more, but my phone rang. It was Hawk.

"Kate, I just got word from dispatch. There was a mix-up with the patrol assignments for Judge Marks' house. The replacement officer was assigned to a different location by mistake."

"How does something like that happen, Hawk?"

"I'm not sure. The dispatch log shows the assignment was changed about ninety minutes ago, but no one can tell me who authorized the change."

Damn! I thought. *Does that mean someone with access to police communications deliberately removed Judge Marks' protection, leaving her vulnerable at exactly the moment our killer was ready to strike?* I sure as hell hoped not.

"Hawk, I need you back here. And I want you to

check with dispatch about any other unusual assignment changes or communications during the past few hours."

"Already on my way," he replied.

Corbin came downstairs and joined us in the living room. "Everything's secure, but there are a lot of potential entry points. This house wasn't designed with security in mind. What d'you want me to do, Kate?"

I looked at the Judge who was sitting on her couch clutching one of the commitment files.

"Look at her," I whispered. "She's a bag of nerves. We should move her."

"Yes, but where?" Corbin asked. "And I'm not sure it would do any good anyway. Not if this person is monitoring our every move."

Maybe he was right. Maybe it wouldn't make any difference, but I gave it a try anyway.

"Judge Marks," I said. "I think you should consider staying somewhere else tonight. Maybe a hotel, or with family."

"No," she said firmly. "If someone wants to confront me about these commitment orders, then maybe it's time I faced the consequences of my decisions."

"Facing consequences and getting murdered are two different things," I replied. "This woman isn't about justice or closure. She's about revenge."

"Maybe it's what I deserve," she whispered.

I knelt down beside her chair. "Look," I said, gently, "you made legal decisions based on professional psychiatric evaluations. You didn't know those evaluations were fraudulent or that the treatment program was abusive. The guilt belongs to the people who deceived you, not to you."

She looked at me with tired eyes. "But those children suffered because of orders I signed. Doesn't that make me responsible?"

"No! It makes you a victim of the same conspiracy that hurt them."

My phone buzzed with a text message from an unknown number: "I can see you through the front window. Two inside and two in the cop car. More than I expected."

I stood up and showed the message to Corbin. "Geez," he muttered, and went to the window, "She's out there watching us right now."

I joined him and looked out around the neighborhood, trying to figure out where she could observe the house without being detected. *Geez, she could be anywhere,* I thought. The mature trees and neighboring houses provided plenty of opportunities for concealment.

Samson joined us at the window and stood on his hind legs, his front paws on the sill. Then he growled low in his throat. He was looking to the right and far away, down the street. I saw movement. A figure in dark clothing was walking quickly away. Was it our killer? I looked at the blue and white. It was facing the wrong way. I looked again for the figure, but it was gone.

And then my phone rang. It was an unknown number.

"Captain Gazzara," a calm, professional-sounding female voice said. "You beat me to it. Well done."

"Who is this?" I asked.

She laughed, a musical tinkling laugh, then said, "I think you're beginning to figure that out. I've been following your investigation with great interest. You're very good, very thorough. I'm impressed."

"If you want to talk, surrender yourself, and we can discuss whatever grievances you think you have through proper legal channels."

"Ah yes, legal channels?" she said. "Captain, I spent three years in that vile place, because Judge Marks signed the commitment forms without bothering to get proper expert opinion. No, Captain, she sent me there on the word of that charlatan, Holloway. It was all about the money, as you've probably realized by now. Your precious legal system failed me when I was sixteen years old. Why would I trust it now?"

"Because murder isn't justice. It's just more violence." It wasn't much of an answer, but it was all I could think of in the moment,

"Tell me, Captain, what would you call what they did to us? Medical professionals torturing children for research grants? Judges signing orders based on fraudulent psychiatric evaluations. Federal officials covering up medical abuse because it was politically expedient?"

The voice was intelligent, controlled. Not emotional or unhinged, but coldly rational.

"I would call it criminal abuse that should be prosecuted to the full extent of the law," I replied.

"And how's that working out for you?" she asked. "Even now, your federal agents are trying to bury it, aren't they? Eight people are dead, and the system is still protecting the criminals that ran that hellish place."

Eight? I thought. *Geez, I only know of five.* "If you surrender now," I said. "I'll make sure the truth about the experimental program comes out, I promise. Full public disclosure, media attention, congressional hearings if necessary."

"Captain, I think you're a good police officer, but you just don't understand how these things work. There are too many important people involved, too much political liability. The truth will be buried along with the evidence, as it always is."

"Then help me prove it," I said. "Surrender and provide testimony about what happened. Be a witness instead of taking the law into your own hands."

The line was quiet for a long moment. Then: "Judge Marks is sitting in her living room right now, reading commitment orders from the 1990s, isn't she? She's trying to remember which of the children she sent to hell, and you're protecting her."

"We're protecting her, yes," I replied.

"And that's why I'm walking away tonight. But know this, Captain, it isn't over. There are forty names left on my list."

"You need to stop," I said. "This is not the way to do it. How many more people are you planning to kill?"

"As many as it takes." And the line went dead.

I looked at Corbin, who had been listening to my side of the conversation. "She's gone," I said, "but she'll be back."

"So what do we do now?" he asked.

"We keep Judge Marks safe, and we figure out who

we're really dealing with." *Geez, what a frickin' mess,* I thought.

Hawk arrived a few minutes later and, as we set about establishing a more secure perimeter around the house, I realized that tonight had been a warning more than an attack. Our killer had wanted to demonstrate that she could reach her targets despite police protection, but she'd also shown restraint when the situation became tactically unfavorable which made her an even more formidable adversary.

That combination of capability and restraint made her more dangerous, not less, because it meant she was thinking strategically, not just acting on impulse.

Judge Marks was safe for now, but forty other people were still in danger. And somewhere out there, someone with a plan twenty-five years in the making was deciding who would be next.

16

Federal Interest

Monday Morning, 8:15 AM

THE FOLLOWING MORNING, MONDAY, I WOKE AT SIX AS usual, but feeling like death warmed over, which was unusual. After Sunday night's close call with Judge Marks, it was after midnight when I'd finally gotten to bed. So, I reset my alarm for seven and dropped back onto my pillow for what I hoped would be another hour of sleep. It was a forlorn hope. The habits of a lifetime are not easily set aside, and I lay there for the hour with my mind in a whirl and at the end of it all, I rose from my bed at seven feeling almost as whacked out as I had an hour ago.

Samson, however, seemed to appreciate the extra hour. We skipped our usual run in favor of coffee on the back porch—for me, not him—in my PJ's, and then a quick cold shower after which I dressed in jeans, a black Tee, and black leather shell jacket. Then I fed Samson, ate two slices of toast, and arrived at the department at a little before eight-forty-five.

I entered the building through the rear entrance, sneaked past the chief's office door, only to be intercepted by Christy before I could reach the elevator.

"Kate, Chief Johnston wants to see you immediately. And..." she drew it out, "he's in a terrible mood, and he's got someone with him, so tread carefully."

Geez, I thought, *what a way to start a Monday, much less a new week.* I sighed, then said, "Tell him I'll be just a minute." Then I took Sammy upstairs, left him with Tracy and headed back down to the chief's office, where I found Johnston seated behind his desk across from a woman I didn't recognize.

"Kate, this is FBI Agent Sarah Gleave," Johnston said. "She's here to consult on the Holloway case."

Agent Gleave stood and extended her hand. She was about my age, in her early forties, with short brown hair and the kind of professional demeanor that suggested she was used to being the smartest person in the room. Her handshake was firm, her smile polite but not warm.

"Captain Gazzara, I've heard excellent things about your work on this case. The Bureau is very interested in your progress."

"Agent Gleave," I replied, settling into the chair across from her. "What kind of consultation are we talking about?"

"The interstate nature of these murders brings them under federal jurisdiction," she said, consulting a folder.

"We understand you've connected killings in Chattanooga and Memphis, possibly others across the Southeast."

"Chattanooga and Memphis, that's correct; the Southeast? I'm not so sure. But we're handling the investigation through existing mutual aid agreements with other agencies."

"Of course. But given the sophistication of the crimes and the potential for additional victims, the Bureau thinks federal resources might be helpful."

I studied her carefully. Gleave's questions and statements were phrased... I'll say professionally, but something about her presence felt wrong. Federal agents didn't usually show up to "consult" on local cases unless there was something they wanted to control or contain.

"What kind of resources?" I asked.

"Database access, behavioral analysis, coordination with other field offices. The Bureau has extensive experience with serial killers who operate across state lines."

"At this point," I said, "we don't know that this killer has crossed any state lines."

Chief Johnston leaned forward. "Kate, Agent Gleave is particularly interested in the evidence you've gathered about the experimental program."

"Is she, now?" I asked, looking directly at Gleave. "Why would that be?"

"Medical abuse involving federal healthcare funding falls under Bureau jurisdiction," Gleave replied smoothly. "If this experimental program received federal grants or involved federal facilities, there could be civil rights violations that need to be investigated."

"So you're here to investigate the experimental program, not to catch the killer?"

"Both, actually," she replied. "But understanding the historical context is crucial to predicting the killer's next moves."

I wasn't buying it. Gleave's interest in the experimental program seemed much more focused than her interest in preventing additional murders.

"You said there have been similar cases in other states," I said, watching her carefully. "What can you tell me about those cases? If the Bureau's been tracking this pattern killer, you must have intelligence we could use."

She hesitated slightly. "We're still analyzing potential connections. That's part of why your evidence would be so valuable."

"What evidence specifically?" I asked, already amused.

"We understand you've obtained documentation from the experimental program. Patient files, staff records, that sort of thing."

And there it was. She wasn't here to help with the investigation. She was here to assess what evidence we had and probably ensure it didn't become public.

I leaned forward. "I appreciate the Bureau's interest, Agent Gleave, but we're in the middle of an active investigation. Any evidence sharing would need to be coordinated through proper channels."

"Of course. But given the federal implications, it would be helpful if we could review your materials sooner rather than later."

I glanced at Chief Johnston. He looked uncomfortable. "Kate, Agent Gleave has proper authorization for federal oversight of this case."

"I understand that, Chief. But I'm sorry. I'm not sharing evidence in an active murder investigation without a clear understanding of how it will be used."

Gleave's professional smile became slightly strained. "Captain, I think there might be a misunderstanding about the Bureau's role here."

"Is there?" I said. "Because it seems to me, you're more interested in containing information about the experimental program than in catching a serial killer."

The room went quiet for a moment. Chief Johnston cleared his throat.

"Kate, why don't you bring Agent Gleave up to speed on our current investigation status? She might have insights that could help."

I spent the next twenty minutes giving Gleave a carefully edited version of our investigation. I covered the basic facts - five murders, medical staging, evidence of connections to the experimental program - but I didn't mention Elena's safe deposit box, the encrypted communications, or the specific details about our killer's surveillance capabilities.

"Very thorough," Gleave said when I finished. "What's your next step?"

"We're following up on leads related to the experimental program staff. Trying to identify potential targets and establish protective measures."

"And the evidence from the experimental program itself?"

"We're still analyzing it." I replied.

"I'd like to review that analysis when it's complete."

"I'll consider it," I said.

Agent Gleave closed her folder and stood up. "Captain, I hope we can work together productively. The Bureau has resources that could be very helpful to your investigation."

"I'm sure we can find ways to cooperate," I replied.

After Gleave left, I looked Johnston in the eye and said, "She's not here to help us solve this case. She's here to bury it. That's not going to happen this time."

"I understand," he replied, thoughtfully. "But, Kate, if we don't show real progress soon, the feds are going to step in and take over completely."

"How much time do we have?" I asked.

"I don't know," he replied, uncomfortably. "Days, maybe only hours, especially if there's another murder."

"Then I'd better get on with it," I said, standing up.

I left the chief's office and headed back to the situation room, where I found Jack hunched over his computer with a triumphant expression on his face that suggested he'd found something important.

"You look perky, Jack, what do you have?"

"Something weird," he replied without looking up from his screen. "I've been monitoring for any new intrusions into our systems, and I found something interesting."

"More database hacking?"

"Yeah, but not ours this time. Someone's been accessing the FBI's databases."

I felt a chill. "Our killer?"

"That's what I thought at first. But look at this." He

pulled up a log of database queries. "Whoever's doing this has been accessing files on unsolved murders across the Southeast. All with the same pattern, all during the past two years."

"How many cases?" I asked, leaning over his shoulder.

"At least a dozen that I can identify. Memphis, Atlanta, Birmingham, Nashville, even one in Jacksonville. All similar methods, all victims connected to psychiatric facilities or medical research."

"So our killer has been active longer than we thought?" I said.

"Or they're researching similar cases to understand law enforcement patterns," Jack replied. "Look at the timing of these database queries. They correspond with our own investigation milestones. Every time we discover something new, someone accesses the FBI files to see what the feds know about related cases."

"So what you're saying is our killer is tracking multiple federal investigations?"

"I'm saying someone with serious hacking skills is staying ahead of multiple law enforcement agencies across several states. And they're doing it by monitoring the monitors."

I studied the data Jack had compiled. If our killer had been operating for two years instead of two weeks, that changed everything about the scope and sophistication of their operation.

"Jack, can you trace these FBI intrusions?" I asked.

"I'm working on it, but whoever's doing it is using... Well, you know. It's going to take time."

"How much time?"

"Maybe days, maybe weeks. This person is operating at a level I've only seen from professional intelligence agencies."

My phone buzzed with a text from an unknown number: "Agent Gleave asks some interesting questions, doesn't she? I hope you were smart enough not to trust her."

I showed the message to Jack, whose eyes widened.

"She's monitoring our federal contacts now?" he muttered.

"Looks like it," I said. "She certainly knows I had a meeting with Agent Gleave."

"Kate, this is getting scary. If she can monitor individual FBI agents, she can monitor anyone."

"We know from Elena's evidence cache that she knows all about the personnel assigned to Greenbriar," I said. "That's not such a big deal. What is a big deal is that she knows I've just met with Gleave."

I thought about Gleave's questions and her obvious interest in controlling evidence about the experimental program. "Jack, I want you to run a background check on Agent Sarah Gleave. If you have to hack... No, don't do that. Find out what cases she's worked, what her specialties are, and who she reports to."

"You think she's not legitimate?"

"Oh, I think she is, but I also think she's here for reasons that have nothing to do with catching our killer," I replied.

As Jack began his research, I realized Gleave's presence wasn't a coincidence; it was damage control.

But if federal agents were trying to contain information about the experimental program, that suggested the conspiracy went deeper than medical abuse at a single facility. It suggested ongoing cover-ups at the highest levels of government.

My phone rang. It was Corbin.

"Kate, we've got a problem. Dr. Fletcher just called. He's received another threatening message."

"What kind of message?"

"Someone left medical equipment on his car windshield. A cardboard box containing some old electroshock therapy devices and restraints. It has to be her, right?"

I nodded to myself. "Did she leave a note?"

"Just one word, written in red marker on his windshield: 'Remember?'"

"Where's Fletcher now?" I asked.

"In his office with two patrol officers outside," Corbin replied. "But Kate, he's terrified."

"No kidding," I said, dryly. "Okay, I'm on my way."

As I headed for the elevator, I had the feeling that Gleave's arrival and this new threat to Fletcher weren't coincidental. Someone was applying pressure from multiple directions, forcing us to make decisions about evidence sharing and witness protection.

But she'd made a mistake. By threatening Fletcher while Agent Gleave was in town, she'd revealed she was monitoring federal involvement in real time.

As Samson and I drove toward Fletcher's office, I couldn't help but feel I was being watched by more than just our killer. Gleave's questions, the FBI database intrusions, and the timing of Fletcher's new threat; it all suggested that multiple parties were interested in controlling my investigation.

But whoever was pulling the strings had underestimated me: I wasn't going to let political considerations interfere with catching a killer. Federal pressure or not, we were going to solve this case and bring justice to the victims of both the current murders *and* the experimental program, even if it meant me going up against the FBI itself.

17

Digital Warfare

Tuesday Morning, 9:45 AM

THE COFFEE WAS COLD, THE DONUTS WERE STALE, AND Jack North looked like he'd been mainlining caffeine for the past eighteen hours, which he probably had. When I arrived at the police department on Tuesday morning, I found him in the conference room surrounded by print-outs, laptops, and enough energy drink cans to power a small aircraft. But the look in his eyes told me he'd found something big.

"Please tell me you have good news," I said, settling into a chair while Samson found his usual spot beside the conference table.

He sucked air in through his teeth and said, "Define good." It was one of his favorite responses, and I shook my head as I watched him rubbing his eyes. "Because what I found is definitely important, which is good, but it's also terrifying, which is bad."

I'd been expecting something like that. Ever since Agent Gleave's visit yesterday and Fletcher's new threatening message, I'd had the feeling we were dealing with something much larger than a single revenge killer.

"Talk to me, Jack," I said. It was one of *my* favorite sayings.

Jack pulled up a complex network diagram on his main screen. "I've been working on tracing those database intrusions, and I finally broke through some of the encryption. I found the digital identity behind all this surveillance."

"Subject23?"

"That's what she calls herself in some of the communications, but she's been using multiple identities for years. The primary one is sophisticated beyond anything I've ever seen."

He clicked through several screens showing financial records, social media profiles, and what looked like surveillance logs. "See? She's been systematically tracking every person connected to the experimental program," he said, then turned and looked at me.

I said nothing. Instead, I raised my eyebrows and waited.

He got the message. "She knows where everyone lives, where they work, their financial situations, their family members, their daily routines. Look at this." He pulled up a spreadsheet. It showed names, addresses, employment records, even photos of houses and office buildings.

"So we're back to 'they?'" I said. "And this is Elena's target list," I said, recognizing some of the names.

"Plus, about twenty more people we haven't identified yet," he said, leaning back in his chair. "But here's the scary part: they've been monitoring these people for years, not weeks. Long before the murders started."

Jack opened another window showing social media monitoring logs. "They've been tracking Facebook posts, LinkedIn updates, professional licensing renewals, property tax records, even online shopping patterns. If Dr. Fletcher bought a coffee at Starbucks and paid with a credit card, this person knew about it."

"What about us?" I asked. "Our investigation?"

Jack's expression became grim. "Ah, well, yeah. That's where it gets personal." He pulled up another set of files. "They've been monitoring your digital footprint for the past month, Kate. Your emails, your online searches, your credit card activity. They know what you had for dinner last Thursday."

"What the hell?" I said, unable to believe what I was hearing, seeing. "How is that even possible?"

"They're using law enforcement databases, social media scraping, financial monitoring services, even traffic camera and facial recognition. It's like having a private intelligence agency focused solely on tracking 'their' targets."

"And I'm a target?" I asked, incredulously.

"You're the lead investigator on the case that threatens their mission," he said. "Of course you're a target."

Jack clicked through several more screens. "They

know about your morning runs with Samson. They know you stop at Dunkin' Donuts on Tuesdays. They know you go to the shooting range Sunday afternoons. They've been building a profile of your behavior patterns."

The thought of being watched that closely was unsettling, but not surprising. We'd already known our killer had sophisticated surveillance capabilities. What bothered me more was the implications.

"Jack, how is one person managing this level of surveillance on dozens of targets?"

"That's what I've been trying to figure out. The computational resources alone would require significant funding and technical infrastructure. But then I found something else."

He opened a new set of files. "Financial records. Anonymous payments to medical facilities, housing assistance programs, legal aid societies. All connected to survivors of the experimental program."

"Our killer is helping other victims?" I asked.

"Not just helping. Supporting. Look at these payment amounts." Jack highlighted several transactions. "Fifty thousand dollars to pay off a medical debt for a former Greenbriar patient in Atlanta. Twenty-five thousand for housing assistance in Memphis. Fifteen thousand to a legal aid fund for victims of medical abuse."

I studied the payment records. "How much total?"

"Over the past three years? Nearly half a million dollars. All anonymous, all routed through various charitable organizations, all specifically targeted to help survivors of the experimental program."

"So while they're killing the perpetrators, they're also supporting the victims," I muttered.

"And it gets even more interesting," Jack said, pulling up another screen. "Some of these payments are ongoing. Monthly assistance for survivors who can't work due to ongoing health problems from the experimental treatments. Housing assistance for people who can't maintain stable employment. Medical care for conditions that resulted from the abuse they suffered as teenagers."

I leaned back in my chair, trying to process what Jack had discovered. Our killer was providing systematic support for other survivors while eliminating the people who had hurt them. *Or could it be more than one patient doing the killing?* I wondered.

"Jack, where's all this money coming from?"

"The payments are being made through a network of legitimate businesses and investment accounts. Whoever Subject23 really is, they have significant financial resources."

"How significant?" I asked.

"Based on the payment patterns and account structures, I'd estimate they have access to several million dollars. Either through personal wealth, business success, or financial crimes we haven't detected yet."

"Any idea what kind of businesses?" I asked, my brain already hurting from the information overload. *No wonder the feds want to shut it down,* I thought, savagely.

"Medical consulting, pharmaceutical research," he replied, "healthcare administration. All legitimate, all profitable, all connected to the healthcare industry."

That made sense. Someone who had survived the

experimental program might have been motivated to build a career in healthcare, either to help others or to gain access to the resources needed for revenge.

"Jack, have you been able to trace any of these financial accounts back to a real identity?"

"I'm working on it," he replied, "but the account structures are complex. Multiple shell companies, offshore banking, investment partnerships. It's going to take time to unravel."

"Jack," I said. "You're doing an amazing job. Thank you, but I'm wondering, how the hell do we communicate securely?"

"We don't," he replied. "At least not electronically. Any digital communication can be intercepted by someone with these capabilities."

I thought about the implications of that. If our killer was monitoring all our communications, she knew about every aspect of our investigation, and yes, I was still going with a female killer. She knew which witnesses we were planning to interview, which evidence we were analyzing, which protection details we were establishing.

"Jack, I want you to keep working on tracing those financial accounts. And I want you to monitor for any unusual activity around Fletcher's location."

As I prepared to leave, Jack called me back.

"Kate, there's one more thing. Since I found evidence that they've been researching you personally, I got to thinking you'd better be careful. They have all they need to go against you, when you're least expecting it."

I nodded. It wouldn't be the first time someone had tried to kill me. I could think of at least half a dozen times. I'm only alive now because of Samson and Harry Starke.

As Samson and I headed for the elevator, I couldn't help but think how our investigation had become a chess game where our opponent knew all our moves before we made them and I couldn't even see the board. Subject23 had been watching us, learning from us, staying ahead of us, monitoring our every communication and action.

But maybe something was about to break. By helping other survivors financially, she'd created a paper trail that might lead us back to her real identity. And by monitoring our investigation so closely, she'd revealed the scope of her capabilities, which told us we were dealing with someone with significant resources and technical skills.

The question was whether we could trace those clues back to her before she completed her mission. Because based on what Jack had discovered, Subject23 was someone with the financial resources and technical capabilities to operate almost like a private intelligence agency. And she was focused on eliminating everyone connected to the experimental program, including the investigators who were trying to stop them.

And then I had another thought: sometimes the best way to catch someone who thinks they're always one step ahead is to let them believe they have the advantage; until you spring the trap.

18

Federal Interference

Wednesday Morning, 9:00 AM

AFTER A ROUGH NIGHT AND A SHORTENED RUN, I ARRIVED at the station the following morning, Wednesday, at nine o'clock to find Chief Johnston waiting for me in the conference room with a stack of official-looking documents and the kind of expression that meant my day was about to get considerably more complicated.

"Kate, we need to talk," he said without preamble. "Agent Gleave was here an hour ago with a federal seizure order for all evidence related to the experimental program."

I felt my stomach drop. "A seizure order?"

"Every document, every file, every piece of physical evidence," he said, handing it to me.

I looked at the papers. The legal language was dense,

but the message was clear: the federal government was attempting to take control of our investigation and bury the evidence we'd been collecting.

"Chief, we can't let them do this. The evidence is crucial to understanding what's driving these murders."

"Kate, I don't have a choice. This comes from the Justice Department. If I don't comply, they'll send federal marshals to seize everything and probably suspend our department's federal funding."

I studied the seizure order more carefully. The timing was suspicious: it had come just as we were getting close to identifying our killer and exposing the full scope of the experimental program conspiracy.

"Chief, how did Agent Gleave know exactly what evidence to request? This order lists specific files and documents that we haven't shared with anybody."

"That's what bothers me too," he replied. "Someone's been feeding information to the feds."

Before I could respond, Jack North appeared in the doorway carrying his laptop.

"Kate," he said, dropping into a seat at the conference table and opening his computer. "I've been monitoring federal database queries related to our case, and I found something disturbing."

"What kind of disturbing?" Johnston asked, glancing at me.

"Agent Gleave has been accessing files that go way beyond normal inter-agency cooperation. She's been researching the personal backgrounds of everyone here, everyone connected to the experimental program investigation, including current financial status, family members, and recent communications. You, Kate. Me, Corbin, Tracy, Hawk, even Coop."

Jack pulled up a series of database queries on his screen. "Look at this timeline. I'm assuming every time we interview a witness or discover new evidence, Gleave gets a notification somehow, and accesses federal files to see what other agencies know about the same people."

"So she's been monitoring our investigation in real time?" Johnston said, obviously disturbed by what he was hearing.

"More than monitoring," Jack replied. "She's been using federal resources to stay ahead of our discoveries and probably sharing information with people who want us shut down."

Chief Johnston leaned forward to study Jack's screen. "Are you saying Agent Gleave is working for someone other than the FBI?"

"I don't know; not for sure," he replied. "What I'm saying is she's been in contact with people connected to the experimental program who have a vested interest in keeping it buried," Jack replied.

Jack opened another window showing communication logs. "I found encrypted communications between Gleave and what appears to be a law firm that represents several pharmaceutical companies. The same companies that funded the experimental program in the 1990s."

"Do tell," I said, knowingly. The pieces were starting to come together. Of course they were. Agent Gleave was here to protect Big Pharma.

"Jack, what else have you found?" Johnston asked.

"Financial records showing payments to various officials for 'consulting services' related to medical research oversight. Including payments to federal agents who were supposed to be investigating institutional abuse."

"Gleave was being paid by the pharmaceutical companies?"

"I can't prove direct payments to Gleave," Jack said, "but I can prove that several federal officials involved in the oversight of psychiatric treatment programs have received substantial consulting fees from companies that benefited from the experimental program research."

My phone rang. I glanced at the screen. It was Tracy.

"Kate, I'm at Chattanooga General Hospital with Dr. Pierce. She's received another threatening message, but this one is different. It's not from our killer. It's from someone warning her to stop cooperating with our investigation."

I felt a chill. "Go on."

"A phone call, this morning, telling her that continued cooperation with police could result in federal charges related to her involvement in the experimental program. The caller knew specific details about her conversations with us."

"Someone's trying to intimidate our witnesses?" I said.

"That's what it looks like," she replied.

"Okay," I said. "Leave it with me." And I hung up.

I looked at the chief and said, "That was Tracy. Dr. Pierce has received a phone call threatening federal charges if she continues to cooperate with us."

He stared at me for a moment, then said, "I'm not

surprised. They've been all over it almost from the start. What to do about it, though? That's the question."

Johnston studied the seizure order again, muttering, "So they're using federal authority to bury evidence of federal crimes? Why am I not surprised?"

"Kate," Jack said, "the financial networks we've been tracking are too complex for one person to manage alone. The digital surveillance capabilities... It's not one person. The resources and technical expertise are beyond what a single individual could develop."

"Any ideas?" I asked.

He shrugged. "I don't know. It's hard to tell. It goes pretty deep, but it looks to me like we're dealing with someone who's receiving support from all sorts of people and institutions."

Chief Johnston looked at the evidence Jack had compiled. "Kate, if there's an organized effort behind these murders, why haven't we seen evidence of coordination between attacks?"

"Because the coordination happens at the planning and resource level," I replied. "Our killer's operating independently, but there's a coordinated effort at the federal level to shut down our investigation."

"And you think Agent Gleave is part of it?" he asked, frowning.

"I don't know," I replied. "I don't know what she knows, but I do know she's trying to shut down our investigation."

Chief Johnston was quiet for a long moment, studying the seizure order and the evidence Jack had compiled.

"Kate, what are you thinking?" he asked, finally.

"I'm thinking we ignore the federal seizure order and complete our investigation. If Gleave wants our evidence, she can get a legitimate warrant based on actual federal crimes, not political pressure from the pharmaceutical companies. And even if she does burst in here and confiscates everything, we have backup copies, right, Jack?"

Jack nodded.

Johnston stared at me for a moment, then said, "That's a risky position to take, Kate. This isn't a private office. This is a city police department. I can't imagine the repercussions if that was to happen."

"It won't happen, Chief. One, I don't think she has the authorization to make such a move. Two, I don't think she has the balls. And three, if we turn over our evidence to people who are working to protect the perpetrators, it will disappear into the federal bureaucracy and will never see daylight."

Jack looked up from his computer. "Kate, someone's been in contact with the media. It looks like they're preparing to go public?"

"Geez," I muttered. "Are you sure?"

He nodded.

"All right, Chief," I said. "It comes down to this: we have a choice. We can comply with Gleave's seizure order, or we can complete our investigation. What d'you want me to do?"

Johnston stood up and walked to the window overlooking the parking lot. "How much time do you need?"

"Twenty-four hours," I said with my fingers crossed.

"Maybe less if we can identify and locate our suspect. I think we're close to a breakthrough. And I think our suspect knows it."

Jack looked up from his screens. "Kate, someone at the federal level is shutting down our access to the databases and communication networks. I still have access but—"

"How long do we have?" I snapped.

"Maybe a couple of hours before they lock us out completely."

I looked at Johnston, who was still staring out the window. The decision he made in the next few seconds would make or break our investigation.

"Chief?" I said.

He turned back toward me. "Kate, you have your twenty-four hours. After that, I'll have to comply with federal pressure."

"And Agent Gleave?" I asked.

"I'll tell her the evidence is being cataloged and will be transferred tomorrow. That should buy you some time."

"Are you sure, Chief?" I said. "This could end your career." I was deeply concerned.

"Don't worry about it, Captain. It's about time I retired anyway," he said, smiling, something I hadn't seen him do in months. "Just do your job and nail these bastards."

Against the Clock

Wednesday Afternoon, 1:30 PM

WITH LESS THAN EIGHTEEN HOURS BEFORE CHIEF Johnston would be forced to hand over our evidence to Agent Gleave, the conference room had taken on the atmosphere of a war room. Maps, photographs, and documents covered every available surface, while Jack, surrounded by three laptops, worked quietly monitoring federal surveillance of our activities.

"All right, everyone," I said, standing at the white-board where I'd mapped out our remaining time. "We have until tomorrow morning to identify our killer and arrest her."

Jack looked up from his laptop, where he'd been cross-referencing survivor networks with current medical licenses, and said, "Kate, I've been thinking... If our killer really has support from an organized network of survivors, we're not just dealing with one person, are we?"

"What do you mean?" I asked.

"I mean the financial resources, the technical capabilities, the intelligence gathering, it's too sophisticated for a lone actor."

Cooper, who was examining the timeline we'd constructed of the killer's activities, jumped in and said, "Which explains how they've stayed ahead of us. If they've got people monitoring our investigation, tracking our movements, probably even feeding them information about federal interference..." he trailed off, frowning, then said, "Jack, how are they getting this information in real time?"

"I've been wondering the same thing," Jack replied. "Based on the timing of these messages, they're either intercepting our communications directly, or they have someone feeding them information from inside law enforcement."

"Inside source? Hah," I said. "A leak. Why am I not surprised?"

"And, speaking of federal interference," Jack said. "They just cut off our access to the databases."

"Geez," I muttered. "How can they do that?"

"Multiple ways," Jack replied, his fingers flying across his keyboard as he monitored the federal systems. "First, they'll revoke our credentials to federal databases - FBI, NCIC, DEA systems, all the inter-agency stuff we use for background checks and case coordination."

"How quickly can they do that?"

"They're doing it right now. A few keystrokes and our department login credentials become worthless. Then they'll block our IP addresses from accessing any federal law enforcement networks."

I shook my head. *This can't be happening,* I thought. "That it?" I asked.

"Uh, uh," he replied. "They'll take away our access to their communication systems. They can cut us off from federal radio frequencies, secure networks, real-time intelligence sharing. Basically, they'll isolate us from any federal resources."

"What about our local systems?" Corbin asked.

"Those they can't touch directly," Jack replied. "Local databases, our own communication networks, evidence we've already collected, that stays with us. But Kate, we rely heavily on federal cooperation. Without access to the FBI databases, interstate criminal records, federal forensic labs..."

"I get it," I replied. "We're flying blind on anything that crosses state lines."

"Exactly. And given that our killer appears to have been operating across multiple states, losing federal access severely limits our capabilities."

"How long before we're completely cut off?"

Jack glanced at his screens. "Database access is already gone. Communication systems... not so easy. Maybe by tonight. They're moving faster than I expected."

And the pressure was intensifying faster than I'd expected. Agent Gleave and her associates were already cutting off our resources. Me? For once in my career, I was feeling just a little helpless, and aware that everyone was staring at me. *Uneasy lies the head that wears the crown,* I thought, then turned again to Jack.

"What can you tell us about this so-called survivor network?" I asked.

"Yeah, that," he said. "I've been analyzing the financial patterns and communication networks. The support structure is sophisticated. Multiple funding sources, encrypted communications, even what appears to be safe houses and identity management services."

"Safe houses?" Corbin asked, his brow deeply furrowed.

"Properties purchased or leased through shell companies," Jack said without looking at him. "Great for people who need to disappear. I'm betting they've been preparing for just this scenario for years."

Corbin was studying the target list we'd recovered from Elena's research. "If, as you say, this network has been planning to punish the program's staff, they know where everyone is, right?"

Jack looked up and nodded.

"Locations, security arrangements, and daily routines," I added.

The scope of what we were dealing with was becoming clearer. Our killer was part of an organized resistance movement bent on the destruction of their abusers.

"All right," I said. "If we're dealing with an organized network, we need to think strategically. What would their next move be?"

"Acceleration," Corbin said. "If they know federal

agents are about to shut down our investigation—and from what Jack's said I'm sure they do—they'll move to complete their mission before they can be stopped."

"Which means more targets, more quickly," Tracy added.

"Geez," Jack said, suddenly straightening up in his chair, and switching his attention back and forth between all three screens. "Kate, someone's accessing the security systems. They're downloading employment schedules, even family information. And some of the subjects they're researching aren't on Elena's original list…"

He trailed off, staring at the screens as the data continued to scroll.

"Talk to me, Jack," I snapped. "What does it all mean?"

"Someone's downloading…" he paused, then continued, "I'm seeing searches about federal agents, pharmaceutical company executives, even some congressional staff members who I'm guessing must have been involved in oversight of the psychiatric treatment programs."

So, I thought, *the network is expanding their target list to include the people who are currently protecting the perpetrators of the original crimes.*

"Jack," I said, "can you identify any specific targets?"

"Agent Gleave, for one," he replied. "Several pharmaceutical company executives and at least two federal officials."

It was at that moment my phone rang. It was Chief Johnston.

"Captain, you need to come to my office immediately.

Agent Gleave is here with four federal marshals. They want the evidence transferred immediately, and they have the authority to seize everything if I don't comply."

"So, they're not waiting until tomorrow—"

"That's correct," he snapped.

I looked at my team. "Very well, Chief, I need thirty minutes to secure some of the files."

"I can give you fifteen minutes," he replied. "After that, I'll have to allow them access to everything."

I hung up and said to Jack, "How quickly can you backup and secure the rest of the files?"

"Already done," he replied. "I've been preparing for this since yesterday. Everything important is secured in multiple cloud locations they can't access without my passwords, all of them twenty-five randomized characters."

"Tracy, Cooper, I want you to start reaching out to potential targets. Anyone on Elena's list who might be in immediate danger needs to be warned."

"Isn't that obstruction of a federal investigation?" Cooper asked, obviously a little uptight.

"At this point, saving lives is more important than federal cooperation. If we have to choose between protecting victims and appeasing Agent Gleave, we choose the victims."

I thought about that as I prepared to face Gleave and her federal marshals.

"All right, everyone. Here's what we're going to do. Jack, you continue monitoring network activity and federal surveillance. Tracy, start contacting potential targets and warn them about the immediate danger.

Cooper, you coordinate with Patrol to establish protection for anyone who wants it. Corbin, you're with me."

"Where are we going?" he asked.

"To face Gleave and her marshals."

As we prepared to leave, my phone buzzed with another text: "Captain, the choice is yours. Work with us to expose the truth, or with the federal authorities to protect the people who tortured children in exchange for research grants. Either way, justice will be served."

Federal Confrontation

Chief Johnston's office felt like a courtroom when Corbin, Samson, and I arrived. Agent Gleave stood behind the chief's desk like she owned it: feet apart, chest out, hands behind her back, chin up, while four federal marshals in tactical gear flanked the doorway. The message was clear: this wasn't a negotiation.

"Captain Gazzara," Gleave said without preamble, "I trust your team has completed cataloging the evidence."

"It's ongoing," I replied, remaining standing near the door with Corbin to my left and Samson to my right. "We're not quite prepared to transfer anything yet."

"I'm afraid that's no longer your decision, Captain." Gleave gestured to one of the marshals, who stepped forward with an official document. "This is a federal seizure order signed by a federal judge thirty minutes ago. All evidence, files, and investigative materials related to the Greenbriar experimental program are now under federal custody."

"Kate, I'm sorry," Johnston said. "My hands are tied."

"No problem, Chief," I replied, studying the seizure order. The federal government was about to take full control of our investigation.

"On what grounds?" I asked, looking at Gleave.

"Interstate criminal activity, federal healthcare fraud, and potential terrorism threats," Gleave replied smoothly. "This investigation has expanded beyond local jurisdiction."

"Terrorism threats?" I said, smiling. "Are you serious?"

"Captain, we have reason to believe the person you're pursuing has connections to organized groups planning attacks on federal facilities and personnel. This is now a matter of national security."

I almost laughed out loud. It was bullshit, and we all knew it. But it was official bullshit backed by four federal marshals and a signed court order.

"Agent Gleave," I said, patiently and with a little sarcasm for good measure, "this is a *local* murder investigation. Five people are dead, and we're close to identifying the killer."

"Which is exactly why federal oversight is necessary. Captain, your investigation has been compromised from the beginning. Critical evidence has been mishandled, witnesses have been intimidated, and there are indications that someone within your department has been leaking information."

"Hahahaha!" This time I actually laughed at her. "That's ridiculous and you know it."

"Is it? How else would you explain the killer's ability to stay ahead of your investigation? Their knowledge of your investigative procedures? Their access to information that should have been confidential?"

Gleave was turning our own competence against us, suggesting that our thoroughness was evidence of internal corruption.

"How d'you know all that?" I asked. "Could it possibly have been someone on your team that's been leaking information?"

She didn't answer. Instead, she looked at Marshal Davidson and said, "Please coordinate with Captain Gazzara to ensure the orderly transfer of all materials."

"Agent Gleave," I said, "I need to ask you something directly. Are you here to catch a killer, or are you here to protect the people who covered up medical abuse in the 1990s?"

For the first time, Gleave's professional composure slipped slightly. "Captain, I'm here to ensure that federal crimes are properly investigated by appropriate authorities."

"That's not an answer," I said.

"It's the only answer you're going to get," she snapped.

Johnston cleared his throat. "Captain, I need you to comply with the seizure order."

"Chief, if we turn over our evidence now," I replied, "this investigation disappears into federal bureaucracy. The killer escapes, and the truth about the experimental program gets buried forever."

"Captain," Marshal Davidson said, stepping forward, "we're prepared to take custody of the materials with or without your cooperation. Cooperation would be... easier for everyone."

It was a polite threat, but a threat, nonetheless.

"How much time do I have to finish gathering our files?" I asked.

"Thirty minutes," Gleave replied. "After that, my team will be conducting a complete search of your facilities."

I looked at Johnston, who nodded grimly. There was nothing he could do to stop it, and we both knew it.

"All right," I said. "Thirty minutes it is."

And with that, we left the chief's office. Me? I was sick to my stomach. Gleave had outmaneuvered us completely, and, by the time we finished gathering the files, our investigation would be over, and the killer would disappear... but would she?

As we walked along the corridor toward the elevator, my phone buzzed with a text from Jack: "Everything's secured in the cloud. They can take our files, but they can't take our knowledge."

"Corbin," I said quietly, "we're not done. Not by a long shot."

"How so?" he asked, looking at me as we walked.

"I mean, Agent Gleave has made a critical mistake. She's so focused on protecting her pharmaceutical company contacts that she's forgotten we're actually trying to catch a killer."

"She's cut us off at the knees," he said. "So, what do we do now?"

"No, she hasn't," I replied, smiling to myself. "We let them have the files. And then we solve this case without federal resources."

When we returned to the conference room, I found the rest of my team already preparing for the federal seizure. Tracy and Cooper were boxing files, and Jack had ensured that our most sensitive intelligence was secured beyond federal reach.

"How much do they get?" Tracy asked.

"Everything official," I replied. "Case files, evidence logs, witness statements, forensic reports, those computers... You haven't deleted anything, have you, Jack?"

Jack grinned and shook his head. "No, ma'am. But all they'll get is sanitized versions of everything."

"What about the survivor network intelligence?" Cooper asked.

Jack shrugged. "If the feds want to protect the perpetrators, so be it. That's their choice. I have it all in the cloud. We're not going to let them bury evidence of ongoing crimes, are we, Cap?"

He finished just as Gleave appeared in the conference room doorway with two marshals. "Captain, how are we progressing?"

"Almost finished," I replied.

"Excellent. Marshal Davidson will need to interview each team member to ensure complete transfer of materials."

"Interview them about what?"

"To verify that no evidence has been withheld or destroyed. Standard procedure in federal seizures."

She could do as she liked, but I wasn't worried. It was all there for them to find, if they knew where and how to look. We'd made backup copies of everything, and we'd hidden nothing.

"Agent Gleave," I said, "once you take custody of our files, what happens to the active investigation?"

"The investigation continues under appropriate federal supervision. Any local involvement will be determined by federal authorities."

"Meaning we're cut out completely," I said.

"Meaning that federal resources are better equipped to handle complex cases involving interstate criminal activity and potential terrorism," she replied.

There was that terrorism allegation again. Gleave was building a narrative that would justify any level of federal control.

"That's one hell of a stretch," I said, "and you know it."

She ignored me and twenty minutes later, the marshals began removing the boxed-up files while Gleave supervised the transfer and the sum total of our investigative work disappeared into federal custody, leaving our conference room looking stripped and empty.

"Captain Gazzara," Gleave said as the last boxes were loaded onto carts, "thank you for your cooperation. We'll be in touch if we require any additional assistance."

"What about the active threats to potential victims?" I asked.

"Federal protective services will handle that aspect of the case," she replied.

"And the killer?" Corbin asked.

"Will be apprehended by appropriate federal task forces," she replied.

After the federal agents left, the five of us sat in the empty conference room, looking at the bare tables and whiteboard where our investigation had been mapped out.

"So that's it?" Cooper asked. "We just let them bury everything?"

"Hell no," I said. "We have a killer to find."

"What do you mean?" Tracy asked.

"I mean, Agent Gleave just gave us the perfect cover. Officially, we're off the case. Unofficially, we're free to pursue leads without federal oversight or interference."

Jack was already setting up his personal laptop on the empty conference table—the three department laptops having been seized along with the files. "Kate's right," he said grimly. "They got our official files, but they didn't get the backups, and they definitely didn't get our understanding of the case."

"Plus," Corbin added, "we know something they don't know. We know they're not really interested in catching the killer."

"So what's our next move?" Tracy asked.

I looked around at my team. We'd been through complex cases before, but never one where we'd had to work around federal interference.

"Our next move is to solve this case before the feds can bury it completely. Jack, what's the status on our suspect's ID and location?"

"Still working on it," he replied. "And Kate, I'm seeing increased internet activity around the potential targets. It looks like the network knows about the federal seizure. Thirty minutes ago, encrypted communications spiked across all the channels I've been monitoring. Someone sent out a mass alert about federal interference. I think they're intending to complete their mission before the feds can stop them. And Kate, some of their targets now include federal agents."

"Including Agent Gleave?" I asked.

He nodded. "Oh yeah, Agent Gleave, for sure."

If it hadn't been so serious, I might have laughed at that. Gleave had just made herself a target by protecting the people the survivor network was trying to eliminate.

"All right, everyone. We have maybe hours before this situation implodes. Tracy, you continue reaching out to potential victims and warn them about immediate danger. Cooper, coordinate with patrol to provide protection for anyone who wants it. Jack, keep monitoring both the network and federal activities. Corbin, you're coming with me and Sammy."

"Where are we going?" he asked.

"To find our killer before she decides that the feds are just another obstacle in her path to justice."

But before we could leave, my phone buzzed with a text from whom I believed to be our killer: "Captain, those federal agents just made a serious mistake. You have 24 hours. After that, everything goes public."

I showed the message to the team.

"She's giving us one last chance," Jack said.

"No, she's not," I replied. "She's playing us. She's giving herself one last chance. She wants to complete her mission, whatever that is. We have to find her and stop her."

"But in twenty-four hours, the network is going to release everything," Tracy said.

"No, I don't think so," I said. "I think it's an empty

threat. I think she and/or the network have been playing us." I shrugged. "So what if they do release everything? What difference does it make, other than expose a lot of people who deserve to be exposed? We have a killer to catch. Let's frickin' do it."

I turned to Jack and said, "How long before we lose all communication with the law enforcement networks?"

"Hard to say," he replied. "They might go completely dark now that the feds have taken over. What are you thinking?"

"I'm thinking that someone who's spent twenty-five years planning this operation isn't going to let a little federal interference stop them. But I'm also thinking they might be willing to work with law enforcement that they trust."

"You want to make contact with them directly?" he asked, obviously stunned.

"I want to give them an alternative to violence. But first, we need to figure out who our suspect is and where she's planning her final confrontation. Come on, Corbin. Let's go."

As we walked to my car, I realized something: Gleave's actions had fundamentally changed the dynamics of our case. We were now caught between an organized survivor network seeking justice and a federal task force bent on protecting the perpetrators of institutional crimes. It was a nightmare I didn't want to live through; could we find a path to justice without allowing either side to destroy the other?

I loaded Sammy into the back seat, knowing there were innocent people out there who deserved protection, that the truth needed to be exposed, and that the legal system that was supposed to ensure justice for all had just failed spectacularly. And we were now preparing for a confrontation where justice would be decided by violence rather than the law.

But I sure as hell hoped not!

21

Hidden Identity

Friday Morning, 8:30 AM

FRIDAY MORNING DAWNED WITH A GRAY SKY THAT matched my mood - overcast, ominous, and full of the promise that something significant was about to happen. We had less than twelve hours left before the killer's support network's deadline and, despite working through most of the night, we still didn't have a solid lead on our killer's identity or current location. But as Samson and I walked into the situation room at eight-thirty that morning, I could tell by Jack North's expression that something had changed.

"Please tell me you have something," I said, settling into a chair with Samson at my feet.

"Yeah, I have something," Jack replied. He sounded

tired, and no wonder. By my reckoning, he hadn't been to bed for almost forty-eight hours.

"I finally cracked the encryption on those financial accounts we've been tracking," he said, leaning back in his chair and stretching his arms above his head.

By then, the rest of my team had gathered around Jack's workstation. Somehow, from where I'd no idea, he'd managed to find two more laptops, and all three screens were displaying support network diagrams, financial records, employment histories, and what appeared to be a comprehensive timeline of digital activities spanning several years.

"So what have you got?" I asked.

He leaned forward, tapped a few keys, and brought up a complex flowchart on his main screen. "I've been working backward from the Patient Advocacy Research Foundation account, tracing every financial transaction, every shell company, every digital identity our killer has used over the past five years."

"Okay," I said. "So?"

"I found the pattern. Look at this." He highlighted a series of connections between various medical facilities across the Southeast. "Our killer has been working short-term contracts at hospitals and medical centers throughout Tennessee, Georgia, Alabama, and Mississippi. Always six-month assignments, always in positions that provide access to patient records and medical supplies."

Tracy leaned forward to study the timeline. "Wow, that's amazing," she muttered.

"She's a nurse practitioner specializing in trauma

counseling and patient advocacy. Sometimes working in emergency departments, sometimes in psychiatric units, occasionally in administrative roles that provide access to historical medical records."

"That would give her everything she needed," Corbin said. "Access to drugs and equipment, legitimate reasons to research patient files, and the ability to move between different locations without attracting attention."

"Exactly," Jack said.

"So while she was working as a legitimate medical professional, she was also planning her mission," I said.

"That's what it looks like," Jack replied. "Now for the good stuff, Kate. I found this." He tapped a key and the black screen on the central laptop lit up to reveal what appeared to be an employment record.

"Kit Morrison," he said. "Nurse practitioner at Chattanooga General Hospital. She's been working there for five months. Her references and credentials are impeccable."

I felt the adrenaline kick in. "This is her?" I asked, hardly able to believe what I was seeing and hearing.

"Yep!" he emphasized the word by making the P pop with his lips.

"You've gotta be kidding me," I muttered, staring at the screen. We finally had a name and a current workplace. "Kit Morrison. What else do you have on her?"

Jack took a deep breath, nodded to the right, once, then said, "Everything, and it looks completely legit." He scrolled down through personnel records. "She has a nursing degree from Vanderbilt, a nurse practitioner certification from Emory, specialized training in trauma counseling and patient advocacy. Performance reviews describe her as exceptionally skilled, and particularly effective with patients who have experienced drug abuse and trauma."

"It all fits the profile," Tracy said. "And it seems she specialized in what she knows best, from personal experience."

"The reviews also mention her extensive knowledge of psychiatric treatment protocols," Jack continued. "A note here talks about her ability to identify signs of medical abuse that other medical professionals might miss. Her supervisors praised her dedication to patient rights and her advocacy for trauma victims."

Cooper was examining the employment timeline Jack had compiled. "So, Kit Morrison was working at Chattanooga General during the entire period when the murders began?"

"Her contract started a little less than six months ago—nine days, to be exact," Jack said, nodding. "Right around the time we think the planning phase of her operation shifted from planning to active surveillance and targeting," Jack said. "She would have had access to the hospital computer systems, medical supplies, staff directories, and patient databases."

"What about her living situation?" I asked.

Jack pulled up another screen showing lease agreements and utility records. "She's been renting an apartment on the north side of town under the Kit Morrison identity. The utilities are in her name. She has a clean credit history, and no red flags that would attract attention."

"And her background before the Chattanooga contract?"

"She worked a six-month contract at a trauma center in Memphis," he said. "Before that, at a psychiatric facility in Atlanta, before that, a medical center in Birmingham."

I studied the employment history Jack had compiled. Kit Morrison, if it was her that had been moving around the Southeast, had built separate identities for each contract, all with almost identical credentials and references. She'd spent years establishing those identities. It was impressive... I was impressed.

"Have you been able to connect the Kit Morrison identity to the Greenbriar experimental program?" I asked.

"Ah, now that's where it gets tricky," he said, pulling up another set of files. "The Kit Morrison identity was created about seven years ago, with a completely clean background and legitimate educational credentials. But the financial networks that support this identity connect back to older accounts that might be tied to the original patient records."

"Meaning?" I asked.

"Meaning someone with access to significant financial resources spent years creating a completely legitimate professional identity for Kit Morrison. Medical school transcripts, nursing certifications, employment references, everything you'd need to work in healthcare without anyone questioning your background."

Hawk, who had been quietly reviewing the surveillance reports, looked up and said, "Kate, this level of identity construction would require serious resources and connections. We're not talking about someone who just changed their name and got fake documents."

"What do you mean?" I asked.

"Look at the timeline," Hawk said, pointing to Jack's employment history. "Kit Morrison didn't just appear seven years ago with fake credentials. She went to a real nursing school, completed real clinical rotations, and passed real licensing examinations. She is what she appears to be, an extremely well qualified medical professional. Someone invested enormous time and money to create her persona."

Jack nodded and pulled up an additional screen. "Hawk's right," he said. "I've been digging deeper into the educational records, and they're not forged. Kit Morrison actually attended Vanderbilt University's nursing program, completed clinical rotations at multiple hospitals, and graduated with honors."

"So she became a real nurse practitioner using the Kit Morrison identity?" Cooper muttered.

"That's what it looks like," Jack replied. "And then there's this: the financial records show that someone was paying for her education, living expenses, and professional development costs throughout the entire process."

"How much are we talking about?" I asked.

"Conservative estimate?" He shrugged. "About three hundred thousand dollars over six years. Tuition, housing, medical expenses, living stipend, even money for professional conferences and continuing education."

Tracy whistled softly.

"But where did that money come from?" Corbin asked.

Jack switched to another screen showing a complex web of financial connections. "That's where the trail gets really sophisticated," he said. "The money came from what appears to be a trust fund established in the early 2000s, right around the time the experimental program ended."

"A trust fund?" I asked. "How—"

"Multiple trust funds, actually," Jack said, cutting me off. "Set up through offshore banking, managed by a series of shell companies, all designed to provide long-term financial support. And Kate, the amount of money involved suggests this was a comprehensive plan to create a specific professional identity over a specific timeline."

I felt pieces of a larger puzzle starting to come together. "Jack, who had the financial resources and legal connections to set up that kind of trust fund structure?"

"That's what I've been trying to figure out. The legal work was done by a prestigious law firm in Nashville, the banking was handled through established financial institutions, and the ongoing management has been top-grade."

"So we're talking about someone with serious money and connections?" I said.

He nodded. "Someone or some entity, like a network, who gained access to serious money through legal settlements, insurance payouts, or other compensation related to the experimental program."

Hawk leaned forward. "Kate, what if the trust funds

were set up as part of legal settlements for families of the experimental program's victims?"

"You mean someone sued the medical establishment and used the settlement money to fund Kit Morrison's education?"

"It's possible," Hawk replied. "A lot of institutional abuse cases from the 1990s and before, and after, for that matter, were settled quietly, with non-disclosure agreements and sealed records. If someone received a substantial settlement and wanted to use that money to create a specific kind of revenge, this would be exactly how they'd do it."

Jack was already pulling up more records. "I can check for legal settlements and insurance payouts related to the experimental program, but those records might be sealed or confidential."

"Do what you can," I said.

Jack's fingers flew across his keyboard for several minutes, accessing various financial databases and probate records. "Kate, I think I found it," he said, pulling up what appeared to be legal documents. "There was a substantial amount of money involved, but it's not what you'd think."

Jack scrolled through the documents. "These are court records," he said. "And, according to them, Morrison received a substantial settlement from a wrongful death lawsuit she brought against Greenbriar Behavioral Health Center on behalf of her sister. The case was settled in 2009 after four years of legal battles."

"Her sister?" I frowned.

"Yeah, Kelly Morrison, Katherine's—Kit's—older

sister. Both were patients in the experimental program. Kelly committed suicide in 1999. Katherine was discharged two months later. She sued Greenbriar in 2005, claiming the experimental treatments were the direct cause of her sister's death. The case was finally settled out of court." He looked at me, his eyebrows raised.

"And there's her motive; her sister's suicide. Go on, Jack," I said. "What kind of settlement?"

"The settlement documents show Morrison received approximately three point eight million dollars, but it came with strict conditions. Sealed records, non-disclosure agreements, and the money was placed in a restricted trust fund specifically for her education and what the court called 'rehabilitation and future life establishment.'"

Tracy leaned forward. "So Greenbriar paid her off. They paid for her nursing education to keep her quiet about what they did to her and her sister?"

"That's exactly what it looks like," Jack replied, nodding. "And according to the trust documents, Morrison had 'complete discretion' in how to use the funds once she completed her education."

"The settlement essentially gave her permission to seek justice," I muttered.

Corbin was examining the settlement documents. "This explains how Morrison could afford to fund years of preparation and help other survivors."

"And it explains Morrison's sense of mission," Hawk added.

Jack pulled up more financial records. "The money

has been carefully managed through legitimate investment accounts. Morrison has been using the income to
fund her various identities, help other trauma survivors,
and build the capabilities needed for her mission... Why
are we calling it that, by the way?"

I didn't know. Someone had called it that, but I
couldn't recall who it was, so I didn't answer. Jack? He
just shrugged and continued.

"Morrison seems to have been using the money
responsibly from a financial standpoint. She's main-
tained the principal through sound investments while
using the income to fund her activities. She's also made
anonymous donations to trauma treatment programs
and survivor support services."

I was about to respond when Jack suddenly straightened in his chair, staring at his computer screen with an
expression of recognition.

"If I remember correctly, we found a Katherine
Morrison in the patient files." Jack pulled up the experi-
mental program records. "Yes! Here it is: Katherine
Morrison, admitted to the Greenbriar Behavioral Health
Center in 1995 at age sixteen. She was discharged
September 27, 1999. Her sister committed suicide two
months earlier on Sunday, July 18."

Tracy leaned forward to look at the screen. "So we
found her. Katherine Morrison."

"The records show that Katherine and Kelly
Morrison were in the program at the same time for
about three years" Tracy said, reading over Jack's shoulder. "And Katherine was discharged two months after
Kelly's suicide. They were both subjected to the same

experimental treatments - electroshock therapy, experimental medications, and prolonged isolation. And... they were separated."

"So they were isolated from each other," I said, trying to imagine what that must have been like for them.

"According to these notes, yes," Jack replied. "And the separation appears to have been particularly traumatic for Katherine, who was younger and dependent on her sister for emotional support."

"What do the files say about Katherine's specific treatments?"

Jack opened Katherine Morrison's individual file. "She was considered one of the most challenging cases because of her resistance to treatment. The treatment notes describe Katherine as 'highly intelligent, manipulative, and resistant to standard therapeutic interventions.' They subjected her to increasingly aggressive treatments to try to break down her psychological defenses."

I was stunned by what I was hearing.

Jack scrolled through the medical notes. "She was subjected to experimental antipsychotic medications, electroshock therapy administered multiple times per week, prolonged isolation in what they called 'reflection rooms,' and something called 'behavioral modification protocols' that sound like psychological torture."

"And her sister Kelly was receiving similar treatments?"

"Similar, but Kelly appears to have broken down first. The notes describe her as becoming compliant and docile after about eighteen months of treatment, while Katherine continued to resist for the full three years."

Hawk was studying the timeline Jack had constructed. "So Katherine Morrison watched her sister deteriorate under experimental treatments," he said. "And she was separated from Kelly when she needed support, and then she lost her to suicide. That's a recipe for murder if ever I heard one."

"According to Kelly Morrison's suicide note, she specifically mentioned the experimental treatments and blamed them and the medical staff for destroying her life."

"Did Katherine Morrison have access to her sister's suicide note?"

"The records show that Katherine,was Kelly's next of kin—they were orphans. Their parents were killed in an auto accident in 1996—now nineteen, having reached the age of consent, would have been responsible for handling her sister's affairs after her death and would have received her personal belongings. The note was addressed to her, Katherine, so yeah, she would have seen it. She probably still has it."

Tracy was examining Kelly Morrison's medical records. "These treatment notes describe someone who was completely broken by what happened to her. She was suffering from severe anxiety and depression and still they kept treating her. What kind of animal does that?"

"Dr. Holloway," I muttered. "And Katherine Morrison spent the next twenty-odd years building the skills and resources necessary to ensure that everyone responsible for her sister's death would face the consequences."

I studied the file photographs of both sisters.

Katherine looked defiant and determined even as a sixteen-year-old, while Kelly appeared to be just an innocent young kid.

"Tell me about the lawsuit," I said.

"The medical establishment closed ranks," Jack said. "Defense experts testified that the experimental program was legitimate research conducted according to accepted standards, and that Kelly Morrison's suicide was the result of pre-existing mental health issues rather than institutional abuse. But Katherine's lawyers proved otherwise. They also named specific defendants, including Holloway and several other doctors, nurses, and administrators who had participated in the experimental program."

"The same people we're now protecting," I said.

"Holloway was specifically named for his role in designing and implementing the experimental treatments," Jack continued. "Judge Marks was named for signing the committal orders on flimsy evidence, Dr. Pierce for administering experimental drugs, and Elena Vasquez was mentioned as a potential witness who could have testified about the abuse but chose to remain silent. There are more, of course, including the King sisters, but these are the ones we're most familiar with."

"How many people were named in the lawsuit, Jack?" I asked.

"Forty-seven defendants total. Including medical staff, administrators, pharmaceutical company representatives, and judicial officials who had participated in or enabled the experimental program."

I could only shake my head at the enormity of it all.

But I also knew that the hunt was entering its final phase, and I had the uncomfortable feeling that Katherine Morrison had always known this day would come. She'd been preparing for a final confrontation not just with her targets, but with law enforcement, federal agents, and anyone else who might try to stop her from honoring her sister's memory. *She's on a suicide mission*, I thought. *And, in a few hours, we'll face someone who'll stop at nothing to avenge her sister's death, the most dangerous adversary a law enforcement officer can face.*

"Jack, what's the address for Kit Morrison's apartment?"

He consulted his files and gave me the address. It was on Frazier Avenue.

22

Confrontation

Friday Afternoon, 1:00 PM

"CORBIN, TRACY, YOU'RE WITH ME," I SAID. "COOPER, YOU coordinate with Patrol to establish a perimeter around the building. Jack, keep monitoring for any digital activity associated with Kit Morrison or any of her other identities."

"Kate," Jack said as we prepared to leave, "if Kit Morrison has abandoned her legitimate identity and gone underground, she might be preparing for something... final. Someone who's spent years building a professional cover doesn't throw it away unless they're planning to complete their mission and accept the consequences."

"You think I don't know that?" I snapped, then thought better of it. "Sorry, Jack. Stay in touch, okay?"

He grinned at me, then at Sammy, who looked back at him with his head tilted to one side, and I had the distinct feeling that some kind of message passed between them.

The drive to Kit Morrison's apartment took fifteen minutes through the early Friday afternoon traffic that seemed determined to slow us down. During the drive, I found myself thinking about the photograph Jack had shown us. Kit Morrison looked competent, professional, trustworthy; exactly the kind of person you'd want caring for trauma victims. But she was also someone who wouldn't hesitate to kill to further her quest for revenge, and I had a feeling this meeting wasn't going to go well.

The apartment building on Frazier Avenue, just a short distance from the Veteran's Bridge, was a modest four-story structure in a quiet neighborhood, the kind of place where people minded their own business and didn't ask too many questions about their neighbors. Nothing about it suggested it had been home to a serial killer, but then, they never do, do they?

I parked across the street and spent a moment studying the building and surrounding area. Kit Morrison had chosen this location carefully. I knew the building, and I also knew there were multiple exit routes, good sight lines to approaching vehicles, and the kind of anonymous urban environment where someone could come and go without attracting attention.

"Third floor, apartment 3B," I said as we exited the car and prepared to approach the building entrance.

A middle-aged woman was checking her mailbox in

the lobby. She looked up as we entered, taking note of our badges.

"You need some help?" she asked, stridently.

"Yes, ma'am," I said. "I'm Captain Gazzara, Chattanooga Police. We're looking for Kit Morrison in apartment 3B. Have you seen her recently?"

"Kit? No, not for several days. What you want with her? She's a nice girl, very friendly, always says hello when we pass in the hall. But no, I haven't seen her since..." She thought for a moment. "Maybe Tuesday evening when she was on her way out. Seemed to be in a hurry, carrying a large bag."

"What kind of bag?"

"I dunno. Like I said, a large black bag. She said she had to go help a patient who was having a crisis. She's a nurse, you know?"

Tuesday evening would have been right after Elena Vasquez's murder. I figured Kit Morrison had probably been cleaning up evidence and preparing to abandon her identity.

"Can you describe Ms. Morrison?" Corbin asked.

"Professional looking woman, late thirties, early forties I should say. Always dressed nice, like she was going to work at a hospital or medical office. Very polite but kept to herself mostly. She mentioned once that she worked with trauma patients and sometimes had to respond to emergencies."

"Did she have many visitors?" Corbin asked.

"Not that I noticed," she replied. "She seemed to live a quiet life. But she was obviously successful, always paid her rent on time, drove a nice car, seemed to have her life together."

"What kind of car?" I asked.

"Small. Dark blue, I think. Nothing flashy, quite new, I think."

Corbin was taking notes as the woman talked. "Did Ms. Morrison ever mention family or personal relationships?" he asked.

"Noooo." She drew the word out. "She told me she traveled a lot for work, consulting at different hospitals. She mentioned once that she didn't have much family, that her work was her life. I got the impression she'd been through some difficult times but had built a good career for herself."

"Has anyone else been asking about Kit Morrison?" Tracy asked.

"No, but now I think of it, the custodian... I should say the building manager, I guess. He said she called Wednesday morning to say she had a family emergency and would be away for an extended period. She said someone would be by to collect her belongings and settle any outstanding issues with the lease."

"And did anyone come by?" I asked.

"I don't think so," she replied. "Her apartment has been quiet since Tuesday night. But I did notice that the cleaning service was here Wednesday afternoon."

"Cleaning service? What cleaning service?" Corbin asked, looking up at her.

"Oh, it was a professional cleaning company. They brought a lot of equipment, spent several hours working in her apartment. I thought it was unusual for someone to have professional cleaning done when they were moving out, but maybe she wanted to get her security deposit back."

That would explain any lack of forensic evidence, and I figured we were probably wasting our time, but... you never can tell. Me? I was certain Kit Morrison had arranged for professional cleaning to eliminate any traces that might lead back to her real identity or activities. *Smart woman*, I thought.

We took the elevator to the third floor and found apartment 3B at the end of a narrow hallway. The door was locked, but the building manager provided a key after we explained the situation and showed our warrant.

The apartment wasn't just empty. I mean, it was *empty!* No furniture, no personal belongings, no indication that anyone had lived there recently. The rooms smelled faintly of cleaning chemicals, and the carpet had been steam-cleaned and vacuumed.

"Geez," Corbin said as he was examining the spotless kitchen. "They didn't miss a thing, did they?"

He moved on into the living room. It was bare. Then, "Hey, Kate, come and look at this," He called from the bedroom. He was standing in front of the window that looked out over the parking lot at the rear. I went and looked.

"Perfect view of the street and multiple exit routes," he said, nodding across the parking lot. "That one opens up onto Tampa, that one to the left to Frazier, the one to the right, also to Frazier. She chose this apartment carefully."

I walked through each room, looking for anything

that might give us a clue about Kit Morrison's current location or future plans. The bathroom medicine cabinet was empty, the kitchen cabinets contained no food or personal items, even the closets had been stripped bare.

But the apartment layout told a story. I could see faint impressions in the carpets that told me the furniture had been arranged to provide clear sight lines to all entrances and exits. The bedroom was ideal for monitoring the parking lot while remaining concealed. Even the kitchen had been set up to allow quick movement between rooms without being visible from the windows.

"She thought of it all, didn't she?" I muttered, more to myself than to Corbin.

Two minutes later, "Kate," Corbin called from the kitchen. "I found something."

He was standing at the kitchen counter holding a slim manila folder. "I found this taped to the bottom of that drawer." He nodded at it as he handed me the folder. "It's addressed to you."

"Geez, really?" I said with a half-laugh, wondering how the hell she could have known I would be the one, and that I would find it, which I hadn't. I shook my head and opened the folder. Inside I found a handwritten note and what appeared to be several photographs.

The note read: "Captain Gazzara. You're a good cop and I know you'll have found this folder. By the time you read this, I'll be preparing for the final phase of my objective. The photographs will help you understand why I'm doing this. But more than anything, I want to thank you for conducting a thorough and unbiased investigation. Bless you. I hope you will continue to do so. The truth about the experimental program must come out. - K.M."

The first photograph showed a group of teenagers in hospital gowns, all looking hollow-eyed and defeated. It appeared to have been taken in some kind of recreation room, with clinical white walls and institutional furniture. At the bottom of the photo, someone had written in pencil: "Greenbriar Behavioral Health Center - Subject Group 1996."

The second photograph showed what appeared to be a medical procedure room with restraint equipment and electroshock therapy devices. Handwritten notes in the margin indicated dates and patient numbers, suggesting this was documentation of specific treatments.

The third photograph was the most disturbing. It showed a teenage girl strapped to a medical table, obviously unconscious or heavily sedated, with electrodes attached to her head. Written at the bottom was *Subject 23 - Session 47.*

Geez, I thought, *that's her. That's Kit Morrison.*

I studied the faces in the group photograph. All teenagers, all showing signs of trauma. But one face stood out: a thin girl with dark hair and who seemed to be staring directly at the camera with an expression of cold determination and... hate.

"That's her," I said, pointing to the girl in the photograph. "That's Kit Morrison at sixteen years old."

"She looks..." Corbin started, then stopped.

"She looks like a frickin' demon," I finished. "They must have really put it to her. I don't see anyone who looks like her sister, though." I handed him the photo.

"No wonder she's after the people who did this to her and Kelly."

Corbin handed the photo back to me and I looked at it again, and then I saw it: a faint reflection in the window in the background of what appeared to be another teenager taking the picture.

"Corbin, look at this," I said, pointing to the reflection. "There's someone else there, someone taking the picture."

"You think Kit Morrison had an accomplice?" He asked, frowning.

"No, I think this was a fellow victim. Maybe, even back then, someone was helping her. There were what, sixty-odd victims, that we know of? Maybe some of those fellow victims might still be helping her now."

"Sixty-seven," Corbin muttered.

"What did you say?" I asked, staring at him.

I said, "there were sixty-seven victims, that we know of."

I was about to answer him when my phone rang. It was Jack.

"Kate, Kit Morrison just used her medical credentials to gain access to the old Greenbriar Behavioral Health Center."

"What?" I said, my mind in a whirl.

"Kit Morrison just used her med—"

"Geez, Jack," I snapped, interrupting him. "I heard you the first time."

"Oh, yeah, sure. Anyway, it's her. The security cameras caught her entering the building about an hour ago."

"You sure it's her?" I said. "Is she alone?"

"She matches Morrison's description," he replied. "And she wasn't trying to hide her face. And no, she wasn't alone. There was a woman with her. I couldn't see her face. She's a little taller than Morrison. And I picked up communication just a few minutes ago, that Dr. Pierce from Chattanooga General left the building in the middle of a consultation more than two hours ago and hasn't returned. What do you want me to do?"

"Give me a minute to think," I said. Then, "D'you think it could be Pierce with Morrison, that she took Dr. Pierce to the abandoned facility?" It was a stupid question. Jack had never met Pierce and, as far as I knew, had never seen a photo of her, but it was all I could think of at the time.

"It's possible," he replied. "Dr. Pierce was one of the administrative staff who helped coordinate the experimental program at Greenbriar. If Morrison is planning some kind of show."

"Or she might be planning to eliminate her," I said.

I looked at Corbin and Tracy. "We need to get to the old Greenbriar facility immediately. If Kit Morrison is planning something, that's where it's going to happen."

As we headed for the elevator, I thought about the photograph Kit Morrison had left for us. Even as a sixteen-year-old victim of medical abuse, she'd been planning ahead, thinking strategically, vowing revenge. That level of intelligence and determination, combined with years of medical training and professional resources, made her an extremely dangerous adversary.

But it also suggested that she wanted to tell her story,

to be understood. By leaving the photograph and the note for me, she was ensuring we'd follow her and that we'd know why she'd committed these murders and what had driven her to seek revenge instead of justice.

As we raced through the traffic toward the abandoned Greenbriar facility, I realized that we, that is I, was trying to prevent Kit Morrison from destroying herself completely. I also hoped I could convince her to take the high road, to quit the killing, and that she could get her revenge by exposing the rest of the gang of forty-seven and ruining them.

And so, the hunt was about to end where it had begun, in the place where a sixteen-year-old girl had been transformed into a killer, and her sister had been driven to suicide by years of medical torture disguised as treatment.

THE ABANDONED Greenbriar Behavioral Health Center squatted on fifteen acres of overgrown land in Northeast Chattanooga like a monument to institutional failure. As our convoy of police vehicles approached the facility, I could see why Katherine Morrison had chosen this place to make her final stand. The three-story brick building was isolated, defensible, and filled with the ghosts of medical abuse that had reshaped her entire life.

The facility had been closed for over five years, but the bones of the institution remained: barred windows, reinforced doors, and the kind of institutional architecture designed to keep people in rather than welcome them. Weeds had grown up through cracks in the parking lot, and graffiti covered the lower walls, but the building itself stood solid and ominous against the gray October sky.

"Secure the perimeter," I said to the patrol officers who'd followed us and were now gathered around my car. "Nobody gets in or out without my authorization."

Corbin was studying the building through binoculars. "Three floors, multiple wings, probably dozens of rooms. If Morrison knows this facility, which I'm sure she does, she could move around inside without us being able to track her."

"Oh yeah," I said, more to myself than to my crew. "She spent three years in this stink hole as a patient. I guarantee she knows every corridor, every hiding place, every exit."

Tracy, Cooper and Jack had arrived with the patrol officers and Corbin was examining the security camera footage Jack had sent us.

"See? The cameras show Morrison and a woman who could be Dr. Pierce entering through a service door on the north side about two hours ago," Jack said. "There's been no movement since then."

"Could they have left through an exit the cameras don't cover?" Corbin asked.

"Possible, but unlikely," Jack replied.

"There's a small blue Nissan sedan in the parking lot," Tracy said. "And apart from the security SUV, there are no other vehicles anywhere."

"You want me to talk to them?" Corbin asked. "The security people?"

"Maybe," I replied. "In a minute. We need to try to figure this thing… Ah, here's Hawk."

"Kate," he said. "I have the floor plans from the city building department. The facility has three main wings - administration, patient housing, and treatment areas."

"Where would Morrison most likely take Dr. Pierce, I wonder?" I said.

"If I were planning a confrontation," Hawk replied, "I'd choose somewhere with good sight lines and a way out. Probably the administration wing on the first floor."

I studied the building plans Hawk had spread across the hood of my car. The facility was larger and more complex than I'd expected.

"Jack, any luck with communications inside the building?" I asked.

"No. Not yet, but I have established a personal hotspot."

"So, we're going in blind." I said.

"That's about the size of it," Jack said.

Corbin was checking his weapon and radio equipment. "So what's our entry strategy?" he asked.

"Three teams," I said, staring down at the building layout. "Tracy and Cooper, you take the north entrance where Morrison entered. Hawk, you take two patrol officers and secure the south exit. Corbin, Samson, and I will take the main entrance and head directly to the second floor. We proceed carefully and assume she's prepared for our arrival. Morrison is smart and she's had hours to prepare. She knows we're coming."

As we prepared to enter the building, my phone buzzed with a text from an unknown number: "Hello,

Captain Gazzara. I can see you. I'm on the second floor. Come to Room 237. Come alone. Dr. Pierce is unharmed, but her safety depends on your cooperation."

I showed the message to the team.

"Room 237," Hawk said, consulting the building plans. "That's here, in the east wing, second floor," he pointed to a spot on the layout. "It was the facility's main conference room."

"She wants to talk," I said.

"It's a trap," Corbin replied immediately.

"Maybe. But Dr. Pierce is in there, and Morrison has had hours to hurt her, if that was her intention. No! She wants something else."

"You think?" Corbin asked, skeptically.

"I think she wants to tell her story," I said. "To someone who will understand it and make sure it's heard."

Tracy, too, looked skeptical. "Kate, you can't go in there alone. Morrison has already killed five people. She won't hesitate to kill again"

"She's also someone who's waited twenty-five years for this confrontation. If she wanted Dr. Pierce or me dead, she's had plenty of opportunities."

"What if you're wrong?" Hawk asked.

I smiled, looked down at Samson, and said, "I'll have Sammy with me. Failing that, you breach the room and take her down. But I don't think that will happen. As I said, I think she wants to talk."

Against the protests of my team, I entered the building through the front door with Samson at my side, leaving Corbin out front with two officers as backup, while Tracy and Cooper went to the north entrance and Hawk to the south.

The main entrance was unlocked. I stepped inside and wrinkled my nose. The lobby smelled of mold, dust, and institutional disinfectant that lingered years after the building's closure.

The interior was exactly what I'd expected: long corridors with rooms on both sides, lighting fixtures hanging from stained ceiling tiles, and the kind of oppressive atmosphere that comes from years of human suffering. Graffiti covered some of the walls, but underneath I could see the pale green institutional paint that had been chosen to create a "therapeutic environment."

I took the stairs to the second floor, my footsteps echoing in the empty stairwell, Samson taking the stairs two steps at a time. The east wing corridor was dimly lit by sunlight filtering through dirty windows, and several of the office doors stood open to reveal empty rooms stripped of furniture and equipment.

Room 237 was at the end of the corridor, and the door was closed. I could hear voices inside - one calm and professional, the other frightened but not hysterical.

I knocked on the door. "Katherine, it's Captain Gazzara. May I come in?"

"It's not locked," came the reply. "Please come in slowly with your hands where I can see them."

I opened the door and stepped into what had once been the facility's main conference room. The long table that had once dominated the center of the space, and all but one of the chairs that had surrounded it, were long gone. Dr. Pierce was sitting in the one remaining chair, close to one of the windows, her hands zip-tied but otherwise appearing unharmed.

Katherine Morrison stood beside one of the windows, silhouetted against the gray afternoon light. She was smaller than I'd expected, probably five-six or five-seven. She wore dark slacks and a white blouse, and her long, dark brown hair was pulled back in a neat ponytail.

"Captain Gazzara," she said, turning to face me. "Thank you for coming. You've brought Samson with you, I see."

I remained standing near the door, keeping my hands visible but ready to reach for my weapon should it become necessary. Samson stood beside me, his flank touching my right leg, staring at Morrison, but was otherwise quiet. I could feel him breathing steadily.

"Are you all right, Dr. Pierce?"

"I'm fine," Pierce replied, though her voice was shaky. "She hasn't hurt me."

Katherine Morrison smiled slightly. "Dr. Pierce has been very helpful," she said. "She's filled in some of the details about the administration of the experimental program I hadn't considered."

"Katherine," I said, "you don't have to do this. We know about Kelly and what happened to both of you here. We understand how you must feel."

"Do you?" Katherine asked, moving away from the window. "Do you really understand what it's like to be sixteen years old, orphaned, and placed in a facility where medical professionals are allowed to torture you in the name of research?"

"No, of course not," I replied. "But I know what happened to you and Kelly was wrong. Criminal, even. But murder isn't the answer."

"Captain, I spent two years watching my sister deteriorate from the treatments she received here. I watched her struggle with neurological damage, depression, and PTSD until she couldn't take it anymore and she killed herself. Then I spent two years in a sort of hellish limbo, trying to expose what was going on here, but nobody would listen to me."

She moved back to the window and gestured to a stack of several manila folders on the sill. "These are the files Dr. Pierce has been helping me review. They contain documentation of the deaths they covered up."

I looked at Pierce. She turned her head away. "How many deaths?" I asked, looking again at Morrison.

"Twelve," she replied. "All children who were supposed to get better but instead died as a result of the experimental treatments, medication interactions, or suicide induced by psychological trauma."

Dr. Pierce spoke up from her chair. "Captain, I didn't know—"

"Oh shut up, Doctor," Morrison snapped, cutting her off. "You say you didn't know. Well you damn well should have known…" She stared at her for a moment and then turned again to me. "She was just a coordinator. She didn't design the treatments, nor did she participate in what went on in the labs, but she had access to the administrative records that confirms what happened here was the systematic exploitation of vulnerable children."

I looked at the stack of files, then looked at her and said, "If you have evidence of criminal activity, we can pursue it through proper channels. *I'll* pursue it, but you have to stop killing people. Why don't you turn Dr. Pierce loose and we get out of here?"

"Hah! Proper channels, you say?" Her voice carried a note of bitter amusement. "Captain, time and again I tried proper channels. Evidence disappeared. Medical licensing boards ignored my complaints. Professional organizations protected their members. Even the media wasn't interested in allegations against respected physicians."

"Things are different now," I said. "There's more awareness of institutional abuse, more protections for victims."

"Are there?" she asked, her voice tinged with sarcasm. "And what about Agent Gleave? She's trying to stop your investigation even as we speak. The medical association is threatening legal action against your department. Federal officials are pressuring you to focus on catching me rather than exposing the experimental program."

She was right, and we both knew it.

"What is it you want, Katherine?" I asked, quietly.

"I want the truth to come out in a way that can't be suppressed or buried. I want the families of the children who died in this program to know what really happened to them. And I want to make sure that the people responsible for Kelly's death understand what they took from the world when they destroyed her."

"And then what? You surrender? Disappear? What's your endgame?"

Katherine was quiet for a moment, looking out the window at the facility grounds where she'd spent three years of her adolescence being subjected to horrendous torture.

"My endgame is to ensure that Kelly's death meant something. That the suffering she endured serves a purpose by preventing future victims."

"Katherine, killing people doesn't prevent future victims. It just creates more tragedy."

"Does it?" She asked. "How many medical professionals will think twice about abusing vulnerable patients if they know there might be consequences? How many administrators will be more careful about approving experimental treatments if they understand that someone might hold them accountable?"

I could see the logic in her argument, and the fiery determination that had helped survive three years of institutional abuse and build a successful medical career. But I could also see the grief and anger that had driven her to seek revenge.

The room was quiet except for the sound of wind rattling the old windows. Katherine Morrison stood at the window staring out across the lot. Dr. Pierce sat silently, having witnessed a conversation that would probably haunt her for the rest of her life.

"So, what happens now, Katherine?" I said finally.

"Now, Captain Gazzara, you have a choice. You can arrest me, and this evidence will disappear into the legal system where it will be buried by the people who want to protect the medical establishment. Or you can let me complete my mission, and the truth about the experimental program will be exposed in a way that forces real accountability."

"I can't let you continue killing people."

"Then we have a problem," Katherine said, her hand moving to something at her waist. "Because I've spent twenty-five years working toward this moment, and I will not let institutional protection and legal technicalities prevent justice for Kelly and the other children who died here."

I felt Samson tense as I reached slowly for my radio, but Katherine stepped quickly to Pierce's side and shook her head.

"I wouldn't do that, Captain," she said, quietly. "Dr. Pierce's safety depends on how this conversation ends."

23

Bad Memories

Friday Afternoon, 3:30 PM

THE SILENCE IN ROOM 237 STRETCHED BETWEEN US LIKE A taut wire ready to snap. Katherine Morrison stood beside Dr. Pierce, her left hand resting on her shoulder, a long, thin-bladed scalpel in her right hand. Dr. Pierce sat frozen in her chair.

"Katherine," I said carefully, "You don't need to do this. Dr. Pierce has been cooperative. She's helped you document the evidence. There's no reason to hurt her now."

"I have no intention of hurting Dr. Pierce unless you do something stupid," she replied. "Neither you nor the dog can move fast enough to stop me inflicting a fatal wound. I cannot allow this investigation to be buried the way everything has been buried for the last twenty-five years."

"Then help me understand what you want," I said. "What will it take for you to surrender peacefully?"

Katherine looked out the window and nodded. "Captain, do you see that building over there?" She pointed to a squat, single-story structure about fifty yards from the main facility. "That was the isolation unit. Children who resisted treatment or asked too many questions were taken there for what the staff called 'reflection therapy.'"

"What was reflection therapy?" I asked, frowning.

"Solitary confinement in a room with no windows, no furniture except a toilet, and no human contact for days or weeks at a time. The staff told us it was to help us think about our behavior and attitudes."

I could hear the pain in her voice, even after all these years. "How long were you in isolation?"

"In total, forty-seven days, over multiple stays. The longest single period was twelve days when I was seventeen. Kelly was in isolation for sixty-one days total. The staff said she needed more reflection because she was influencing other patients to resist treatment."

Dr. Pierce looked up from her chair. "Katherine, I never knew about those isolation periods. That wasn't in any of the administrative records I saw."

"Because it wasn't officially part of the treatment protocol," Katherine said. "Dr. Holloway and the other physicians kept those records in files that were destroyed when the facility closed."

"But—" I began but was cut off as she continued.

"I remember every single day," she snapped, "every

injection, every electroshock treatment, every moment of terror and every moment of helplessness. And I remember watching Kelly deteriorate until she couldn't function in the outside world. Bad memories, Captain, all of them, but they are all I have."

I could see tears in her eyes. But her voice remained steady and controlled.

"After Kelly's suicide," she continued, "I tried to honor her memory by building a life that would help other trauma victims. I became a nurse, then a nurse practitioner. I specialized in treating people who had been abused by institutions and medical professionals. I thought if I could help enough people heal, it would somehow balance the scales. Eventually, I filed a wrongful death lawsuit against Greenbriar. But I was young, too young. The lawyers got together and persuaded me I couldn't win, and they offered me a deal. They paid me off, and I let them," she finished bitterly.

"But that wasn't enough?" I said.

She shook her head. "For the next ten years, I tried to make peace with what happened to us. I helped survivors, I donated money to advocacy groups, I even testified at conferences about institutional abuse. But the people who destroyed Kelly's life were still out there, still practicing medicine, still respected members of the medical community."

"What changed?" I asked.

Katherine was quiet for a moment, staring out over the grounds. "Two years ago, I was working at a trauma center in Atlanta when a teenager was brought in. She'd been sexually abused at a residential treatment facility, but the staff there had convinced her family that she was lying because she had a history of behavioral problems."

"Similar to what happened to you and Kelly," I said.

She nodded. "It was the identical pattern. A vulnerable child, a family crisis, placement in an institution, abuse disguised as treatment, the victim blamed for reporting the abuse. When I saw that girl, I realized then that nothing had really changed. People were still doing the same things to children, but with better legal protection."

I could understand how witnessing that kind of abuse might have triggered Katherine's decision to take matters into her own hands. But I said nothing. Instead, I waited for her to continue.

"I decided that Kelly's death had to mean something more than just another tragedy to be covered up and forgotten," she said. "I decided that the people responsible for destroying her life needed to face the consequences and... I sentenced them to death."

Geez, I thought, then said, "But that's not going to solve anything, is it? Killing people doesn't honor Kelly's memory. It just creates more victims."

"Does it? Dr. Holloway will never abuse another patient. And I'd be willing to bet Judge Marks will never sign another commitment order based on fraudulent psychiatric evaluations. And the people who are still alive that took part in the experimental program will think twice before harming other vulnerable patients."

She held up the scalpel for me to see. "Captain, this is a grafix scalpel, the same type of instrument Dr. Holloway used to perform invasive procedures on teenage patients without proper anesthesia. He called it 'teaching them to tolerate discomfort—'"

"Captain, are you okay?" Corbin's voice over my radio interrupted her flow.

"Yes, I'm talking to Ms. Morrison. Stay back. I'll call if I need you."

"You used his own methods against him."

I looked at her and said, "How d'you think this is going to end, Katherine? You know I'm not going to let you go on killing. It has to end here."

"The original lawsuit named forty-seven defendants. I've eliminated eight. Dr. Pierce has provided information that confirms the involvement of six more staff members who are still alive and *still* practicing." She emphasized the word still.

"So, you think I'm going to let you kill six more people?" I said. "It's not going to happen. You need to put that thing down and turn Dr. Pierce loose."

"I realize you're not going to let me go," she replied. "No, I'm planning to ensure that everyone who participated in the systematic abuse of children understands that actions have consequences."

I thought about the federal interference, the political pressure to end the investigation, and the institutional forces that would bury Katherine's evidence if she was simply arrested and processed through the legal system.

"Katherine, what if I could guarantee that the evidence you've collected would be made public, that the truth about the experimental program would be exposed?"

"Can you guarantee that?"

"I can promise to try."

"Captain, with respect, I tried for twenty-five years. Legal action, media attention, professional complaints, advocacy work - none of it created any real accountability. The system protects its own. You know that, from personal experience."

"Then help me change the system. Surrender, provide testimony, work with me to ensure this evidence reaches the right people."

Katherine was quiet for a long moment, considering my offer. Then she shook her head.

"Captain, do you know what happened to the other patients from the experimental program?"

"Some of them. We've interviewed several survivors."

"Twelve committed suicide. Eight died from drug overdoses, probably related to addiction issues stemming from the experimental medications they received as teenagers. Six are in long-term psychiatric care. Three have disappeared entirely. Of the original sixty-three patients, fewer than twenty are living anything resembling normal lives."

The scope of the damage was staggering. Katherine and Kelly Morrison had been part of a systematic destruction of young lives that had continued for years, even after the facility closed.

"Katherine, those statistics make your case for legal action even stronger. With that kind of documentation, prosecutors would have to take notice."

"Would they? Or would they find reasons to dismiss the evidence, just like they did twenty-five years ago?"

She had a point. The institutional forces that had

protected the experimental program in the 1990s were still operating today, as evidenced by Agent Gleave's attempts to control our investigation and the medical association's threats of legal action.

"What would convince you to work with me, through legal channels?" I asked.

"Honest answer?" she asked. "Nothing. I've seen how the system works, Captain. The people responsible for Kelly's death will be protected by lawyers, professional organizations, and federal officials who are determined to avoid scandal or public accountability at all costs."

I looked at Dr. Pierce, who had been listening to this conversation with growing understanding of the scope of the conspiracy she'd been part of, however unknowingly.

"Dr. Pierce, is there anything you can tell her that might change her mind about this course of action?"

Pierce looked directly at Katherine. "I'm sorry. I had no idea how extensive the abuse was or how many children were hurt. If I had known..."

"If you had known, would you have done anything different?" Katherine asked.

Pierce was quiet for a moment. "I'd like to think so. But honestly, I was a young resident, and I trusted the medical professionals to know what they were doing."

Katherine stepped closer to the window and picked up one of the files. "This was Jennifer Walsh, age fifteen," she said. "She died from a seizure induced by an experimental medication. The death certificate listed the cause of death as a pre-existing neurological condition."

She picked up another file. "Timothy Harper, age

sixteen. Suicide three days after being discharged. His family was told he had underlying mental health issues that couldn't be treated."

"Katherine—" I began.

"Shut up!" she snapped. "Sarah Martinez, age fourteen. Developed severe neurological damage from electroshock treatments. She's been in a care facility for twenty-five years because she can no longer speak or care for herself. And there are more, many more, just like them. So, Captain, as I said, I'm going to give you a choice. You can arrest me now, and this evidence will disappear into the legal system where it will be buried by people who want to protect the medical establishment. Or you can walk away and let me complete my mission."

"I can't let you continue killing people."

"Then we have a standoff. Because I can't let the people responsible for Kelly's death escape accountability again."

She stepped back again, closer to Dr. Pierce's chair, the scalpel still in her hand. "Dr. Pierce has been very helpful, but she's also a witness to this conversation. She knows about the evidence, she knows about my plans, and she knows that the medical establishment has been covering up systematic abuse for decades."

"Dr. Pierce isn't responsible for what happened to you and Kelly," I said. "Don't make her pay for other people's crimes."

"I'm not planning to hurt Dr. Pierce. But I also can't let her leave here to report this conversation to Agent Gleave or the medical association lawyers."

"What are you proposing?"

"A trade. Dr. Pierce's freedom for an honest conversation about what really happened in the experimental program and what needs to happen to prevent future victims. And then… Well, we'll see."

She was offering me exactly what I'd been hoping for. But she was also making it clear that she wouldn't surrender, wouldn't abandon her mission, and wouldn't allow the truth to be buried again.

"And if I agree, will you release Dr. Pierce unharmed?"

"I'll release Dr. Pierce once I'm confident the truth about the experimental program will be properly exposed."

"And then?" I asked, already knowing the answer.

"I walk away and complete my mission."

"Katherine, I don't want to kill you, but I will if I have to."

She looked out the window at the facility grounds where her nightmare had begun. "Captain, I died in this place twenty-five years ago. Ever since then I've been on borrowed time leading to this moment."

I reached for my radio, but Katherine shook her head.

"Not yet, Captain."

24

The Truth Will Out

Friday Afternoon, 4:45 PM

"CAPTAIN GAZZARA," KATHERINE SAID, HER VOICE TAKING on the professional tone I'd heard her use when discussing medical procedures, "before you decide what to do about my mission, I want you to understand exactly what happened in this facility. Not the sanitized version in the official records, but the truth that Kelly and I and sixty-one other children lived through."

I remained standing near the door with Samson at my side, keeping my options open, but also showing I was willing to listen. "So, tell me," I said.

Katherine stepped over to the window and sorted through the files until she found the one she needed.

I looked down at Samson. One word from me and...

but I hesitated. She turned away from the window, the file in her hand.

"This facility was officially called the Greenbriar Behavioral Health Center Experimental Treatment Program. It was funded by a combination of state money, federal grants, and pharmaceutical company research contracts. The stated purpose was to develop innovative treatments for severely disturbed adolescents who hadn't responded to conventional therapy."

"And you're going to tell me the real purpose?" I said.

"To test experimental medications and treatment protocols on vulnerable children who had no legal advocates and whose families had essentially abandoned them to the system" she said, opening the folder. "This file contains research proposals. The pharmaceutical companies were paying the facility to test drugs that hadn't been approved for adolescents, or even for human use in some cases."

I moved closer to examine the documents she was showing me.

"Stay back," she said, holding up the scalpel.

I stopped. She took a step forward, reached out, handed me the file, then stepped away.

The file contained technical and clinical research proposals, but the basic premise was clear: use institutionalized teenagers as test subjects for experimental treatments.

"Most of the children had been sexually abused," she said, "physically abused, or neglected by their families. They were already traumatized when they arrived here."

"And the experimental treatments made them worse," I said.

"Much worse. The medications caused seizures, neurological damage, and permanent cognitive impairment. The electroshock treatments were administered without proper anesthesia because the doctors wanted to study the psychological effects of pain and fear. The isolation procedures were designed to break down psychological resistance."

Dr. Pierce spoke up from her chair. "Katherine, I coordinated some of those treatment schedules, but I was told they were standard psychiatric interventions."

"The standard interventions were used as a baseline," Katherine replied. "But each patient was also subjected to experimental protocols that weren't disclosed to the families or even to most of the staff." She pulled out another set of documents. "These are the real treatment records, kept separate from the official files."

"How did you get access to these records?" I asked.

"Dr. Holloway kept copies in his personal files. When Elena Vasquez was fired from the facility, she managed to obtain photocopies of some of the experimental protocols. She was different. She'd been documenting what she witnessed during her night shifts. Elena knew what was happening was wrong, but she didn't have the resources or legal knowledge to do anything about it. When I contacted her years later, she was still carrying guilt about not being able to protect us."

She picked up another file, reached out and exchanged it for the one I was holding. This one contained photographs. "These were taken during treatment sessions. Kelly somehow managed to get hold of a small camera."

The photographs were disturbing - teenagers strapped to medical tables, electroshock equipment being used on conscious patients, children in isolation cells that looked more like prison cells than medical treatment rooms.

"Kelly took these pictures?"

"Kelly was older. She'd been in the system longer. She hid the camera and took pictures whenever she could."

"Katherine, this is evidence of criminal abuse. Why wasn't it used in your original lawsuit?"

"I tried to use it. But the defense attorneys argued the photographs were taken without consent and violated patient privacy laws. The judge ruled them inadmissible as evidence. The legal system protected the institution and the perpetrators."

She picked up another file and handed it to me, taking the one I was holding from me. "That's a small sample from Timothy Harper's medical records. Look at the report on his brain scan taken after his final electroshock treatment. 'Significant damage to the hippocampus and frontal cortex.' Then look at this psychological evaluation done two days before his discharge. 'Severe depression, confusion, and memory loss.'"

"So, what you're saying is the electroshock treatments caused brain damage?" I asked.

"I am. The doctors knew the treatments were causing neurological damage. They documented it in their research files. But they continued the treatments because they wanted to study the long-term effects."

I was beginning to understand the scope of the medical crimes that had been committed in this facility.

"Katherine, what did they do to Kelly?"

Katherine's composure wavered for the first time during our conversation. She was quiet for a moment, then pulled out another file labeled "Morrison, Kelly - Patient 22."

"Kelly was my older sister. She'd been in the juvenile system for two years before we were both placed here after our parents died. She was seventeen when she arrived. I was just sixteen. We were each other's only family."

"What treatments was Kelly subjected to?"

"Everything. She was part of multiple experimental protocols because she was considered a 'high functioning' subject who could provide detailed feedback about the treatments' effects." Katherine opened Kelly's file. "Experimental antipsychotics, electroshock therapy, isolation therapy, sleep deprivation studies, even experimental surgical procedures."

"Surgical procedures?"

"Dr. Holloway performed what he called 'investigative procedures' to study the physical effects of psychological trauma. Minor surgeries designed to create controlled pain so he could study patient responses."

I felt sick. "They were performing experimental surgery on teenagers?" I asked, not knowing what else to say.

"With no anesthesia sometimes, because they wanted

to study the relationship between physical pain and psychological resistance. Kelly underwent four separate procedures over two years."

"And no one questioned what was happening?"

Katherine picked up a document. "This is a memo from the facility administration to all staff, dated six months before the program ended. It explicitly states that staff members who ask questions about experimental protocols will be terminated and blacklisted from future medical employment."

I shook my head. I just couldn't understand how they could get away with it.

Katherine caught my look and smiled. "They were protecting a multibillion-dollar—that's billion, with a B—research program that was providing data to pharmaceutical companies and federal agencies. And substantial grants to the doctors performing and evaluating the procedures and also administering the medications. Individual staff members who raised concerns were threats to be eliminated."

"But the experimental program was terminated," I said. "Why?"

"Elena Vasquez was partly responsible for that," she replied. "Even though she was fired, she continued working to expose what was happening at Greenbriar. She contacted families, spoke to reporters, filed complaints with medical licensing boards. Eventually, she provided enough documentation to force a federal investigation."

"And the investigation shut down the program?"

"It wasn't quite as simple as that," she said. "The investigation, if you can call it that, concluded that some treatment protocols had been 'overly aggressive' and recommended better oversight for future research. No criminal charges were filed. No licenses were revoked. The facility was closed, but the staff moved on to other institutions to continue practicing medicine and, in some cases, like that of Dr. Holloway, to continue the experimental procedures."

"So, you're telling me that it's still going on today, and that there's been no accountability?"

"None. Dr. Holloway received a letter of reprimand that was sealed and never made public. Judge Marks was commended for her cooperation with the investigation. The pharmaceutical companies that funded the research claimed they had no knowledge of the specific treatment protocols. And the government grants... Holloway was still receiving them."

Katherine walked back to the window overlooking the facility grounds and replaced the files on the sill. "Kelly and I were discharged when the program ended," she said. "Kelly was twenty years old, and I was nineteen. We had no family, no resources, no education, and she was suffering severe psychological trauma from three years of experimental abuse."

"But not you," I said. "How did you survive?"

"I don't know. Barely. It took me a long time to recover from... The truth is, Captain. I was the strong one, which was, in one way, an advantage; in another it made me that much more interesting to the likes of Dr. Holloway. Kelly, however, couldn't function in the outside world. She had panic attacks, seizures from medication withdrawal, and memory problems from the electroshock treatments."

Katherine pulled out a photograph from Kelly's file. It showed the two young women, one looking defeated and damaged. The other, biting her lip, was looking at her sister.

"And then Kelly killed herself," I muttered.

Katherine nodded, tears visible in her eyes for the first time. "She left a note saying she couldn't live with the memories, that the doctors had taken away her ability to be human. She specifically mentioned Dr. Holloway and the surgical procedures he'd performed on her."

"So, what did you do after Kelly died?"

"Not much," she shrugged. "I was devastated by Kelly's death, and I was so glad to be out of there, but as the years passed, I began to think about what I needed to do to put things right. I filed the wrongful death lawsuit, contacted reporters, spoke to medical licensing boards. Everything Elena had tried, plus additional evidence I'd gathered. Eventually I realized that the system was designed to protect institutions and medical professionals, not the victims. Then I met a hacker online." She smiled at the thought. "He was something of a savant. He taught me what I needed to know, so I decided to build the capabilities necessary to seek justice through other means."

She looked me in the eye and said, "Captain, I want you to understand that everything I've done has been motivated by my love for Kelly and determination to save other children from suffering as we suffered."

"Katherine," I said, gently, "I understand why you're angry. I understand why you don't trust the legal system. And I also understand that you're not an evil person. I think you, too, are suffering from the damage done to you by the experimental treatments. I think *you* need help. You've spent years helping other trauma victims, providing financial assistance to survivors, building a legitimate medical career focused on healing. Now it's your turn to get the help you need."

"And none of it was enough to balance what happened to Kelly," she snapped.

"Maybe not. But it proves that you're capable of seeking justice through means other than murder."

Katherine was quiet for a moment, considering my words. Then she shook her head.

"Captain, I've tried healing. I've tried helping. I've tried working within the system. None of it prevented other children from being abused by the same people who destroyed Kelly's life."

"How do you know other children were abused?"

Katherine picked up another folder from the window sill. "Because I've been tracking the careers of everyone who worked in the experimental program. Dr. Holloway was conducting experimental treatments to this day. Judge Marks has continued signing commitment orders based on questionable psychiatric evaluations, to this day. Elena had documented at least six other cases of institutional abuse involving staff members from this facility."

She picked up another folder. "This contains documentation of ongoing abuse by experimental program staff at facilities across the Southeast. Pharmaceutical companies continued using the research data from this program to develop treatments that were tested on institutionalized patients at those facilities. Federal agencies continue funding similar research at those facilities."

As I watched Katherine Morrison standing at the window, her arms folded, the scalpel still in her right hand, staring out at the buildings in which her life had been destroyed, and surrounded by evidence of systematic medical abuse and institutional cover-ups, I realized I was dealing with someone who had spent most of her adult life in a kind of mental fog, building the capabilities and gathering the evidence to ensure that the people responsible for her sister's death would face the consequences of what they'd done, and to ensure that future victims would be protected.

"Kate, talk to me," Corbin said over the radio. "What's happening? SWAT is on the way."

"Damn it, Corbin," I snapped. "We don't need them. Tell them I said to stand down. I have it in hand."

But had I?

The Final Choice

Friday Afternoon, 6:00 PM

IT WAS SIX O'CLOCK IN THE EVENING AND ROOM 237 WAS in shadow. Dr. Pierce sat silently in her chair, having witnessed a conversation that revealed the true scope of the conspiracy she'd unknowingly participated in. And I stood facing a decision that would define not just the end of this case, but possibly my career.

"So, Captain Gazzara, now you know the truth about what happened in this facility and why legal justice will never happen. The question is: what are you going to do with that knowledge?"

I looked at the stack of evidence on the window sill. The scope of the crimes was overwhelming, and Katherine was right about one thing: the legal system had failed these victims completely.

"Katherine, the evidence you've shown me could still—"

"No, it couldn't," she snapped, interrupting me. "I tried all of those approaches. I spent twenty-five years trying. Elena tried. Other survivors have tried. Don't you get it? The system is designed to protect the institutions and medical professionals, not to provide justice for the victims. It's all about money, big money, and politics. It doesn't work, not for people like us, or even you. Yes, you. You could lose your job if you make the wrong decision. Don't you know that?"

The problem was, I did know. But I still had faith in the system and that it could work even for her, even after all she'd done.

"But things have changed," I said, desperately fishing for answers. "There's more awareness of institutional abuse now, more protections for victims, more willingness to hold medical professionals accountable."

Katherine turned again to the window and looked out. "Three doors down the corridor, on the left, is what once was Holloway's office. He would bring patients there for what he called 'private consultations.' They were private all right. Behind the locked door, he performed experimental procedures without any oversight or official documentation."

"Katherine—"

"Kelly was taken to that office seventeen times over the three years she was here. Each time, she came back traumatized and injured. When she tried to tell the staff what Holloway was doing to her, they said she was having paranoid delusions caused by her mental illness."

I could hear the pain in Katherine's voice, even after all these years. "That's exactly why we need to expose this through proper channels," I said, pleading with her. "So Kelly's story can be heard and believed."

"Kelly's story was heard, Captain. I provided detailed testimony about Holloway's abuse during my lawsuit. I told you. The court ruled that Kelly's allegations were unreliable because she had been diagnosed with psychiatric disorders. I can still see that judge's face as he said it."

She moved away from the window, back to stand behind Dr. Pierce, the knife still in her hand. "Captain, I have documentation covering the past five years that proves ongoing abuse by members of the experimental program staff working at other facilities, Including Dr. Holloway."

"Dr. Fletcher, whom you've been protecting, has continued conducting experimental treatments on adolescent patients at his private practice. Three teenagers have been hospitalized with severe reactions to off-label medications he prescribed without proper oversight."

"Do you have documentation of that?" I asked.

"I do. Medical records, pharmacy records, insurance claims. All obtained through my work as a nurse practitioner, work that provided me with access to medical databases. Dr. Fletcher's experimental treatments caused one teenager to develop seizures, another to attempt suicide, and a third to suffer permanent neurological damage."

"Why wasn't this reported to the medical licensing boards?"

"It was. Dr. Fletcher received a letter recommending 'enhanced oversight of prescribing practices.' No license suspension, no criminal charges, no public disclosure."

She smiled at me.

"Judge Marks continued signing commitment orders for the experimental program until it was shut down," she said. "After that, she continued approving placements at other facilities with questionable treatment programs. Residential treatment centers that use isolation, restraints, and experimental medications on teenagers. Facilities that recruit patients through the juvenile justice system by offering treatment as an alternative to incarceration."

"And you have documentation of that, too, I suppose?"

"I do. I have court records and facility reports documenting ongoing abuse at institutions where Judge Marks had sent vulnerable teenagers. Seventeen children committed suicide after being placed in facilities she approved. Their families were told the suicides were the result of pre-existing mental health issues."

Geez, I thought. *If what she's telling me is true...*

"When Greenbriar closed, these so-called medical practitioners simply moved to other locations with the same staff and the same protection from legal account-ability and, coincidentally, the same grants," she said, bitterly.

"Katherine, if you do have this documentation, it

could be used to build a federal case against these facilities and the staff members involved."

"Could it, Captain? I believe that Agent Gleave is, at this very moment, trying to bury this investigation, and she has been since the moment she arrived. And isn't the medical association threatening legal action against your police department? Hah! And you expect me to believe... what, that they'll just roll over and do nothing? Don't make me laugh, Captain."

I knew she was right, but I had to try.

"What would it take for you to work with me to expose them?" I asked.

Katherine was quiet for a long moment, considering my question. "Honest answer? A guarantee that the evidence would be made public in a way that couldn't be suppressed or buried. Congressional hearings with national media coverage. Federal prosecution of everyone involved in the ongoing abuse. And public acknowledgment that the legal system failed victims like Kelly."

"You know I can't guarantee any of that but—"

"No buts, Captain. I know. In fact, I probably know the system better than you do. And that's why I have to complete my mission."

Katherine held up the scalpel between two fingers and waggled it at me. It wasn't a threat, but she was making it clear she was prepared to use it.

"So, you have a choice," she said. "Try to arrest me, in which case Dr. Pierce might be hurt and the evidence will certainly disappear into the legal system where it will be buried forever. Or you can simply walk away."

"You know I can't do that," I said. "Murder is murder. It doesn't matter how justified you think it is."

"Doesn't it, Captain? Then tell me this: If you knew Dr. Fletcher was planning to abuse another teenager tomorrow, would you walk away and let it happen?"

"That's not the same thing," I snapped. I was getting tired of the verbal swordsmanship. I was in an impossible position. Katherine Morrison, a confessed killer, was demanding I let her go to kill again. *Maybe I need SWAT after all.*

I looked at Sammy who was now lying down and seemed to be snoozing, and no wonder. It was time to wrap it up.

"Katherine, what about Dr. Pierce? She's been cooperative, she's helped you document the evidence. There's no reason why you shouldn't let her go."

She looked at Pierce, thought for a moment, then stepped over to Dr. Pierce's chair and carefully cut the zip ties restraining her hands. "Dr. Pierce, you're free to go. Take the files with you, but I want you to understand something: if this evidence disappears, is buried, and the abuse continues, you'll be responsible for every child who suffers because you failed to do what's right."

Dr. Pierce rubbed her wrists, stood up slowly, backed up to the window, and picked up the stack of files. "I'm sorry, Katherine. I truly am. Don't worry. I'll keep them safe," she said. "I promise."

"You can do better than that," Katherine said. "You can tell the truth about what you witnessed, regardless of the consequences. You can support the families of victims who try to seek justice. And you can refuse to participate in any system that prioritizes institutional protection over patient safety."

Pierce looked at me, then back at Katherine. "I will. I promise."

Katherine nodded and turned back to me. "Dr. Pierce is free to leave, Captain. Now you need to decide what you're going to do about me."

"I need you to come with me," I said, reaching for my cuffs.

She shook her head. The long-bladed scalpel still in her hand.

"Samson here can take you down," I said. "I just have to say the word."

She looked at him, smiled and said, "He seems like a nice dog. I'd hate to have to gut him. You want to take that chance?"

"Put it down, Katherine." I put my hand on my weapon.

She smiled. "You won't shoot me, Captain. I know the rules as well as you do. You have to be in fear of your life, and you're not, are you? And I know you're a good cop, so you won't lie and say you were."

By then she was backing up to a door at the end of the room.

"Here's what's going to happen, Captain, I'm going to give you thirty minutes to leave this facility with Dr. Pierce. After that, I'm going to complete my mission."

"What mission? There's no one else here."

Katherine took out her phone and read me a text message from Dr. Sarah Walton. 'Will be there in forty-five minutes.' I sent her a message telling her if she didn't come, I'd expose her. She's coming alone."

"Dr. Walton wasn't even part of the original experimental program," I protested.

"No, she wasn't, but she's been covering for Dr. Holloway, and she, herself, has been conducting off-label research. She received payments from two different pharmaceutical companies, and I can prove it. The evidence is in those files."

"So, you're planning to kill her when she arrives?"

"I'm planning to confront her with the evidence of her complicity and let her choose how I respond."

"And if she doesn't respond the way you want?"

"Then she'll face the same consequences Holloway faced."

"Katherine, I can't let you kill Dr. Walton."

"Then shoot me, Captain. But understand that if you do, this evidence will disappear, and the abuse will continue."

I looked around the room one more time and as I did so, Katherine Morrison turned and walked calmly to the door at the back of the room. I drew my weapon, pointed it at her back as she opened the door and walked out, closing the door behind her, never once presenting anything to me but her back.

I looked at Pierce waiting by the door. "Go," I said. "And take those files with you."

I ran to the door. Grabbed the handle and tried to open it. It was locked.

"Damn," I muttered. Then to Sammy, I said, "Well, I screwed that one up, didn't I, boy?"

She said thirty minutes, I thought. *I wonder if she meant it.*

Pierce had left by the other door, the one I'd used when I entered the room. I took a minute to decide what to do. *I could call Corbin*, I thought. *I could call for reinforcements. This is a huge building. She knows it well, and she has a head start.*

I looked at Sammy. "You think we can find her?"

"Woof!"

Yeah, right, I thought. "Come on then, let's see how good you are."

I took him over to the window where she'd spent most of the last several hours. I figured if there was anywhere in the room where he could pick up her scent, that was it.

He sniffed around the sill then took off for the door through which she'd exited.

"No, that's not it, Buddy," I said, wondering if I could bust the door down, but it opened inward, toward me, so I would be working against the frame, not just the lock.

"This way, Sammy," I said, and we exited through the door through which we'd entered, out into the corridor which was both long and disturbingly quiet.

"Find her, Sammy," I said.

He raised his nose, sniffing the air, then took off running along the corridor.

26

Justice and Aftermath

Friday Evening, 7:15 PM

I<small>T TOOK</small> S<small>AMMY ONLY ABOUT FIFTEEN MINUTES TO FIND</small> her in a small, single-story concrete structure adjacent to and just to the north of the main Greenbriar facility. The entrance door was cracked open just a little, and the hinges squealed as I pushed it open and stepped inside to find myself in a narrow corridor that smelled of mold and damp.

Samson once again took off running along the corridor, almost to the end, where he stopped in front of a door with a faded sign on which was written in flowing, white-painted letters, a single word. Electrotherapy.

I listened for a moment but could hear nothing. I looked at Samson. He stared up at me, then turned his head to stare at the door.

I knocked, then listened. Nothing!

I took a deep breath. "Heel, Sammy," I whispered, then drew my weapon, grabbed the door handle, turned it, pushed the door wide open and stood for a moment, listening.

"Come on in, Captain. I'm... I'm... Just come on in."

I stepped inside the room. It was small, with a single window to the right that let in just enough light to be able to see Katherine Morrison sitting on the floor beside what was obviously a rusted treatment... I'm not going to call it a table, because it wasn't. It wasn't a chair either. I can't describe it accurately, but it looked a lot like an extended recliner set on a pedestal with a foot pedal to raise and lower it. The actual shock equipment had been removed. Only the... chair remained.

So, this is where she and her sister were tortured, I thought. *Geez!*

It was a fleeting thought because my attention was almost immediately drawn to Katherine. She looked exhausted; not just physically but emotionally drained in a way that suggested she'd finally reached the end of a journey that had consumed her entire adult life. The scalpel lay on the floor beside her, and her hands were empty, palms turned upward in a gesture of surrender.

"I knew you'd find me here," she said without looking up. "This is where it all started, Catherine." Then she looked up and smiled weakly. "It seems appropriate we have the same name, don't you think?" She looked away at the object of her misery beside her and continued. "This is where Holloway first explained to me that pain was a necessary part of healing. Can you believe that? I lost count of the hours I spent in this chair."

I approached slowly, Samson padding quietly beside me. "Katherine, where's Dr. Walton?" I asked as I holstered my weapon.

"She's not coming. I sent her a message." She looked up at me and, in the dim light, I could see tears on her cheeks. "I'm tired, Kate. Twenty-five years is a long time to carry this much anger."

"Yes, it is," I replied. "But what changed your mind?"

"You did," she said and sighed, looking sideways at the instrument of her torture. "You and Dr. Pierce. When she apologized, when she promised to help expose the truth, I realized that maybe the legal system might work if enough people were willing to speak up."

I sat down on the floor in front of her, keeping my distance, but showing I was willing to talk. Samson lay down beside me, his head between his paws.

"Tell me about Dr. Walton, Katherine. You said she was part of the cover-up?"

She nodded, then said, "She knew Holloway was continuing experimental treatments at their practice. She helped him hide the documentation when patients suffered adverse reactions. But when I looked again at this"—she looked at the chair—"I knew killing her wouldn't bring Kelly back or prevent future abuse. I knew I had to be given the chance to tell my story where it can be heard by everyone in court. So I decided to give myself up."

She leaned against the chair, her eyes closed. "Kelly would have been forty-four years old today," she murmured. She opened her eyes and looked at me. "She should still be alive, maybe married, maybe with children of her own. Instead, she's dead and all because of people like Holloway and Walton."

She sat up, reached into her jacket, and pulled out a manila envelope. "This contains my notarized statement, Captain, and a key to a safe deposit box at 1st Horizon bank at Hamilton Place. In addition to what Dr. Pierce has, the box contains everything you need to expose these people. Complete documentation of the Greenbriar experimental program, evidence of ongoing abuse by former staff members, financial records showing pharmaceutical company payments, and recordings I made of conversations with other survivors."

I took the envelope carefully. "Why didn't you use this years ago?" I asked, squinting at her. "If you had, you wouldn't be in this mess today."

She heaved a huge sigh, then said. "It wouldn't have worked, Kate. The pressures to cover it all up were too great. I tried again five years ago when I discovered Dr. Fletcher was still experimenting on teenagers. The medical licensing board sent him a warning letter and sealed the records."

She was quiet for a long moment, studying the treatment chair where she'd suffered so many years ago. "I thought if I eliminated enough of them, the others would stop out of fear. But that didn't work either. The system just circled the wagons and tried to protect them. And then Gleave showed up, and you know what that's about."

I sat for a moment in that stinking room—the horrors

that had taken place there I could only imagine—thinking about the repercussions of what I knew I had to do next.

"So?" I said, finally.

"So now I surrender," she said. "I gave you the evidence you need to expose them, and I trust that you'll fight to expose the truth harder than the federal agents will fight to bury it."

She sat up, struggled to her feet, and held out her hands. "I'm willing to face the consequences. But Kate, I need you to promise me something."

"What's that?" I asked as I, too, stood up.

"Promise me that the evidence I've given you in that envelope will reach the public. That the families of children who died in the experimental program will finally know exactly what happened to them."

I looked at the envelope, then at her and said, "I promise I'll try. But I'm not going to make a promise I may not be able to keep. I'll do my best."

"I want you to know that I never intended to become a serial killer," she said. "Each time I killed, it was supposed to be the last one. I kept thinking that surely that will force the system to respond, but it never did."

"Katherine Morrison, I'm arresting you for the murders of Dr. Marcus Holloway and Elena Vasquez. You have the right to remain silent..."

As I advised her of her rights, in almost complete darkness, in that nasty little room, I was filled with conflicting emotions. On the one hand, this woman was a cold-blooded killer. On the other, she was the victim of three years of unimaginable horror right where I was standing. Never before in my career had I faced anything like it. She wasn't born this way. The people that had abused her had created her. And I realized this case challenged everything I thought I knew about justice, accountability, and the responsibility of law enforcement to protect the public.

No, I didn't cuff her. I took her arm and walked her out of the building into the fresh air to the parking lot where my team was waiting.

At my car, she turned and took one last look at the buildings where she'd spent three years of her adolescence.

"Kate," she said quietly, "do you think Kelly would understand why I did this?"

I thought about Kelly Morrison, a young woman who had survived years of experimental abuse, only to kill herself because she couldn't live with the trauma. I thought about the suicide note blaming Holloway and the other medical professionals who had destroyed her.

"Yes, I think Kelly would understand," I said finally. "I think she'd be proud that you never stopped fighting for her."

Katherine Morrison smiled for the first time since I'd met her. "Then it was worth it," she said, and slipped into the back seat of my unmarked cruiser. Samson jumped up onto the seat beside her and she laid her head on his shoulder.

EPILOGUE

SIX MONTHS LATER, AS I WAS WALKING SAMSON THROUGH our usual route in East Chattanooga, my phone rang. It was Michelle Tester, the prosecutor who had handled Katherine Morrison's case.

"Kate, I thought you'd want to know. The judge just handed down Katherine Morrison's sentence."

"Of course," I replied. "What did she get?"

"Fifteen years to life, with the possibility of parole on each of eight counts to run concurrently. As you know, she confessed to three more murders. The judge took into consideration the years she'd suffered at the hands of her victims, her cooperation in exposing the medical abuse scandal and for the exceptional circumstances that led to her crimes."

It was a lighter sentence than I'd expected, but the judge had clearly been influenced by the evidence and her forthright testimony. Katherine's defense team had pleaded that there were mitigating circumstances, Tester had agreed, and the judge had obviously taken them into consideration, too.

"What about the federal investigation?" I asked. "How's that going?"

"Congressional hearings start next month. The Justice Department has opened investigations into fourteen facilities across the Southeast. Three doctors have already had their licenses revoked, and two pharmaceutical companies are facing federal charges for illegal human experimentation."

"Any word on Agent Gleave?"

"Transferred to a desk job in Washington after it came out that she'd been trying to suppress evidence on behalf of certain medical industry contacts. It turns out the federal government is interested in accountability when enough public pressure is applied."

After I hung up, I continued walking slowly with Samson padding along beside me, thinking about the case. Chief Johnston had supported me throughout. The medical association's threats had backfired when the evidence Morrison provided was made public, leading to media coverage that made it impossible for federal officials to continue protecting the perpetrators.

My team had emerged stronger from the complex case. But most importantly, the evidence Katherine Morrison had gathered had finally reached the public. Her revelations had led to investigations at multiple facilities, policy changes in psychiatric treatment oversight, and federal legislation strengthening protections for institutionalized patients.

As we turned and headed for home, Samson looked up and gave me what I'd decided was 'that knowing look' that suggested he understood that once again we'd completed something important together. The hunt for Katherine Morrison was over, but the memories would linger for a long, long time.

"Come on, boy," I said, reaching down and scratching behind his ears. "Let's go get something to eat, shall we?" And he took off, bounding away toward home. Me? I smiled to myself, already wondering what I would do without him, and what the next case would be.

Because in a city like Chattanooga, there was always a next case, another victim who needs someone to fight for justice and the truth. The hunt never really ended. It just evolved. And that's exactly how it should be.

As I settled in for the evening with Samson beside me on the couch, I looked at him, frowned, and said, "Whew, you stink. It's time you had a bath."

"Eeewe," he whined and covered his eyes with his paws.

I laughed, leaned over, and kissed the top of his enormous head. He let one paw slide a little and looked at me with one eye. And I melted.

THANK YOU SO MUCH FOR READING, *BAD MEMORIES*, THE TWENTY-SECOND BOOK IN THE KATE GAZZARA MURDER FILES. WE HOPE YOU ENJOYED THE BOOK AND WILL CONTINUE READING MORE OF BLAIR HOWARDS STORIES.

Y<small>OU CAN FIND A FULL LIST OF HIS BOOK ON THE NEXT PAGE,</small>
<small>INCLUDING A FEW NOVELLAS AND A BRAND NEW</small>
<small>STANDALONE MYSTERY FEATURING</small> K<small>ATE AND</small> H<small>ARRY!</small>

Short Stories and Novellas
Buried Secrets(Harry Starke)

The Painted Lady(Kate Gazzara)

Stand Alone
Hunter's Moon(Kate & Harry)

Series

The Harry Starke Genesis Series
9 Books in Series as of 2025

The Harry Starke Series
25 Books in Series as of 2025

The Lt. Kate Gazzara Murder Files
22 Books in Series as of 2025

Randall And Carver Mysteries
4 Books in Series as of 2025

The Peacemaker Series
3 Books in Series as of 2025

The O'Sullivan Chronicles: Civil War Series
5 Books in Series as of 2025

Science Fiction From Blair C. Howard

The Sovereign Star Series
7 Books in Series as of 2025

also available in German

ABOUT THE AUTHOR

Blair Howard is a retired journalist turned novelist. He's the author of more than 50 novels including the international best-selling Harry Starke series of crime stories, the Lt. Kate Gazzara series, and the Harry Starke Genesis series. He's also the author of the Peacemaker series of international spy thrillers, The Sovereign Star & The Predecessors Science Fiction series, and five Civil War/Western novels.

Visit www.blairhowardbooks.com.
Email: BlairHoward@BlairHowardBooks.com

You can also find Blair Howard on Social Media